French Letters

ABOUT THE AUTHOR

Bruno Bouchet is a Sydney-based writer with a cultural background even more horribly mixed than Greque-en-Provence. Born in Spain of British and French parents, he recently discovered he had an Italian grandmother—all of this makes creating his national dish very complicated. His father lives in Provence and doesn't know anything about this book.

You can contact Bruno via his website
www.brunobouchet.com

BRUNO BOUCHET
French Letters

HODDER

A Hodder Book

Published in Australia and New Zealand in 2004
by Hodder Headline Australia Pty Limited
(A member of the Hodder Headline Group)
Level 17, 207 Kent Street, Sydney NSW 2000
Website: www.hha.com.au

Copyright © Bruno Bouchet 2004

This book is copyright. Apart from any fair dealing for
the purposes of private study, research, criticism or
review permitted under the *Copyright Act 1968*,
no part may be stored or reproduced by any process
without prior written permission. Enquiries should
be made to the publisher.

**National Library of Australia
Cataloguing-in-Publication data**

Bouchet, Bruno.
    French letters.

    ISBN 0 7336 1813 8 (pbk.).

    I. Title.

A823.3

Text design and typesetting by Bookhouse, Sydney
Printed in Australia by Griffin Press, Adelaide

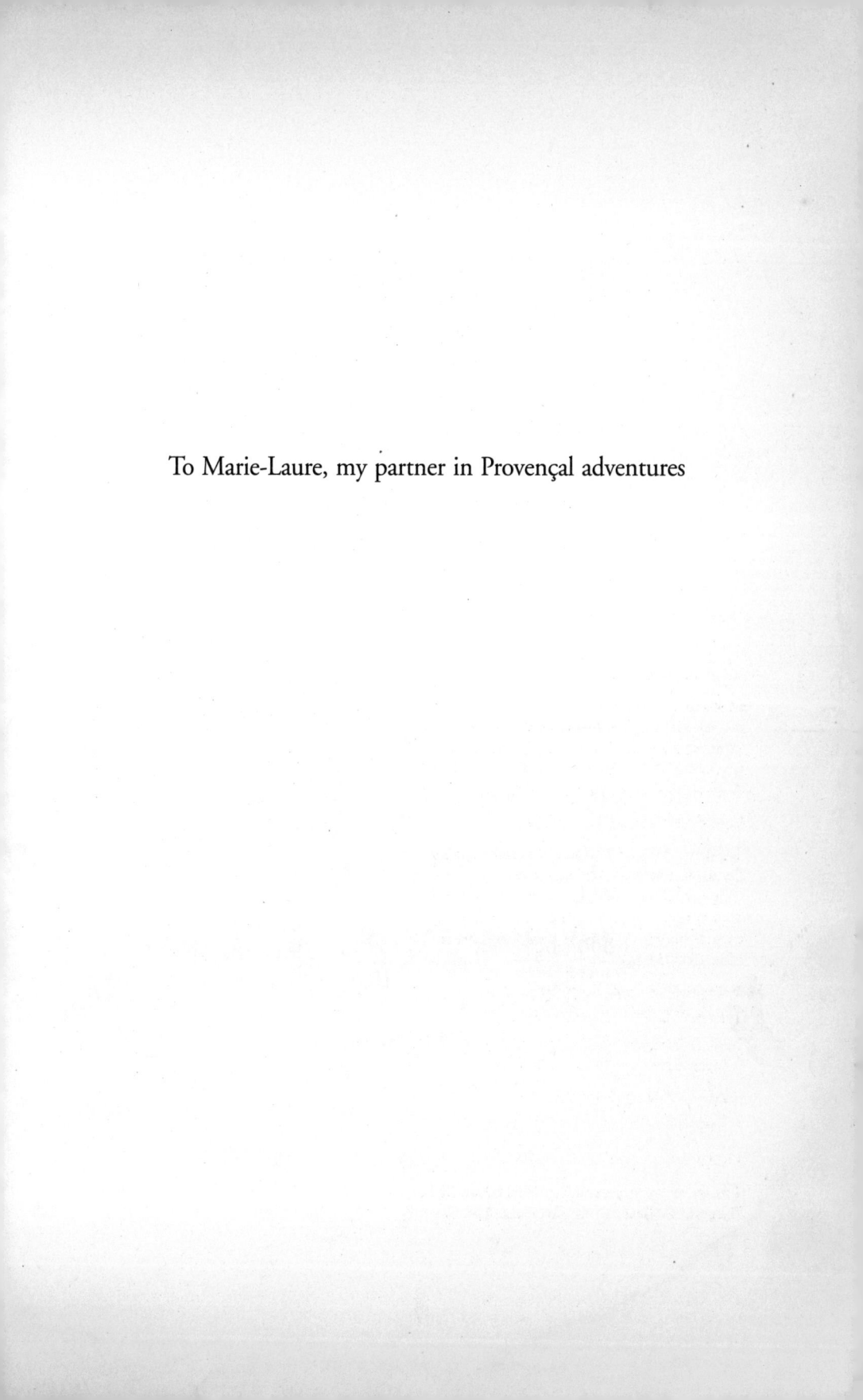

To Marie-Laure, my partner in Provençal adventures

THE NOIRELLE MEN

an ill-fated bunch

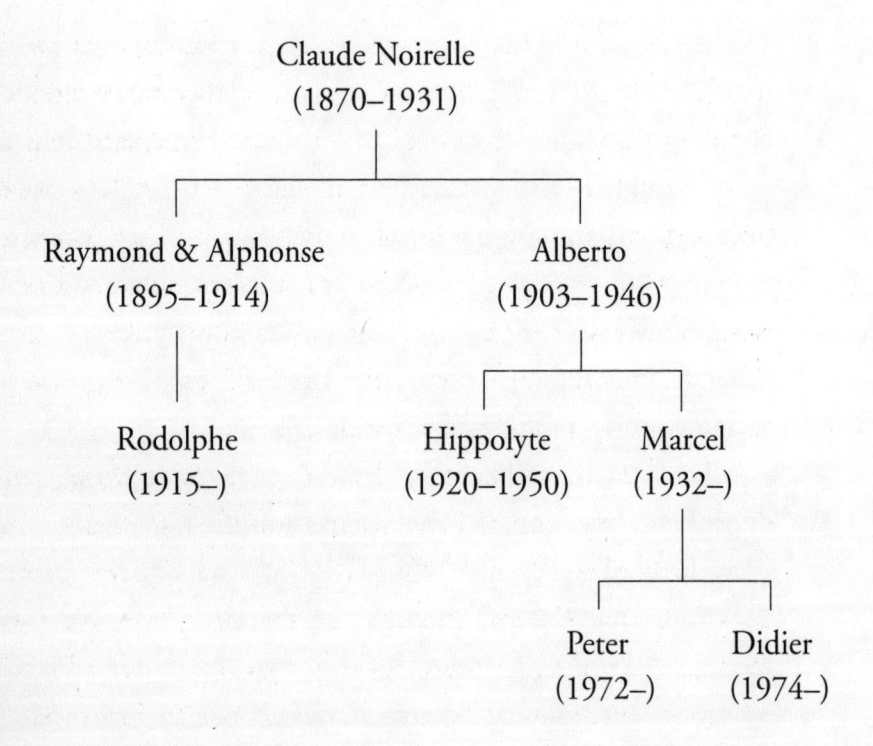

Claude Noirelle
(1870–1931)

Raymond & Alphonse   Alberto
(1895–1914)   (1903–1946)

Rodolphe   Hippolyte   Marcel
(1915–)   (1920–1950)   (1932–)

                          Peter   Didier
                          (1972–)   (1974–)

When the first letter arrived, I sensed straightaway that it was a biggie, but I didn't think it would be life-altering. I didn't think my life needed any altering.

I have to admit I had it pretty easy. I was a trendspotter and ideas man in New York. My firm paid me to predict future trends and come up with ways of cashing in on them. I predicted that cargo pants would lead to a reduction in the sale of wallets—nobody needed them any more with all those pockets. One Japanese car manufacturer paid us $100 000 a year to know what sort of heels would be on women's shoes in three years' time. Stilettos were one thing, but my real area of expertise was food: predicting new tastes and identifying products that would take off.

I didn't do client handling. I didn't do copy approval, creative direction or any kind of supervision. I was the fashionable creature at the heart of the 'creative economy'. God bless whoever it was that decided people like me shouldn't be shackled by everyday office routine. According to them, I needed to live in an unrestricted bohemian environment because I couldn't operate at my best in a nine-to-five situation. I wasn't even confined by a title. It might have limited my thinking. I did spend six regrettable months with 'Success

Catalyst' on my business card but that just goes to show even the best ideas guys have bad days.

I had to be out absorbing the public, creating new ways of reaching into their pockets and grabbing the contents. To justify my existence I had to come up with at least one brilliant, market-altering idea a year. Last year it was pre-bought frozen sandwiches. You bought a week's supply of frozen sandwiches, removed one from the freezer each day and took it to work. By lunchtime it was defrosted and beautifully fresh. I got a $50 000 bonus for that one. I sent my mother $15 000 because she used to send us to school with frozen sandwiches. I didn't suggest the clients use left-over soup as a sandwich filler like she did, but the concept was hers.

For all the dizzy success of frozen sandwiches, there were some things missing from my life. The easiest to define was my father. He was defined as a bastard—of the 'wasn't there' variety. I used to think the 'wasn't there' variety were the worst kind until I learnt the trouble they cause via their absence is nothing compared with the chaos they wreak when they do crash into your life. Mine must have felt he had a lot of catching up to do, showering me with havoc like a lifetime's birthday presents all at once. The other missing things, at this stage, were shoved into the too-hard basket. I wasn't planning on pulling them out, but I suppose it was inevitable they would emerge of their own accord eventually. Until that happened, I was content to sit at work, flicking through the post, waiting for genius to bless me.

Then, one day, halfway through my second cup of coffee, there it was—underneath an envelope containing 'great news' from *Reader's Digest*—an envelope from France. It was handwritten on airmail paper. I was amazed you could even get airmail paper any more (and noted it would be a great way of getting people to read a direct mail campaign). The address was written in an old-fashioned, neat hand with a slight shakiness. The back of the envelope had no name, just a return address in a town called St-Anastasie-sur-Issole. Quite a name, but it was a tiny village. In France the bigger the name, the smaller the town, probably something to do with the size of the mayor's dick.

Up to moment the letter arrived, I had no idea where the bastard (that's the preferred term of reference) was. He could have been living in New York. He could have been living in the apartment below me for all I knew of my neighbours, assuming he kept two large dogs and had a fondness for blasting out that Hawaiian ukulele version of 'Over the Rainbow'. But he wasn't. Even before I opened it, the envelope told me he was in France, and betrayed that I knew instantly it was from him.

I phoned my brother, Didier. He lived in London—four hours ahead. Usually he was too busy at work to talk. He worked for a charity—they're always the worst employers. You feel guilty if you don't slog your guts out and volunteer half your spare time. The rewards are supposed to be self-satisfaction and a free place in the afterlife of your choice. Yet everyone I know who works for non-profit organisations spends the little spare time they have bitching with an intensity that would have you booked into therapy in my firm. Then again, in New York, stepping in dog shit could have you booked into therapy.

Didier answered the phone.

'Dids, guess what I'm looking at?'

'Letter from St-Anastasie-sur-Issole. I got one too. I've been waiting for your call.'

'Have you opened yours?' I asked.

'No, wait up,' He put me on hold and I heard a message about how I could pay someone's winter heating bill by giving up a cup of coffee a day.

'I'm back.'

'Put me down for the cup of coffee thing. You've got my credit card number.'

'Pete, you don't have to…'

'I know I don't. I want to,' I lied. I did feel I had to.

'Fine.' He only said 'fine' when he was annoyed. We fell silent.

'So shall we?' I asked.

'OK.'

The envelope revealed one sheet of gossamer blue paper.

Mon cher Pierre

'Bastard's writing in French,' I said. I refused to acknowledge any understanding of the French language and my name wasn't Pierre, it was Peter.

'You'll have to translate,' I said to Didier. He didn't respond.

'Dids, what does it say?'

'Read it yourself.' He knew I could.

I had always mucked around in French at school and given the teachers hell. When we were learning vocab and the teacher would get the class to recite *'tant pis'*, I was the one who would pronounce the silent 's'. But somehow, in a complete surprise to my teachers and myself, I'd done well in my exams.

'Very puzzling, Peter, very puzzling,' said my teacher about my Northern Territory Certificate of Education French mark, as if she suspected cheating.

I didn't think of my father every time I wrote or spoke a word of French, but the connection was there. After school I made out I had forgotten all my French, but the words were stuck in my mind like stubborn stains. And while I whooped out loud when they bombed out of 2002 Soccer World Cup, in 1998 I'd secretly been a tiny bit proud.

There were few things I could hide from Didier and my French was not one of them. Still, I was determined to hold on to the myth and make Didier pretend too.

'I can't read the writing, it's dreadful. You read it.'

He began reading.

My dear Didier,

I am writing to both of you at the same time. Although you are in different countries, I hope this letter finds you simultaneously, and naturally in good health and happiness.

I understand this must be a shock for you. I make no excuses for not contacting you since my departure. It is inexcusable. Nothing could justify a man's neglect of his sons. My only wish is that your lives have been the better for the absence of someone as worthless as myself.

'He's laying it on a bit,' I commented.

He did a bunk when I was five. We lived in Croydon, Surrey, at the time; I don't really know why there in particular. Then after a few years, Marcel Noirelle sprinted off, leaving behind a mortgage, unpaid bills and a name that meant I got the shit kicked out of me. Noirelly Nelly. The first register at the start of each school year was always hell. The teacher would stumble over my name, everyone would snigger, then I'd correct the teacher and get into a fight at morning break. This happened every year without fail between the ages of five and fourteen.

'Nice' teachers would rehearse the name beforehand and tell off anyone who sniggered. Nice teachers should be shot on sight. There's no worse way to start off a school year than the teacher sticking up for you.

> *As I write, tears creep into my eyes and words evaporate. None are appropriate, none can excuse. Forgive me, not for the past, but for the present, for the incoherence of an old man confronting the greatest shame of his life.*

Vomit noises from the New York end of the line.

> *I shall be direct. I wish to see you, both of you, having attained the point when I can no longer watch time babble by. I wish for peace, to sleep soundly, and I cannot do that until I see you.*
>
> *Alas, what can I offer in return? Your heritage, perhaps. I talk not of money, but of the legacy of being a Noirelle. This is something that, regardless of your feeling for me, it is imperative you must know. Everyone should know their ancestry. If that much can be done, then I will not have failed completely as a father.*
>
> *Each day I await your visit with increasing impatience.*
>
> *Please agree to pass on my most distinguished sentiments to your mother.*
>
> *I kiss you both very strongly,*
>
> *Marcel Noirelle*

'He can just fuck off!' I was in no mood for reconciliation.

'It seems genuine. Quite beautiful.'

'Plu-eaze. What's with the whole "legacy" thing?'

'It's intriguing,' Didier said. 'Haven't you ever…'

'Don't fall for it; it's just a hook to get us interested. I've seen ads for Persian carpet sales that are more subtle than this. He knows he can't sell the touching reconciliation, "let me make up for the lost years," so he creates a whole different spiel to reel us in. That's the direct marketing done, we can wait for the print campaign to start.'

'Stop it, Pierre.' Didier knew how to silence me with one word—my 'official' French name. I didn't use it. 'Haven't you ever wondered about him? Isn't there anything you'd want to ask?'

'Nup. You want to go, don't you?' I asked.

'I'll only go with you.'

'I might be able to get some time off in a few…'

Didier interrupted. 'Don't pretend you couldn't catch the next flight and no one would bat an eye.'

'The pressure's on. I've got to come up with something big.'

That much was true: I hadn't found my market-altering idea for this year. Genius had not, as yet, slapped me across the face on the subway. So far I'd managed to fob the clients off with a few morsels to keep them happy. My last one was chocolate-flavoured Cheddar cheese ('it's like your favourite foods got married and the reception is in your mouth'). Sadly, when I tried the sample the divorce was loud, painful and in my intestines. The clients liked it but it wasn't going to lift the share price.

I told myself that this was what was missing from my life. I was frustrated at not finding this year's big idea. I tried to ignore the sneaking feeling it might be more than that. I refused to acknowledge that it could be anything more than being a little bored with my easy life. It's amazing what bizarre little negotiations you can have with yourself when you really don't want to think about something.

I pulled up Google on my computer and did a search on St Anastasie. It was in Provence.

'It's in the South of France. You really need me to go?' I didn't wait for a response. 'I could link it into an idea for one of our grocery clients.'

'I'll book flights for Marseille next week and write to him to let him know. All you have to do is get to London.'

I didn't answer. Didier knew me well enough to let me pretend I didn't have a choice. I waited for him to repeat himself and then mumbled, 'Use my card.'

He hung up before I changed my mind. I felt worked over. Didier was already colluding with him against me. He was going to manipulate me into some sick form of touching reconciliation. Didier was remorseless at seeing the good in people. But I wasn't.

I read the letter again for myself, making sure no one could see me. My father's eloquent words were a pretense even thinner than the airmail paper they were written on. He was hiding something.

'Typical,' I said to myself and then stopped. If I had no idea what he was like, how could anything be typical? I was annoyed at being annoyed and I was annoyed at the tiny quiver in my stomach. I refused to find an explanation. If I suggested it was the morning coffee I knew I would be lying. Ignoring it was the strongest option.

If I was going to pop over to France I'd have to run it past Hugo. In theory I could have gone off for two weeks' product meditation in Tibet without telling anyone, but it paid to keep people informed, especially Hugo. A few years ago he would have been my boss, but now the concept of a boss was far too limiting to my creative processes so I worked *with* Hugo, not *for* him. He was the Managing Director and a senior partner in the firm.

We had a good relationship, or as good a one as a man who has a shit load of money and the man who makes it for him can have. On the one hand, it was thanks to me he could afford to buy the single largest slab of granite ever imported from Indonesia to surface the vast kitchen benchtop in his Long Island retreat. On the other hand, I could always take my skills elsewhere or worse (and more likely) demand a partnership in the firm.

It was true, he gave me lots of money for not doing very much… but he gave himself a lot more for doing even less. So all-in-all there was a mutual appreciation backed up by a slow-burning wariness.

He liked to think he was at the forefront of trends, but his current preoccupation had long outstayed its fashionable status. He had vehemently predicted the paperless office a few years back. Instead of gracefully accepting defeat, he'd been determined to prove himself right, in his own office at least.

The design was simple but masculine. A few tasteful artworks, a credenza housing non-alcoholic beverages and a mini-fridge. In the middle of the room was a small but expensive L-shaped desk supporting two computers and a phone.

The computers were part of his 'competitive quotient' theory. He picked it up in India. Most people go there to find spiritual enlightenment—he found business theory. He explained it to me once by drawing a triangle (on screen) and showed how the quotient was the congruence of the right skills in the right place at the right time. He figured in New York right now, the skill to have was time-management. Apparently working on two computers at the same time increased his competitive quotient by four degrees.

He also upped his quotient by answering emails while he shaved in the morning. Efficient for emails, but not too efficient for shaving. This morning, as was often the case, he had a nick on his chin.

'Peter, five minutes, go,' he said. I was used to this process, so quickly stated my business.

'I'm off to London and then Provence to explore some food options for G&K.'

He tilted his head like a robot simulating human thought processes.

'Provence's been done to death,' he concluded.

'Yes, but it's a good place to start understanding gourmet food fads.'

G&K were our big grocery clients. They needed a new brand to characterise the best food available. Their existing brands were too mass market. They were losing the top end of their customer base to boutique food stores. Ash-rolled organic goat's cheese, homemade cevapcici—if it wasn't crafted by a blind grandmother in a stinking shed and delivered by Shetland pony, anyone with any real money wasn't interested. I was playing with the concept of 'mass boutique', communicating exclusivity while selling millions. I hadn't worked out how to do it yet, but when I did, it would be my big idea for the year. Normally my brain would worry away at the idea independently, coming up with 'creative solutions' in quiet moments, but this time round I had to make myself think about it.

'*Stimmt*,' Hugo said. It was German for 'I agree', but took less time to say.

'No pressure, but it's June and we haven't had anything big from you this year,' he added, trying to put me under pressure.

'No pressure at all.' I smiled and added, 'Faith!'

'Time's up.'

That was it. A group email to anyone that might be interested and I was booked onto a flight the following week. My biggest problem was how to stop myself thinking about the trip for the next few days. After all, I was completely indifferent and determined to prove it. My mind started working on an indifference quotient but got stuck somewhere between the congruence of material irrelevance and emotional impartiality.

I had known the minute Didier started reading the letter that we would go. Nobody really mulls over decisions. I think deep down everyone makes decisions instantly, they just spend time justifying them.

I persuaded myself I was going for Didier. It was what he wanted, and what Didier wanted, he got. Didier was incredible, so unsullied by the world. He was like some magic material that no matter how much dirt it got dragged through, it always stayed spotless. He made me feel like our old underpants that Mum used as dishcloths, absorbing filth from everywhere they wiped.

Didier had been too young to know what was going on when the bastard went or, more accurately, stopped coming back. Even I was really. My mother coped pretty well with Marcel's departure. That's how it seemed to me, but I suppose five-year-old boys aren't really that observant. She cried when the person who bought our car drove it away, saying it was because of all the lovely trips we had had in it. I didn't remember any lovely trips.

One night she didn't eat dinner with us.

'I'll have mine later,' she said and allowed us to pick up the chop with our fingers and gnaw all the meat off the bone. That evening I caught her wolfing down a peanut butter sandwich and looking longingly at the jar. She saw me and stopped herself eating an extra spoonful. Years afterward she explained to us that all the money she had on that day could only buy two chops. That was the lowest point she hit. After that we always referred to rock bottom in any situation as the 'two-chop point'. It galvanised her into action.

She moved Didier into my room, rented out his room, got a job and held everything together single-handedly. The first person to move into Didier's room was a student lodger who painted the walls black and helped stage the punk revolution from there. He was cool and I believed him when he said he had brought The Damned together. When Didier and I started spitting at people instead of saying hello, Mum decided he had to go.

It was a good move for us because, after a series of emotionally unstable student lodgers, it brought Frank into our house. Frank was Australian, working in London for a couple of years before he settled down. He seemed old to me—Mum's age. It didn't take long before she decided it was mine and Didier's turn to have a room each. She would share with Frank. We weren't fooled but we didn't mind. The main thing was we got our own rooms back.

It was around then that I decided I couldn't remember anything about my father. I suppose Frank might have filled the void, but then I didn't really have a sense of there being a void in my life. It wasn't like someone had torn down a wall of our bedroom and said, 'That's where your father used to be'.

I nearly used the 'you're not my real father' line with Frank once. I should have been using it all the time. That's what you're supposed to say to stepfathers, but he was never a stepfather, he was always Frank. It wasn't that I didn't want to hurt Frank—I managed that often enough—it's just the 'not my real father' weapon had no power.

Frank was a bastard too because he moved us back to Australia with him, and he lied to get our consent. He and Mum pitched the move on beaches and swimming. Sun, waves, surfing, the usual Australian thing. I should have checked the maps more thoroughly. Then I'd have known it was a long walk from Frank's house in Alice Springs to the beach. Admittedly, they did tell me Alice Springs was in the middle of Australia, but London was in the middle of England and you could still get to the coast in a few hours.

That evening Peony was meant to spend the night at my place, but she cancelled due to work. So I was home alone on the Upper West Side. The location sounds far more impressive than it actually is. Just because you're within walking distance of Central Park doesn't mean you've got views. Which makes it all the harder to distract yourself from what you don't want to think about. I decided to focus on Peony and work out what was going on there. It was the first time I had ever done this and a clear sign she'd dropped a spot on the 'don't want to think about this' top ten.

It was easiest to call Peony my girlfriend, but that made our relationship sound too formal. She was an assistant attorney with the Unlicensed Drivers' Unit at the District Attorney's office in New York, or DANY as it was known.

We'd been seeing each other for about four months, which is one month after the usual make-or-break hurdle. I usually got dumped before then: too uncommitted; too keen; too gentle in bed; too aggressive. I was even too happy once; she wanted someone who understood the true misery of life. Getting dumped is no big deal for a man in New York. You collect your reasons like badges of honour. It's hard to tell which you hear most often here: men moaning 'I got dumped again' or women complaining about the lack of single men.

It didn't bother me. I wasn't prowling the streets panting for commitment. If I met someone I enjoyed being with, I wanted to be with them. If it stopped being more satisfying than being on my own, I didn't see the point of continuing. I hadn't got that far with Peony. I didn't think I ever would. We hadn't even reached the 'where are we going' conversation. I wasn't going to start it and she was always too busy. What she needed from me was a bottle of wine, a good laugh and sex.

During her phone call to cancel our evening's get-together, I did unwittingly reach a relationship milestone. I made a lame joke about her having an affair with Danny. It seems everyone who works at DANY gets the joke from their partner at some stage.

'Does that mean we're serious?' I asked.

'Maybe.'

'I'm leaving the country next week,' I said and she laughed. 'No seriously I am… I've got to go to Europe for work and I'm calling into London to see my brother.'

'Oh,' she said with a hint of disappointment before recovering quickly. 'I thought maybe you'd dodged a fare on the subway again and wanted to run from justice.'

Our 'relationship' had nearly ended before it started when I admitted to having jumped the barrier at the West 96th Street station on the way to our first date. I'd lost my weekly ticket and was running late so I dashed through the side gate as it was buzzed open for a woman with child in pushchair. I thought nothing of it until I told Peony my excuse for being late. She held my gaze in a vice-like grip as she reached slowly for her phone. I must have smiled the right smile, looked contrite or cute or something, because she relented and decided not to report me. She did fine me five dollars on the spot, which she gave to the next street beggar she passed.

'No,' I said, 'I just robbed a bank this time. Look this trip, I…'

Some sort of explanation was required, I thought, even if it was just to say I'd booked it before the DANY milestone comment. I didn't get time to give one.

Another call came through for her and she was plunged back into the mind-numbing pressure of prosecuting driving misdemeanours by people without a valid driving licence.

Nobody would ever make a TV series out of her job. There were no desperate gun battles through the streets to apprehend notorious red-light jumpers. No media scrums to face after a day of sensational evidence in court.

I think I was Peony's all too infrequent escape from her work. Something that was nothing to do with traffic citations. I didn't even have a car. She liked that; no risk of professional compromise if I second-guessed those tricky lights on the corner of Broadway and 93rd. Peony was committed to her work.

For me, she was a connection with the real world and what was truly important. Her life might have been dedicated to bringing unlicensed drivers to blind justice, but it seemed so much more useful than what I did.

DANY kept her busy right up to the night before I was due to depart. We spoke on the phone and I managed to sneak downtown to have coffee with her, but the time we had was so short I didn't get to tell her the real reason for the trip. Even on the night before I left, with my suitcase standing in the living room, I still didn't lay the whole father thing on her. It was part of my strategy of not thinking about it.

'Should I be bothered, upset or something?' she asked. I looked puzzled.

'Aren't girlfriends supposed to be suspicious when their boyfriends take sudden trips without them?'

'Possibly,' I answered, 'but we've never taken a trip together. Do you feel annoyed?'

'Hell, no…I'm no good at this.' I think she meant relationships. 'If my mother found out about you…'

'What about me?' I sensed a 'where are we going' talk and for once almost welcomed it.

She smiled and shook her finger. I wasn't going to get the distraction. 'Believe me, you don't want my mother in this.'

Her thought process shifted to a subpoena she had forgotten to lodge, then she succumbed to the workings of my fingers. Peony had white skin. Didn't believe in sunbathing, didn't have time for it if she had. It was so pure and incredibly soft. I could run my finger down her arm and see it turn red under the pressure, like a pink comet.

I was massaging her neck as we sat in bed. She liked being massaged and relaxed quickly. Peony didn't have time to ease into it. The muscles were rock solid one moment and like jelly the next. She was asleep. I grabbed the glass of wine resting precariously on her thigh. She could fall asleep during anything: dinner, a movie, sex—anything that stopped her thinking about work could trigger sleep.

Peony had once told me that when she fell asleep during sex, I should carry on. Apparently she enjoyed it. The one time I tried it, I didn't. Apart from the blow to my lovemaking prowess, I needed an active participant. The noises she made—a bizarre cross between a snore and a groan—were signs of pleasure but I couldn't help wondering who I was transformed into in her sleep. All up, it wasn't an ego-nurturing experience.

I wasn't in the mood for sex that night but it was good to have her in the bed with me. When the phone rang she didn't even stir. I assumed she was fast asleep.

It was my mother doing one of those telepathically well-timed calls that mothers do. Another part of the failing 'don't think about it' strategy was not calling her. I'd sort of planned to tell her about the trip from Didier's place. He could do the justifying and I'd toss in the bitter jibes so she wouldn't feel betrayed.

Mum still lived in Alice Springs, getting weirder by the day. Her unique selling point was that she got more interesting as she got older. Of late she had passed interesting, was charging through kooky and aiming for deranged. She figured that when the time came for her to go into a home (she had no illusions about us looking after her), a mental health institute was better than a nursing home.

'They have better gardens,' she reasoned.

Frank had died a couple of years ago, taking his wonderfully calming influence with him. She was a dog off the leash now, heading straight for the flowerbeds to wreak havoc.

In her mind she was heading to the Northern Territory parliament. For the last ten years she had stood as an independent candidate in each Territory election. Every time she stood for a different issue. Three elections ago, she was the sole candidate for the Voluntary Euthanasia Party. Then it was Repeal Mandatory Sentences. Last election it was Legal Recognition of Gay and Lesbian Relationships. It was always a good radical cause because that would really piss the neighbours off. I suspect that was the primary purpose: making the Blenkinsaws confront 'Die with dignity' or 'My son is gay; what about your child?' banners during the elections. They were always worded so Mr Blenkinsaw could take it personally.

Mr Blenkinsaw would hobble to the middle of the road, stop, pretend to look at the banner for the first time, feign fury and hobble marginally less slowly to our side of the road. He'd look up again, as if he couldn't believe what he saw, clamber up the two steps and hammer as best he could on the flyscreen.

'Why do you always have to ram your politics down our throats?' As soon as he uttered that line, the election was truly underway.

Mum was gifted at attention-seeking publicity stunts. At the mandatory sentencing election, she had officially handed over the front garden to the traditional Aboriginal owners of the land. There had been a smoking ceremony and the local press had taken some pictures. Some of Mum's Aboriginal friends agreed to send their kids round to wear handcuffs on the lawn for a couple of hours to accentuate the fact that youths were being sent to prison for very minor offences.

For her gay rights election, she got permission from the traditional, and now current owners, of her front lawn to stage a same-sex kiss-in. The same Aboriginal kids came round and kissed each other on the lips. A few genuine gay men and lesbians also popped round for obvious displays of affection. That year Mr Blenkinsaw did not come round to issue the official 'ramming down our throats' line. His wrath was so great it had to be delivered by telephone. Mum recorded it on her answering machine, called me and left it on my machine too. No message from her, just Mr Blenkinsaw's apoplectic rage. It made me strangely homesick.

She never got elected. If the Territory government was really unpopular she'd get up to sixty votes, but normally she hovered around the twenty mark.

Despite her allusions to kookiness and political power, Mum's mind could be razor sharp. Within thirty seconds of talk, she knew something was up.

'Peter, what is it? You obviously want to tell me something, because if you didn't want to you'd hide whatever's bothering you better than this. What've you done now?'

'I haven't done anything!' I had to say that; I think it's a genetically coded reaction to that question. 'We both got a letter from the bastard and we're… sort of going to see him.'

'Oh. Right. When?' I could hear her lips pursing across the world.

'I'm flying to London tomorrow.'

'When did the letter come?'

'Um, last week.'

'Like shit off a shovel! You're not wasting time. He's still got it then!'

I didn't know what she meant. Apparently he was always able to get people running after him. She wasn't angry about us visiting, more resigned to the fact that it would happen at some stage.

'Still saying you don't remember anything?'

'I don't.'

'Fine.' She used 'fine' like Didier did, like we all did.

'Just be careful,' she added, so I promised to look after Didier.

'It's *you* I'm worried about. It'll be hardest for you.'

'Why would it?'

She sighed. We didn't talk about the bastard—he didn't live in our comfort zone.

'Don't go expecting answers to anything. He's…he's…' She was struggling.

'Not too fond of truth?' I offered.

'He'll flirt with it, like he does with everything else.'

As I heard her speak about him in the present tense, I realised he was leaping out of the past. History was coming alive.

'He's all charm.'

'What?' I was shocked that she was paying him a compliment.

'No, literally. There isn't much besides the charm.'

'How come you never saw through him before you married him?'

The question came out before I could stop it. I didn't want to ask about him.

'I did!' she said. 'I knew he was an inveterate charmer, but it was 1970—I was all shaved armpits and tight-fitting bras. When I thought I saw a glimpse of a vulnerable boy under all that charm, it was like a red flag to a bull. I was his woman and I was going to rescue him.'

'Did you?'

She laughed; paused for a moment. 'He makes… he makes life rich. Everything seemed brighter, food tasted better. He can make you believe that life is pure joy, and then he's gone and life seems…dull.'

'Mum,' I didn't know what to say.

'The best rides at the funfair always end before you want to get off.'

Mum's conversation put paid to any sleep that night. Who was he, why bother contacting us and why was I lying awake at 3 a.m. over someone I couldn't care less about? I must have fallen asleep eventually because I dreamed about him.

In the morning Peony kissed me goodbye breezily as she shot out on her way to work. In a minute she was back, knocking on the door (we hadn't exchanged keys).

'I should've given you a bigger goodbye. I'm not dumb. I know this is no business trip.' She hugged me before I could respond. 'Do what you have to do.' She took my hand in both of hers in an almost motherly way. 'Take care, you hear!'

Then she was off to ensure those guilty of running red lights without a licence felt the full wrath of New York justice. I was touched. Perhaps the DANY joke really was a milestone.

Flying to London was weird for me. I'd always thought of it as home, but I hadn't lived there since I was fourteen. We'd both changed, and London, as much as I wanted to belong, made me feel like a foreigner.

I had to take some responsibility for our family leaving London and moving to Alice Springs. I was allegedly 'going off the rails'. All I did was bunk off school with Andrew Holland and get Asda-pissed (that was getting cans of home-brand lager from the supermarket, Asda, and drinking them in the multi-storey car park). Then we lay across the car park exit so no one could get out. Andrew Holland got grounded for one week. I got transported to Australia—I think his parents were a bit soft.

That incident was the deciding factor in our departure. Frank had to move back because his visa was expiring. He couldn't stay in Britain for any longer without marrying our mum. Mum said she couldn't get divorced because the bastard had vanished. In reality I don't think she wanted to remarry anyway. She was over identifying as a wife and mother.

My mother had already been thinking positively about the move to Australia and when I revealed myself to be on the fast track to a life of drugs and crime (I omitted the third key element of getting

Asda-pissed—shoplifting the sixpack), that was it. Decision made, bags packed, Qantas flight boarded.

It couldn't have come at a worse time. I was fourteen and had just got over being 'foreign' in Croydon. My name was almost accepted, I was finally 'from here', when suddenly I was plunged into 'get back to your own country' territory again. In Croydon I had stunk because, according to everyone in my primary school, the French didn't wash. In Alice I was English and I still stunk because now Poms didn't wash.

I didn't belong. I knew then I would always be a dirty foreigner. Luckily I ended up living in New York, where everybody was a dirty foreigner. Nobody cared where I came from, and the crazier my background the better. In New York I was a citizen of the world and I didn't stink. The city did that by itself, especially in summer.

I suppose it's the dirty foreigner in me that makes me good at what I do—the perennial outside observer. People get excited by fads and trends. I don't; I think it's all crap. I can just tell which crap has got legs and which hasn't.

The timing of my flight meant I could arrive at Heathrow, grab a cab and get to Didier's workplace in the afternoon to pick him up. I liked to think I knew London well, but actually I didn't. I wanted to be able to argue with the driver about the quickest route but I couldn't. The driver's friendly question, 'So where are you from?' reminded me quickly I was a foreigner here too.

While I'd moved to New York to be a trend-spotting whiz, Didier had gone back to London as soon as possible. He used his British citizenship to get into uni there, fell in love with a doctor and stayed. He was dedicating his virtuous life to good works. Everyone knew he'd take life in his stride. There was a calmness about Didier. Mum said he slept so still when he was a baby that we had to turn his head from side to side so his soft skull wouldn't get squashed flat.

Didier's office was in Farringdon. He worked for FHC. It was an HIV charity. The letters stood for the Faith Hope Charity. It wasn't a Christian thing, it had been named after a drag queen, Faith Hope, who had died with AIDS. She had amassed quite a fortune in her years as a drag performer and left the money to establish a fund to help people with HIV. FHC (the drag roots were downplayed now) ran support groups and information for positive gay men, education programs on safe sex, self-esteem and good health. Didier was gay with a capital G. I don't mean he was flamboyant, colourful or musical. Quite the opposite; but he lived and breathed being gay. It was a bit hard not to when you worked for FHC and lived in a lesbian cooperative.

I liked going to FHC. There's no bigger ego trip than being a straight brother in a gay office. There's something about a straight brother that gets gay men going. I think it's a joke to get at the gay one, or something about the unobtainable. Didier got his own back with my female friends who made comments like, 'He's so sweet… like you, only nice'.

When I walked into FHC, initially I didn't get much more than a second glance. The receptionist, deep in an important phone conversation, looked at me to say 'your presence has been registered' and continued, 'I tell you it was the blond one… no, not the dumpy one, the pretty boy and he was begging for it… just a moment. Yes?'

'I'm Peter, Didier's brother.' It had the expected effect. The disconnect button was pressed before the words 'call you back' were even uttered.

'I've heard about you... I see you got the looks gene instead of the gay one. Never mind... it is nurture sometimes, not nature.' He winked.

'Just wait a moment there, sir. Let me track him down for you.'

The headset went back on. The receptionist bypassed Didier's voicemail and went straight for the building-wide announcement.

'Didier Noirelle, very attractive man for you in reception, says he's your brother. Come and claim him... before I do.'

Within a minute Didier had shot into reception and glowered at the receptionist.

'Colin, d'you have to be such a stereotype?'

'D'you have to be such a role model?' he retorted.

Didier laughed quickly then grabbed my arm and led me out of the building as fast as possible.

We didn't mention the letter until we were both safely in a cab, cut off from the world and stuck in traffic. There was only one thing for us to talk about and I wasn't going to start.

'The flights are booked, we leave from Stansted. I figured five nights there. If it's unbearable we can bail out.'

'Cool,' I answered.

'Any more thoughts?'

'On what?'

'Don't do this, Peter. We can't just not talk about it.'

He was right; he was always right.

'I know. Let me ease into it, okay? Shit, this traffic.'

It was a short drive from Farringdon through Islington and along Upper Street to Didier's place. Short at four in the morning. At four in the afternoon it was a slow crawl.

At the Angel I looked around, trying to decide if it looked any different from the last time I was there. There was supposed to be a new shopping centre and cinema complex, but I couldn't actually see them.

'If we go right up Essex Road we could head to Clissold Park, where Richard's tree is. We haven't spoken for a couple of weeks and the traffic's jammed on Upper Street anyway.'

I was puzzled, then realised he wasn't referring to me but to Richard, or possibly even the tree. One was dead and the other was a plant, so either way a tough conversation.

'Dids… I don't want to rush in, look at it and sprint off. I'd rather go and have a picnic, spend some time.'

Didier nodded in agreement. As if to prove me right, the traffic jam dissolved as a London jam does. As we drove past the turn-off to Essex Road, he looked back, as if watching someone walk away. Sometimes I hate the fact I always have a ready answer.

Richard was Didier's partner. That's the word he used: partner. He was the doctor Didier fell in love with, only he'd been a final-year medical student when they met. Within a year, they were living together. He seemed a nice, intelligent guy. A bit too controlling, I reckoned. He made all the decisions. The things *he* did became the things *we* did. Maybe I was jealous. I'd been shunted down to the number two spot in the top ten most important men in Didier's life, but he was still number one with me.

Within two years Richard was diagnosed with AIDS. Another year and he was dead—it was before, just before, all the treatments. I only saw Richard once towards the end. I had known what to expect—I had seen photos and that Benetton ad campaign in the '90s, so it wasn't a shock. What I wasn't prepared for was Didier. Here was my kid brother, lifting Richard, wiping his arse, juggling medicines, bills, food, cleaning and more bills. He looked so terrible I thought that he must have it too. I was angry and scared and I blamed Richard.

Didier wasn't HIV-positive, he was just exhausted. I did my usual—helped out by paying bills. Didier was grateful, sort of. He was too drained to make a song and dance about electricity.

I didn't go the funeral. I was too angry at the corpse. All I could picture was Didier wiping Richard's bum and I hated him for that. Didier never said anything to me. Perhaps he understood. I didn't dare ask.

He had a tree planted in Clissold Park, not far from where he lived now, and scattered Richard's ashes amongst the roots. I'd never visited the tree. Every time I was in London Didier gently tried to get me to go but I always got out of it. If I did visit I would have pissed on it. I couldn't let Didier see that.

Richard was the perfect partner. I pitied the guys that tried to compete after him. There were lots of them but no one got anywhere. Didier's relationships lasted about as long as mine, only it was he who did the dumping.

🌳

'Oh...it's you.' Didier's flatmate gave me her usual greeting as we walked into their apartment.

'Be a doll, make us a cup of tea, sweetheart,' I smiled.

'Nothing's changed then.'

You could call Caryn a lesbian man-hater. I always did. She hated me and I was a man, ergo...but I was the *only* man she hated, with the possible exception of her father. That one point in common had not been enough for us to establish a friendship.

She had been a volunteer helper when Richard was ill. After he died, she and Didier ended up moving in together as flatmates. She had been a great friend to him, probably better than me. *Definitely* better than me. When I first met her, after Richard's death, she was sitting at the kitchen table reading the paper. She wore rectangular black-framed glasses with pointy outside corners. Caryn looked hard at me above the rims and then returned her eyes to the paper without a word. She had all the proof she needed.

'So,' Caryn said, sitting herself like a therapist in the living-room armchair, 'you're off to see him then. What does your mother think?'

'We haven't told her yet,' Didier mumbled.

'Actually, she called me…she's okay about it.'

The brief 'Oh' from Didier indicated that perhaps I should have mentioned it before now.

'Are you expecting some big male-bonding thing, Peter?' Caryn asked.

'I'd love to chat, Caryn, but Didier and I have a lot to talk about before we go. We haven't much time.'

'Fair enough.' She got up and walked off to the kitchen.

Didier and I sat still. Neither of us had any idea where to start. I'd just said we had lots to sort out to avoid Caryn's interrogation.

'So what have you been thinking?' I put the onus on Didier.

'I've been quite busy. I suppose I pushed it out of my mind.'

'Look,' I said, 'what's to talk about? We go see him, get this family history thing and push off. I thought we could have a night or two in St Tropez, it's not far. Have a retro '70s chic sort of thing, fry ourselves silly on the beach and get invited onto a oil sheik's yacht.'

'Remember that time you talked us into the *Moulin Rouge* launch after party?'

We giggled. We had held a race of the sexualities to see who could get a come on from the most people. Points were awarded for celebrities and double points for minor TV personalities desperately seeking publicity. Didier had won six to two.

The frivolous reminiscing was interrupted by Caryn wheeling in a whiteboard with a roll of butcher's paper tucked under her arm and a wicker shopping basket full of marker pens, blank labels and sundry stationery.

'I knew this would happen. The two of you are going on the most challenging journey of your life and you think giggling about the old times is all you need to get ready. Well, it's not, and Didier, you know better. It's his fault.' She moved round to point at me with the butchers paper. 'You're dealing with enormous issues, so big you can't even start to comprehend them. I'm going to make sure you do, even if I have to facilitate you to within an inch of your lives. Right, let's do this properly.'

She pulled out a roll of blank labels, wrote Caryn on one, peeled it off and slapped it onto her chest. She passed the roll and the pen to Didier.

'I think we know who we are,' I said.

'It's about process.' Caryn stood with her hands on her hips as Didier slapped a label with my name and a flower drawn on it onto my shirt. I had been ambushed.

'Did you know this was going to happen?' I asked Didier.

'We keep an emergency workshop kit. Never know when a crisis might need processing.'

He put his label on and settled down, smiling at Caryn. She smiled back. This was their territory.

'Right. My name's Caryn. Let's establish some parameters.'

Thirty minutes later I was sitting cross-legged on the floor, trying to list my hopes for the visit. I was supposed to be honest. Caryn looked at my blank sheet and assured me I was in a safe environment. Didier was furiously covering his piece of paper with lots of different coloured words. I started to write some down.

Caryn summarised some of our hopes on the board. Didier had:

There's some sort of recognition
Forgiveness
Explanations
Regret
Some physical resemblance
Peace
Fun

I had:

Let him know he's a bastard
Score this year's big idea
Get away quickly
Didier doesn't get upset

He leaned over and squeezed my hand at that last one. Caryn said it was okay to be negative—I was being honest and that was really important.

Next came the playdough. Caryn made us fashion our father in playdough.

'It doesn't have to be figurative, doesn't have to be human. Just whatever sums him up for you right now.'

I started making a face. For a split second I tried to remember what he looked like, but it didn't work. Art had never been my strong point and I ended up with something that looked like a teapot.

Didier had made a little round paddling pool.

'Mum said it was the last thing he bought for us,' he explained. 'When it was up in the garden in Croydon, I used to look at the still water and try to see his reflection, so I could see what he looked like. But I never could. I couldn't remember him.'

He looked at his empty pool again and I was back there, in Croydon, watching him dip his finger in the water. I had always thought he was watching clouds in the reflected sky.

'Do you remember him?' Caryn asked me.

'No...some vague things, but no.'

'What did he look like?' she asked.

'We don't know,' answered Didier. 'There are no photos of him.'

'None at all?' said Caryn. 'That's weird.'

She was right. There had been none around the house in Croydon. Mum used to show us photos of when we were little, and talk about him having taken this one or that one, or why he liked the photo of us sitting on the bonnet of the car in particular. But he was never in them.

Years later in Alice, I had asked if we had a photo of him. We didn't. Mum said all the photos of him were in the box of lost things. When we went to Australia, a box went missing in the move. From toys to photos to clothes, it was crammed with a wide range of things that all vanished. I imagined it floating in the ocean somewhere—the box of lost things.

'D'you think she got rid of them?' Didier asked. It seemed a logical explanation, except our mother was never interested in pretending the bastard didn't exist. Getting rid of his photos wasn't something she would do. Frank would never have dared throw anything out. It was strange. If he had refused to be in any photos, Mum would have mentioned something about it. *Someone* must have got rid of them all.

'Right. Role-play.' Caryn ended the discussion and moved on.

The role-play didn't go well. I was my father, Caryn was me, Didier was to observe.

'You're a complete shit!' Caryn fired off before I had even said, 'Hello, son'.

'Have we started?' I looked to Didier. He nodded.

'Yes, I am,' I answered her, trying to assume character.

'There were so many times I wanted to speak to you. Wanted you to take me in your arms and tell me everything was okay. You weren't there, you weren't there.' She sank to her knees in front of me and started beating her fists on my thighs.

'I hate you, I hate you, I hate you.'

I stepped backwards, retreating from her pummelling. She shuffled forward on her knees with every step I took back. She chased me back into the whiteboard, knocking it and me to the floor. Tears poured down Caryn's face as I was pinned against the board, wiping it clean with the back of my shirt. She continued to pound my thighs.

Didier came over to bring her arms to rest. She turned to him and sobbed into his shoulder. Suddenly she stood up and said to me, 'You're a cold bastard, you really are.'

We didn't sleep much that night. I was on the floor in Didier's room. Normally we talked when I stayed there. But our chat was foiled by the current David. So many of the men that had become besotted with Didier since Richard had been called David that I'd stopped learning individual names. He could have started a monastery, full of men dedicating their lives to him, all inspired to good works and all called David.

Caryn said Didier was 'boyfriend material'. Every guy he met wanted to settle down, no matter how casual he tried to make it. Didier just wanted fun and sex. He didn't need a relationship, he said. He had Caryn for that: except for the sex, they were like an old married couple…actually, they were *exactly* like an old married couple.

The current David had discovered Didier was heading off to France and had insisted on coming round to play a role in 'our family drama'. He had greeted me with a hug.

'You're so brave going to see Dad like this. Both of you, I'm really proud of you.'

I felt this was a bit too intimate for a first meeting, even for someone from New York where 'Hi, I'm Cheyne, I was abused as a child,' is an acceptable greeting.

The current David grabbed Didier's hand as well as mine and was squeezing us both. I tried to be polite.

'Thanks, Dave, that means a lot.'

'My name's Andrew,' he said.

Didier asked for some time alone with him in his room before I came to bed. I assumed he had to fob him off with some sex. I didn't mind. It was better than him getting horny and trying to do the silent groping thing while I was in there.

After an hour, Didier crept out of the room to explain the situation.

I was wrong. The David wasn't being porked, he was being dumped, very gently, very lovingly, very definitely. It had been on the cards for a while, but the hugging and pride in the kitchen had sealed his fate.

Didier had banked on the David storming off immediately, leaving the room to us. In a rare instance of poor judgment, he got it wrong. The David was insisting on one final night together.

'D'you want me to sleep on the sofa in the living room?' I asked.

'No!' Didier looked alarmed. 'If you're in the room, he'll behave.'

It was a restless night. As I lay on my mattress on the floor, all was quiet on the bed, until a great moan rose like a tsunami and crashed into torrents of sobbing which gradually ebbed into silence.

They were followed by some shuffling in the bed and Didier whispering an assertive 'No'.

'Just one last time, please.'

'No.'

Silence again. I could feel my mind wandering into those bizarre nonsense thoughts that come as you begin to fall asleep when the next round of sobbing began. I can stand having my falling asleep process interrupted twice, but my brain has a 'three strikes and you're awake' policy. The third strike came with the next wave of sobbing.

I switched on the light, made him get dressed, marched him out into the street and flagged down a taxi.

'You're pathetic,' I said to him as I shut him in the cab. 'No wonder you got dumped.' Sometimes the kindest thing you can do is let people think you're a complete shit.

In the morning we were too dazed by lack of sleep to think of anything other than getting to the airport and onto the plane. I hadn't dreamed about my father. I hadn't dreamed about anything. I was just haunted by the sound of the David's sobbing.

As we left the apartment, Caryn took hold of my arm. 'Look after him.'

I nodded in response.

'And yourself,' she added.

'Of course.' I shrugged my shoulders. Caryn pressed her lips together. I think I'd brushed off a nice gesture. It doesn't matter how good you are at reading people, there's always someone you get wrong. 'Sorry.'

Just as the cab began to pull off, Caryn virtually threw herself on the bonnet. I wound down the window.

'Here... I found this on the floor as I was going back in, it must have come this morning.'

She handed through a thick envelope with a French stamp on it, addressed to Didier.

It contained several typewritten sheets. The paper was old and yellowed and it had been written on a real typewriter. All I could read at the top was: *St Hubert, Provence 1894.*

Along with the sheets was another letter from Marcel, again on airmail paper, which seemed a bit silly given all the other paper, but I was still in my flirtation with airmail paper as a marketing concept so I didn't mind.

The letter was addressed to Didier and someone called Pierre. Didier read it out to me anyway.

My dear Pierre and Didier,
With what delight I learned that you will be rendering a visit to me. As I write tears of gratitude flow freely down my cheeks. I am not deserving of this great honour but I will endeavour without cease to ensure your stay with us will be as enjoyable and fruitful as is possible.

Perhaps you would like to start learning of your past. Our family has a colourful history of which you could be proud. In a moment of arrogance I began to write our story down, imagining great things... alas, the great things remain in the past and possibly the future, but not in my ignoble present. This is my poor attempt to tell the story of your great-grandfather as I learned it from those who went before me.

I await your arrival with growing excitement and, if I may say, a little apprehension.

I kiss you both very strongly,
Marcel Noirelle

Didier turned the page over to see if there was any useful information. He'd gone into full travel-organisational mode.

'He doesn't say whether he'll be meeting us. I gave him the flight details. I did book a hire car just in case and I've downloaded a road map of how to get there.'

'The man's mad, that's the second lot of tears we've had—and who's "us". He's not alone. And a story, for God's sake! Must say he's running a good campaign, softening us up before we even get there. Smart.'

'I think it's fantastic. This is our great-grandfather.'

'We don't even know if he's telling the truth.'

Didier rolled his eyes.

At the airport, Didier performed a brutal act of collaboration with the enemy. Pretending to be going off to the toilet, he photocopied the story so we could both read it. On the plane he steadfastly engrossed himself in its pages, refusing to respond to my attempts at conversation. He left me no option but to join in.

ST HUBERT, PROVENCE 1894

Where does legend end and history begin? Perhaps it is where living memory fades into stories of the dead. That misty place is where this story begins. It begins with my grandfather, Claude, and the scent of lavender as I raise a long-dried but headily fragrant posy to my nose.

They laughed when Claude first gave his farm entirely over to lavender. He was too far south, they said, lavender was grown further north. They were wrong. Claude's lavender flourished. His fields were out of the village, higher up the mountains where the land was not so steep. In a large gap in the pine forest there were sunny sheltered fields of purple. Seasons came and went and Claude sold every sprig of lavender he could grow. The land was good, his plants were strong, he was blessed.

His house was in St Hubert, a small village in the hills of Chaine de la St Baume. There were no level streets in St Hubert, everything was either up or down. The slopes were good for everyone's legs. St Hubert was renowned (among its own residents) for well-shaped legs.

It began with Claude, if what was said in the village was true. But if everything that was said in the village was true, then a woman in Brignoles once gave birth to a pig and trees could swallow people.

He was known to be one of the more prosperous farmers but it was not for his lavender that Claude was talked about. It certainly wasn't for his singing. He loved singing. He sang in the church and lost his voice in that of the choir. No one had any problem finding it for him—half a note below everyone else's. They tolerated it because they liked Claude, and felt a little sorry for him.

When a new priest, Father Bonnet, came to the village, he did not feel sorry for Claude. God deserved only the finest voices so Claude was ousted from the choir. Father Bonnet gave him something even better however. He accompanied Claude on his next visit to his buyers in Marseille and bought him a ticket to the Opera Municipal.

The opera was *La Forza del Destino*. Claude was lost once again—the grandeur, the passion and most of all the singing. His voice joined in, following the notes and sounds if not the words. The priest tapped him and put a finger to his lips. Claude learned to soar on the inside.

As he left the theatre, he carried the music in his head like a bucket brimming with water. As he and Father Bonnet rode back to St Hubert the next day, he refused to talk and blocked his ears as he tried not to spill a drop on the journey. He carried it back with him to sing in his lavender fields. There, no one could say his voice didn't soar with the birds.

From then on, every time he went to Marseille, Claude would visit the Opera. He timed his visits to their seasons, determined to be awash with music and to remember as many tunes as he could to sing in the fields.

Walking through lavender fields singing might seem a happy life, but it wasn't, for Claude was best known in the village for his lack of a wife. He met many young girls, danced with them at fêtes, and they were drawn to him but something always went amiss.

He was young, not unattractive, with a good income and the St Hubert legs. In short, a catch, and he wanted to be caught. He was like a fish leaping from the river into the fisherman's net, only to find there was a hole that returned him immediately to the water.

Virtually every girl in the village had considered Claude as a possible partner before they found their actual husband. Either his sweetheart's head would be turned by another man, or her parents would move away and insist on taking her, or she simply lost interest. Whenever he neared the point of proposal, everything fell through.

He was afraid it was his destiny.

'Pah,' said his mother, Mère Noirelle, 'you just don't want it enough. Women like to rescue their men, from wine or from a dirty house. You don't need rescuing.'

'I might need rescuing from loneliness,' he offered.

'Pah,' she answered, but she knew what he needed rescuing from was her. The two of them lived alone. His father was long dead and Claude had been their only child. Outside the bedroom she fulfilled all the duties of a wife. He couldn't cope without her, yet he might not marry while she was still there.

'He's trapped,' she muttered to herself and resolved to get him married.

When Claude announced he was seeing a new girl, Mère Noirelle realised what he must do.

'Say nothing to her. Flirt with her. Let her know you desire her, but don't talk of love or the future. When she turns around in a fit of tears and hates you for no reason, come and tell me immediately.'

It happened soon enough. He'd been teasingly trying to kiss her as he normally did, when suddenly she slapped him and ran off crying.

'Good,' said Mère Noirelle. 'Now wait.'

For four weeks he waited, until the village fête.

'Son, at the fête, you and she must drink plenty of wine. Take her somewhere quiet, kiss her here.' She pointed to the spot behind her ear that had first induced her to succumb to Claude's father. 'Put your hand here... and seduce her.'

'Mother!'

'Do it or die a bachelor'.

At the fête he did as he was told and made love to the girl, Celline. Seduction is easy with a mother's guidance.

It worked. Celline fell pregnant. Her father demanded her seducer marry her. Claude was jubilant.

At his wedding feast he joyously announced he had beaten fate. It drew some sharp looks. They said in the village that no good came from cheating fate.

They *did* a lot of saying in the village. In most villages you never knew who they were. However in St Hubert they were Madame de Beaumarchais, the wife of the publican, and Madame Dupont who owned a small shop stocked with a variety of unnecessary goods. Madame de Beaumarchais' daughter, Yvette, tried to join in, but it would take years before she had the necessary wisdom of her elders.

'They say Claude Noirelle is bringing a fate worse than being unmarried on his head,' said Madame Dupont.

'Yes, I heard only misery will come from tricking fate,' Madame de Beaumarchais agreed.

'Yes, they say she will miscarry,' tried Yvette and was chastised for malicious gossip.

Yvette was wrong and the others were right. Celline gave birth to twin boys, Raymond and Alphonse, but died in the process. Claude was back where he had started but with two sons and his grief to nurse.

A wet nurse was found to feed the boys. An unmarried mother, she'd lost her own child and so loved the twins as her own. They were no ordinary twins, she noted. They cried at the same time, wet themselves at the same time and refused to sleep if they were not in the same cot.

'Like one soul in two bodies,' she foolishly announced in the shop.

They looked at each other. No good would come of it.

The wet nurse was not the most attractive of women, but Claude's mother saw the advantages of an official union. It would be cheaper than paying her and then she could keep house as well. For the nurse it was a step up in life. Marrying Claude meant keeping warm in winter.

They married. She died. She slipped on one of the many steep slopes in the village and rolled all the way down it, coming to a violent rest against a rock. Mère Noirelle cursed the nurse's weakness. She wasn't from St Hubert and didn't have the legs.

'Why, I've slipped a dozen times and lived. The women of today, they're simpering princesses, dying at the drop of hat.'

Now everyone in St Hubert was repeating what they said: Claude was cursed because he'd defied his fate.

'Pah!' said Mère Noirelle. 'Go to Marseille and come back married, and make sure she's strong this time!'

He came back with Giselle.

'What kind of a name is that?' they asked in Madame Dupont's shop. They soon discovered.

Giselle had been a singer with the Opera Municipal. Claude had been transfixed by her voice. In point of fact, it wasn't her voice. His seat was at the back of the theatre and he mistook the woman singing next to her on stage for her. It didn't matter, she could still sing.

'Didn't have time to change after the opera, I see,' commented Mère Noirelle when she first arrived. Giselle liked bright clothes. She liked singing and she liked to feel the sun on her skin.

'They say she's a gypsy.'

'I've heard that she was a whore.'

'She's a wolf transformed into a woman's shape.' Yvette's enthusiasm got the best of her again. Wherever Giselle came from, they decided she was the devil's spawn. That's why she never went to church.

Claude's mother refused to believe the stories. She was relieved to hand the reins over. The twins were six years old, learning all the tricks that twins could play. Giselle looked like a tough one to her and her legs could cope with the streets of St Hubert. It was her job now.

'Right, I'm going,' she announced, removed her apron and went to bed.

In the morning Claude found her dead—smiling, calm, cold. Giselle tried to comfort him by singing but she did not take over where Mère Noirelle left off. Housework was not for her, she was an artist, a spirit. She insisted Claude employ someone. The way he had talked in Marseille of his steady income, she had assumed there would be at least one servant anyway. She got her servant and Claude was rewarded with news of another child.

'If it's a girl, we'll name her after your dear mother,' Giselle announced, looking forward to a girl whom she could dress and make beautiful.

It was a boy. At the news of the birth, everyone came to Claude to offer their condolences, but were shocked to discover Giselle had not died and was up and walking the day after.

'It's not natural,' they said.

'Have you counted the baby's toes?'

The baby, Albert, was anatomically correct. Despite the impending sense of doom, which the entire village felt, nothing dreadful happened for a year. Albert thrived. The twins grew into a world that physically occupied the same space as the village but was also in an entirely different place.

Giselle was still alive. She lay around the house, wanting a daughter but refusing to submit to pregnancy again. She didn't sing any more, always too tired.

'I'm not a performer, I'm a wife and mother.'

Hortense, her servant, gave the bread she was kneading an extra shove.

Claude's life was as close to perfect as it was going to get: a thriving lavender farm, three sons, a beautiful wife. He got no sex and still grieved for his mother, but he figured a bit of grief was part of everyone's life. It was only natural.

Giselle took to bringing him his lunch in his fields, and then wandering off by the river. He enjoyed the attention. He thought perhaps she was getting more interested in him.

Hortense knew different. When Giselle returned from delivering Claude's lunch, she'd sing quietly to herself.

'Something's made her sing and I'll bet a week's washing it's not poor Claude,' she reported to the shop.

Giselle vanished within a month.

'They say she's run off with that doctor who was staying at the inn.'

'She's gone back to whoring in Marseille.'

'Someone saw a wolf slope into the woods the day she vanished.' This time no one contradicted Yvette, they just sighed. The burden of being right was a heavy one.

They said Claude had brought it on himself.

'And his sons too, I'll warrant,' added Madame de Beaumarchais, extending the curse for generations to come.

Claude submitted to fate: three dead wives were hints enough. He resigned himself to raising his sons alone and secured the services of Hortense as a housekeeper. Her only condition was that he never seek her hand in marriage. Given her age and size, it was an easy bargain.

It was an ideal arrangement. Hortense was the perfect surrogate mother. Claude's house was well run on a tight budget and there were no deaths for years. Instead of challenging fate, Claude carefully cohabited with it.

Hortense was one of the few who could tell the twins apart but she wisely never told them how she knew. They examined themselves in the mirror, determined to find the difference.

'It can't be seen in a mirror, I'll tell you that much,' she announced.

She took it upon herself to keep their mother's memory alive.

'She was pretty and had such a smile. It won your father's heart. It could have won the heart of any man, but it was your father that she wanted. You have her smile—use it well.'

The first time she told Raymond and Alphonse that, she knew it wasn't true, but after a while it became true. Their mother became a saint who sacrificed herself for the love of her family.

'What about my mother, was she a saint too?' asked Albert.

'No, she was a free spirit.' Hortense couldn't lie completely but there was no point making the boy miserable with the truth.

'Am I a free spirit too?' he asked, leaping off a kitchen chair and flying with his arms.

'Oh yes,' said Hortense and kneaded her dough harder.

'Would they have liked each other, our mothers?' Raymond asked.

It was a ridiculous question and Hortense said so.

'But if they were both here with us, by magic, would they be friends?'

'They'd be too busy chasing after you three scoundrels to be friends. Off with you all, outside.'

They obeyed. In the garden outside the twins dared Albert to walk on tiptoes between the lines of Hortense's beans. He had to walk sideways to fit.

'Your mother was a witch, you know,' Alphonse said to him, to make him lose his balance.

'That's not true,' he shouted.

'You'll turn into a toad on your tenth birthday,' added Raymond.

'You're lying,' Albert shouted and lost his balance, knocking Hortense's beanpoles over. They laughed as he ran inside to get her sympathy before she discovered the damaged beans.

'You'll not turn into a toad when you're ten,' said Hortense. 'A horror probably, but not a toad.'

More years and still nobody died. It was uncanny, but they were unrepentant. Fate was yet to demand full payment from the Noirelles, they said and settled down to wait.

If one waits long enough, anything will come true.

Sucked in. Just as the story was getting going, he stopped with hints about a long wait.

'"Where does legend end and history begin?" Pompous git!'

'Please,' said Didier, 'is there any chance of you letting up? You're all worked up. You know who you remind me of?'

'Go on.'

'Old Mr Blenkinsaw from across the road, harrumphing his way to our door.'

'No way!'

Turning into your parents is one thing; turning into your grumpy old neighbour is worse.

It was a short flight but the lack of sleep and nerves about the impending reunion made it an anxious one—not helped by the bright orange uniforms ramming trolleys up and down the aisles and flogging refreshments from their matching orange lips.

It was typical that on the one trip when we were in no hurry to arrive, the flight service providers made a bid for world's best-practice status. One dodgy Provençal story and a choc chip muffin and we were in Marseille ahead of schedule, with bags actually waiting for us on the carousel.

As the final set of electric doors swung open into the main hall, Didier was pushing our trolley and I was looking for the car-hire area. The very first thing I saw, like a magnet locking on north, was *him*.

I wanted to not recognise him. I wished we had swept straight by, got our car and arrived in St Anastasie while he was still waiting there. I even wished the only reason I'd recognised him was that he recognised me first and waved. Not a chance.

Sometimes you see someone and you wait until they make the first gesture of recognition before you make one. You don't do it deliberately, and it might be just because you're scared they won't recognise you and you don't want to make a dick of yourself, but it's still a power thing. It only has to be tiny—a smile, a look in the eyes, just something that acknowledges they saw you. This was one of those power games and I lost, big time.

He looked about seventy, with close-cropped white and grey hair—the only man in the entire hall in a suit and tie. I breathed in, my hand started to point at him. He didn't respond, just kept staring at the doors waiting for 'his' people to arrive. I suddenly realised how stupid I had been. He'd mentioned nothing about meeting us. Probably didn't even have a car. I'd made a fool of myself over a complete stranger.

'Shit,' I said to myself. Didier stopped.

'What?'

'Nothing,' I mumbled, 'just shit, that's all.'

If I had only carried on walking, I could have got away with a respectable loss. If I'd only looked ahead, moved on, it would have been all right. But now I understand why there are so many legends about people looking back and losing everything. I did a Lot's wife or whatever her name was from the Bible and turned round. The temptation was too much. As I did, I'm sure his eyes moved off me and back to the swing doors. I swear I caught the end of that movement. It was his attention, his eyes burning into my back that made me turn. I looked at him curiously, trying to see if there was something I recognised. I knew it was him. It wasn't a 'memories flooding back, him tossing me into the air in fields of golden wheat scenario'. I just knew it was him. It was a physical sensation.

Just as I realised I'd been had, he turned slowly and held my gaze. It was a power-play walkover. In that split second his eyes said that he knew I knew.

His eyebrows, the corners of his mouth, his arms, they all rose, as if pulled by the same thread. He tapped the small woman standing next to him and pointed towards me.

I should have accepted defeat then, but no. I had to heap more humiliation on myself. I could have waved back, smiled, thrown a knife, anything but turn around and pretend I hadn't seen him. This wasn't just a loss on points, it was a total knockout. Forced me into the first recognition, pressured me into an own goal and caught me out in my first dissemblance.

'Dids,' I said. He couldn't hear. When I'd stopped to look, he had carried on.

'Didier!' I shouted. He still didn't hear. I had to run after him shouting, knocking a young girl over and triggering French abuse from her parents. I grabbed Didier's arm.

'He's here,' I said through clenched teeth, worried that the slightest jaw movement would be visible from behind. I tried to indicate over my shoulders with one eyebrow and no head movement. It looked like a twitch.

'Really!' Didier looked around enthusiastically, trying to see him.

'What are we going to do?' I continued, clenching my teeth.

'Say hello, I suppose.'

How could he be so calm? But then he was blissfully unaware of the brutal domination game I'd just lost.

As I stood petrified or turned to salt or whatever it was, the little woman who had been standing next to him tapped me on the arm. She was a tortoise. Big eyes in a round face that was the exact width of her wrinkled neck. Her hair, cropped close at the sides and bouffant on top, kept to the same width, so it could all retract into her shell.

'*Venez…vite!*' She looked angry and pulled at my hand to make me follow her. She was strong, but I pulled back harder. She stopped, turned and shouted, 'Too much, you kill him, you kill him!' Then she muttered something I couldn't understand and plunged off as quickly as her waddling legs would allow. She looked back again, threw her hands up in despair and came and grabbed me again. This time there was no resisting. She dragged us to him.

He was sitting down with a security guard standing close by and a crowd of concerned well-wishers. Both hands were clutched to his chest. His red face grimaced. The security guard was trying to undo the top button of his shirt.

'*Mon pauvre Marcel!*' cried the little woman. 'Marcel, Marcel!'

As I stood listening to his name being called I looked at his hands, wondering if they were what mine would look like in years to come. Then it occurred to me that this attack had been very quick. In a few seconds, he had shifted from calmly and brilliantly out-manoeuvring me in the recognition domination match to slumping helplessly against death's door.

I pushed some breath between my lips, flicked my hands in the air and shrugged my shoulders. I stopped the hands mid-motion, wondering why I was being so French when I hadn't been in the country two minutes. It would probably be onion strings and a beret within a day.

Didier knocked one hand out of the way as he rushed forward to kneel down next to him. I remained by the luggage, figuring theft was the biggest risk in this drama.

Didier was crouching next to him, holding his hand, telling him to calm down. He was gulping air, breathing in and out fast. The tortoise was wailing herself into an equally life-threatening state, shouting at the crowd, pushing them back to make space. I could barely understand anything she said. Some of it sounded like French, but most of it sounded like Greek or something.

Didier shouted at me to get a paper bag. I looked at him in exasperation.

'For fuck's sake, Peter, get a paper bag.'

I couldn't believe he was falling for this stupid scene. The whole airport was buying it. Then I realised how the scene looked according to everyone on the planet except me: poor old man dying, evil son refusing to help in order to inherit huge lavender-farm fortune. Didier grabbed a bag held out by a concerned onlooker.

Didier, alone, in the entire hall remained calm. The tortoise was running furiously round in a circle, sure that without her efforts everyone would surge forward and crush *'mon pauvre Marcel'*. The security guard had drawn his gun and was holding it up, scanning for an assassin.

Didier held the bag to the bastard's lips. Air plunged in and out of it, like a steam engine. It wasn't a heart attack, he was hyperventilating. The bag grew moist and gradually the breathing slowed down. All the while his eyes were fixed on me—no blinking, no moving, just staring. It was as if I had positioned myself directly in his line of vision. Eventually his shoulders relaxed. He nodded his head and moved Didier's hand away with an easy movement. I looked at his hand on Didier's. They were touching. Their hands were touching, leaving bits of themselves on each other. He looked at Didier and smiled, exhausted and grateful. His other hand went out to me. I had to move forward and let him touch my sleeved arm.

'My sons,' he said quietly to us. '*Mes fils,*' he said louder to the crowd and then something about us having been returned to him. They applauded. The tortoise rushed to be next to him. Dripping with sweat and panting hard, she had to sit down. The crowd ignored her.

Once everyone had dispersed, the bastard's eyes looked up.

'Let's go!' he said in a French accent.

The tortoise, still slumped down with her elbows resting on her knees and her head hung low, nodded and forced herself up and then helped him to his feet. His shoes were old but meticulously polished, and not by him I suspected. He walked off at a genteel pace, the tortoise scurrying around him, trying to open the automatic doors for him. Didier walked on his other side; I followed with our trolley loaded up with residual doubt.

The bastard and the tortoise talked as if we'd been picked up from an afternoon's shopping not a lifetime's absence.

'We will have to go via Aix,' (Aix-en-Provence, local town of beauty) 'to pick up Alex. She is doing some shopping for the fête. She is trying some of Kiki's recipes,' Marcel tossed in our direction as the tortoise opened the driver's side door for him. We got into the car.

'Australian,' said the tortoise.

I smiled, and tried my first French sentence.

'No, really, we're not. We were raised there after…after…' My first attempt at niceness and I was struggling to find a polite translation for 'the bastard buggered off'. 'After we—'

She cut me off as if she had not heard anything. 'Australian.' She tapped Didier.

'Alex is Australian,' my father explained. He needed a brief pause as the tortoise held the seatbelt out for him from the back seat. Didier was in the back with her. I was riding up the front. He took the seatbelt and continued talking to me, 'She is a chef and writer, Alexandra Beacham. Is that how you pronounce it, Beech-ham? Have you heard of her? She has several books.'

'Alexandra Beacham, yes!' enthused Didier from behind my shoulder.

'What the hell is she doing here?' I asked.

Alexandra Beacham was one of Australia's top-selling culinary writers. She sold a bundle in Australia, had broken the UK market but was virtually unknown in America. She produced gorgeous coffee-table books, full of blurry photographs with one perfectly focused borlotti bean in the foreground and a few recipes that no one ever cooked. Alex Beacham was a culinary pirate, descending on unsuspecting regions of Europe to plunder their finest recipes for a bestselling book. Tuscany, Catalonia and a once unblemished pocket of southern Hungary had all been raided in recent years.

Provence was not the sort of virgin territory she specialised in. I made a mental post-it note to find out what she was doing there. There might be something in it for my clients G&K.

What required more urgent attention was Marcel's driving. He had negotiated us slowly out of the airport and was now touring a roundabout seeking the correct exit. During the second lap he flicked the indicator with a dramatic flourish.

'*Voila!*' he said in triumph, swinging across the path of another car to achieve his desired exit.

Once on the autoroute heading for Aix-en-Provence, he stuck to the middle lane with slow determination. He was the only person in the whole of France who took the speed limit on an autoroute as an upper marker and not a minimum speed. The traffic swarmed around the car like angry bees, drivers and passengers stabbing their fingers at us through open windows.

The chitchat continued oblivious to the fury.

'Maybe the lamb bouillabaisse, she seemed to think that was interesting,' the tortoise wondered, 'or the *Moussaka à la Béchamel de Lavande*.'

I managed to catch Didier's eye in the side-view mirror. His panicked stare gave me a sense of relief. It wasn't just me, this really was weird.

It was as if the life-threatening scene at the airport had not occurred and the biggest thing happening in their lives right now was feeding moussaka with a lavender-flavoured béchamel sauce to an Australian chef. It was confusing. I tried to establish some clarity by turning round to speak to the tortoise.

'Hello, I'm Peter, this is Didier, pleased to meet you.'

She looked strangely at my outstretched hand, then glanced in the rear-view mirror at the bastard.

'*Merde*,' she suddenly cried, as if she'd left something at the airport. 'Of course!'

Ignoring my hand, she grabbed Didier, hugged him and kissed his cheeks five times. Then she finally gripped my hand with both of hers. Tears began to flow.

'So happy... I am your new mother!'

The bastard had been focusing his entire attention on the road, avoiding the embarrassed self-introduction, but then he glanced at me casually and asked with a smile, 'Is your mother still alive?'

'Yes,' I growled.

'Kiki,' he shouted to the back of the car, 'they still have a mother.'

'Oh.' She seemed disappointed. 'I have no children... the Germans during the war.'

'Not now, Kiki,' he shouted merrily. 'Later she will tell stories. Boys, this is Kiki, my wife. She is Greek but has been living in France these last twenty years.'

'Wife?' I queried and caught his eye for the first time since the airport tussle. I silently added bigamist to his honorary title as he shrugged his shoulders.

Seeing as I had now forced us into the conversation, Didier was keen to get some friendliness happening.

'We didn't know you were going to meet us, it was such a lovely surprise.' In my mouth the words would have been a snarling accusation. In Didier's it was an expression of pleasure. Perhaps he was an even better liar than me. Marcel smiled as he studied the road ahead.

'My sons arriving to reunite with me, how could I not... apricots!'

'Of course, apricots,' repeated Kiki. There it was again: life-changing event superseded by a stone fruit.

'Apricots, naturally,' Marcel repeated again. Kiki turned to Didier. I banged my head on the window.

'At airport, we knew we had forgotten something important, but,' and she laughed quite heartily at this, 'we remembered not. Apricots.' That set off another volley of 'Apricots, of course,' from the bigamist bastard.

'Apricots,' Didier joined in. 'I love apricots.'

'The memory,' our driver flicked his eyes in my direction to command my attention, 'is not what it once was.' He leaned forward to concentrate on the turn-off ahead. It could have been the one for Aix so we took it.

It wasn't, so we rejoined the autoroute and barged back into the middle lane.

'How is it you say it...?' he offered an explanation. 'Better safe than sorry?'

Aix-en-Provence is a classic Mediterranean town—all gothic architecture, impossible driving, shouting and smells, with modern technology desperately trying to shove in. The ancient cathedral sat indifferent to the internet café housed in a parvenu two-hundred-year-old building.

As the hunt for the perfect apricot amid piles of fresh produce got underway, the market was beginning to pack up. Marcel examined all the fruit stalls and questioned the stallholders in detail. While they spoke, he watched their eyes and hands, ignoring their exhortations to look at the fruit.

'The secret of the fruit, it is in their eyes,' he said, bestowing upon us his fruit-buying wisdom.

Once the vendor had been selected, he honed in on the fruit.

'Never touch. There is too much emotion in touching. Your hunger will deceive you.'

His hand hovered over the large pile of apricots. I watched his fingers. The nail on his thumb was flat with a slight hollow, like mine only more pronounced. The fingers wavered with a delicate precision, as if tapping the surface of a pond to create the tiniest waves possible.

I'd never really smelled apricots before, I thought they were as bland as fruit got. Now I breathed their flesh. A smile came across his face. He picked one up and held it to my mouth. The smell was insisting I bite it straight out of his hand. I resisted, taking it in my hand and biting as he watched. The flesh collapsed into juice on my tongue as the taste consumed me. One more molecule of sweetness and it would have been too much.

He took the remaining fruit out of my hand, threw it in his mouth and spat out the stone onto the cobbled ground.

'Two kilos,' he said to stallholder, holding up two fingers and ignoring the juice dripping off his chin. This was what Mum had meant. Purchasing the perfect apricot was the most important thing he could do in that moment. I had to admire the intensity.

We moved on to meet Alex Beacham, the chef. She was waiting under the third plane tree from the far end of Cours Mirabeau. Marcel and Kiki were giving her a lift back to St Anastasie. Apricots and celebrity Australian chef were eventually loaded into the car and we set off again. Sadly, only the apricots went in the boot. Marcel lost no time in letting Alex Beacham know we had been raised in Australia. He smiled with satisfaction as her hands shot up in the air.

'Oh, dear! I hate not being incognito when I'm researching. Let's pretend you have no idea who I am,' Alex insisted.

'Yes, let's,' I answered.

St Anastasie was her big find. Fate had made her pull in for petrol at the only service station in town. She'd overheard Kiki talking to the owner and immediately spotted an usual accent. She said that understanding the subtlety of various accents was essential in her 'trade'. I pretended not to know what that was, which didn't amuse her.

'I could smell something exciting,' she declared.

She'd soon 'discovered' that Greeks had been living in that area of Provence for over two thousand years. They had retained their essential Greekness, but isolation from their homeland and centuries of French influence had created a unique culture.

'It's bloody incredible,' she exclaimed.

'Yes, absolutely unbelievable,' Didier replied.

The bastard concentrated harder than ever on his driving while Kiki stared determinedly out of the window. Alex continued explaining the remarkable regional history she had discovered.

'Marseille was originally a Greek settlement, you know: Massillia. Millennia ago. But who would have thought isolated pockets of their descendants would remain. Well, I say pockets, but St Anastasie seems to be the only one. It's too much!'

Even if Alex's sense of smell had been impaired by too much exposure to over-ripe Brie, I could whiff the scam on this one. Kiki revealed everything to me back at their house when I caught her baking the recipes handed down from mother to daughter for generations—literally. She was pulling the sheets of paper out of the oven when I walked into the kitchen. She turned around with the tray in her hands, expecting Marcel. When she saw me, she quickly turned back again and sent the stained, browned recipes fluttering to the floor. Kiki smiled sheepishly as we both bent down to pick them up.

It was Marcel and Kiki's big scheme to bring tourist euros to their village. St Anastasie didn't really have much to attract visitors, so they had concocted a fake Greco-Gallic history and had persuaded the entire village it could trigger a culinary tourism boom. Kiki would run a cooking school and everyone else could do whatever they wanted to cash in. I wasn't sure what Marcel was going to do, other than lounge around looking suitably French and utter a few Greek words.

The plan had barely got off the ground when Kiki recognised Alex at the service station (they got her Australian cooking show on cable TV). It was an opportunity too good to miss so Kiki seized the moment, introduced herself and hastily started creating Greque-en-Provence recipes.

'She's so excited,' Kiki said as we returned the recipes to their tray. 'The truth break her heart. Nice woman, Australian. You do not want to upset her. The village holds fête for her at the weekend. Everyone would be very unhappy. Your father...'

She didn't finish the sentence, realising that was not a good argument with me. I looked at the recipe in my hand. It was for *Dolmades Escargot*.

It was one of those moments when you decide whether to involve yourself or not. If I said anything, my words would form a little thread of interest that Kiki could tie to her wrist and use to attach herself to me. I knew what these threads did. I'd seen clients sitting stony-faced in presentations, but as soon as they made a comment or asked a question, I'd see a thread flying towards me. I'd grab it and reel the client in, trussed up and ready. You could spend your whole life not being reeled in, never being worked over, but believe me, it's really hard work. Sometimes you've got to give in. Submitting to Kiki in the kitchen meant I could hold out when it really mattered. So I sent a thread out. Just one, but who knew better than me: one is all it takes. Of course, it wasn't purely a friendly gesture (I didn't give in that easily): I sensed the idea had possibilities for my 'mass boutique' concept.

'Vine leaves stuffed with snails might be a bit too obvious,' I said.

Kiki perked up. 'She love *Fetta Fondue*.'

Alex's enthusiasm had crushed her judgement like a thrice-pressed olive.

The tortoise had been fobbing Alex off in regard to the recipes, telling her she didn't want to give away her heritage.

'Has she seen any recipes written out?' I asked. She hadn't. I suggested destroying the recipes and pitching them as an oral mother-to-daughter tradition. 'Give her the honour of being the first woman in history to write them down. She'll love it.'

Didier had been with the bastard in the living room while Kiki and I were cooking things up in the kitchen. When I joined them, the silence was solid. Marcel sat still, staring ahead. Didier looked at me and raised his hands in bewilderment at getting the impromptu silent treatment.

'Drinks,' Marcel announced. He offered us a gin and tonic. It was early evening but still hot—perfect gin and tonic conditions. Thrust into the bizarre world of apricots and fetta fondue, something as familiar as a gin and tonic was a haven. And plenty of alcohol was the only way the next few days would be physically possible.

'Sounds great,' I said.

'I'll have the same,' Didier added.

'This,' he held up the gin bottle, 'is the real stuff.' While his back was turned I mouthed 'What happened?' to Didier.

'Nothing,' he mouthed back. 'Hasn't said a single word!'

'They know not how to make gin now. This is the real stuff.'

My dry throat was ready for it. I was waiting for the cool taste to bring relief to the back of my throat…

'Chin chin.'

'Chin chin,' we repeated and drank. No relief. My mouth was filled with a warm sour taste. I wanted to cry. All I wanted was a gin and tonic, an oasis of familiar comfort. It was a mirage.

'Ice kills the gin, it is better without,' he said.

It wasn't just the warmth of the drink. The gin was revolting.

The bastard smiled.

'Made over there.' He pointed to the back wall, towards the house of his friend Louis. Louis had worked for Gordon's for twenty years, so he knew a thing or two about gin and how it was supposed to be. Louis brewed it for the villagers.

'*Merveilleux.*' He smacked his lips and settled back into his chair.

We sat silently, drinking in turn. Marcel would sip, smack his lips and sigh with satisfaction, staring out of the window at Kiki's garden. A minute later Didier would raise his glass to his lips and sip the tiniest amount possible. He looked at his feet. I sipped next, determined to down the hideous gin without a flicker on my face.

I stared at the bastard, challenging him to look at me and explain. Explain the silence, the gin, the letter, our lives. There were plenty of questions now. He had left a trail of them all the way from the airport, like a tomcat spraying up every post.

Perhaps he was doing the alpha male thing, establishing his authority, or perhaps he was an old codger uncomfortable with the emotion of being reunited with his sons. Louis' gin must have been strong, I was feeling more generous than I'd expected on the first day.

We continued to drink in turns—him gazing out of the window, me staring at him, Didier looking around the living room. St Anastasie was a pretty old village, but the house wasn't. Thrown together on the outskirts, it was a late '70s bungalow with an oversized glassed-in front porch. The furniture was old and heavy. It was impossible to walk anywhere without manoeuvering around a chair or tile-top coffee table. The money had been spent on electricals. What did someone of his age need with a vast plasma screen TV, cable, home cinema, DVD system and the latest Bang and Olufsen stereo I wondered from my over-deep armchair. I had to raise my elbows high just to rest them on the arms.

The silence lasted half an hour, until Kiki announced dinner was ready. We were almost comfortable with it. Certainly Marcel was. He leapt from his seat and moved to the table to become the genial *bon viveur*, pouring wine and gorging on life's rich produce. It seemed a more natural role than the strong, silent patriarch. The wine was slightly less local than the gin. He wafted his arm behind his head, indicating the mountains beyond the back of the house. It was real *vin de cave*. You could tell because it came in an old Pepsi bottle. Whatever empties they had on hand when the wine ran out were taken up to the local vineyard and filled up.

Kiki was not impressed. This was a special occasion, she said, he should have fetched some of the good wine. He shrugged his shoulders and let some air rattle his lips. So annoyingly French. I'd never do that.

'We are *en famille*,' he declared, raising his glass to toast Kiki's magnificent steak. It was just another family meal.

I drank the wine. Compared to the gin it was bliss, but after sitting parched I was desperate for water.

'Water?' Kiki looked puzzled at the head of the family.

'Water?' he repeated. 'Do we have any?'

The tortoise waddled off to hunt some down. Cupboards opened and closed.

'I'm sure tap water will be fine,' Didier suggested.

'Tap water...for my sons?' The bastard was horrified. 'No, if you want water, you'll have water. We never drink water. There is no goodness in it. Wine, coffee, tonic, they have nutrients. Water has nothing.'

He took a swig of wine to prove his point.

'Kiki, the water!' he shouted through to the kitchen.

'If it's too much bother, I'll stick to wine.'

'What bother? It is only water. Kiki, Pierre's waiting.'

The sound of Kiki's searching grew more desperate. Pans and '*Merde!*' were being furiously tossed around. They did not concern me.

'My name is Peter.'

'But you were named Pierre. I chose it myself. My choice is not good enough for you?'

'That's not what Peter said.' Didier's hand smoothed the tablecloth. 'Since you...left, he's preferred Peter, it's his choice.'

'He knows that: he addressed his letter to Peter Noirelle,' I blurted out.

'But now I know you speak French so well, we should use your real name, should we not?' he said to me, but shrugged his shoulders at Didier for agreement.

'My name is Peter.'

'But he is still Didier, he did not change.'

'For fuck's sake!' I threw my fork down on the table.

'*Voila!*' Kiki shouted triumphantly from the doorway, holding up a dusty bottle of Evian. She wiped the dust off with her apron, poured some into my near empty wine glass, stood watching as I drank, then clapped and laughed.

'Water!'

'Water,' Marcel muttered in disgust and filled his glass with wine.

The next two hours passed like one hundred and twenty slugs crossing a desert one by one. Marcel gloried in every item of food put in front of him, demanding compliments for Kiki's food before we even had a chance to say anything ourselves.

'Did you enjoy that? Well, tell the woman so!'

When Didier mentioned the story we had read on the plane, I was taking a sip of water, which occasioned a round of evasive bemusement from them. That conversation was throttled at birth. Marcel was not ready to talk. Kiki covered for him, turning the subject to herself. How she came to France, the hardships she had suffered, her adventures, her stories. He listened with devoted attention, reminding her of any bits she may have left out.

'Tell us a little about your life since England?' Didier tried again.

'I have not been to England!' answered Kiki and launched into a mangled story about her childhood in wartime Greece. I thought she was telling us how she had risked her life running sanitary protection past the Germans to the Greek resistance in the mountains. Didier explained later that in French 'tampons' were actually bandages. Shame. The only pleasure of that dinner was the image of Kiki dancing saucily past suspicious Nazi storm-troopers, her hips padded with feminine hygiene products. It could still work as a campaign.

After dinner the table was cleared. We tried to help, but the bastard pinned our hands to the table while Kiki did all the work. Two bottles now sat on the table: a plastic 7 Up bottle of wine that had replaced the finished Pepsi bottle and one empty Evian bottle. Kiki gasped and looked under the table to see if we'd got rid of all the water down there. The bastard shook his head, laughed and looked too. Didier took advantage to nod towards the front door.

'That was wonderful, Kiki. I think I might just take a stroll around the village to walk it off.'

'Great idea. I'll come too,' I replied. We stood up together.

'Very well,' Marcel sighed, wearied at the burden being placed on his poor wife, 'Kiki get the key for the gate and give them a tour of the village.'

Even Didier was worn down by this. We settled for a tour of Kiki's garden instead. She pointed out everything, each description starting with, 'Is dark so you cannot see it, but…'

Not only were we denied any sort of meaningful conversation with the man who had summoned us, we weren't allowed to spend a second on our own. We had to share a room (destiny, obviously) so I thought if we retired for the night, we could get a few moments to talk alone, but even that wasn't possible.

Copious 'Goodnights' followed, along with the fetching of sheets, suggested arrangements for sharing the bed and the blow-up mattress on the floor, and even instructions on flushing the toilet. Every action required one or both of them trotting in and out of the room. I finally eased Kiki out and closed the door. Didier was lying face down on the bed kicking his legs and screaming silently into his pillow. I threw myself onto the blow-up mattress and did the same.

'What the hell have we done?' Didier whispered to me.

We started giggling and shushing. I tried to talk but every time my mouth tried to form words, I'd snort and have to return to the pillow.

'It's a complete—' Didier didn't get to finish his sentence. The door burst open and Marcel entered in his pyjamas. We jumped.

'Mes fils!' He came forward, walking precariously down the gap between the bed and the air mattress like an Australian gymnast on the beam. He leaned over Didier and kissed him on the forehead. He turned to me where I lay on the ground. I could either raise myself up to meet his pursing lips or have him crouch down. As he began to move down, trying to force me to move up, he lost his balance and fell on top of me. His body sprawled over mine, his belly pressed hard against my body. His grey stubbled face scratched my neck. I tried to push him off but he was stuck.

'Kiki!' he shouted, ignoring the fact that he was on top of a living being. 'Kiki!'

I tried to get him off, but pushing meant touching him even more. I couldn't do it. I waited to be rescued like a hooker with a dead client. Didier tried to remove him, but he would not shift.

'Mon pauvre Marcel,' Kiki cried as she entered in her nightdress and pushed Didier aside. Sitting on the edge of the bed she leaned over, grabbed him around the waist, pulled him up and rolled backwards onto the bed so he was sitting on her knee. From there he could stand up and walk out. Kiki followed, closing the door behind her. This time there were no 'Goodnights'.

We didn't speak until we were sure they were in bed.

'I think he's completely mad,' whispered Didier.

'Why was he giving you the silent treatment?' I tried to ask.

'The walls are thin,' Marcel called out from their room. 'If you hear Kiki snoring, hit the wall until she stops.'

The first full day *chez bâtard* and we were thrown out. Kiki needed the men out of the way. Alex came around in the morning so that Kiki could finally succumb to sharing the secrets passed down through the generations. Perched on a stool that Kiki's great-grandfather had allegedly made as a wedding gift for her grandmother, Alex's hand trembled with the honour of being the first person ever to write down the recipes of Greque-en-Provence. The tortoise gave her an hour of inter-cultural female bonding and even managed a few tears as the *Dolmades Escargot* ingredients were revealed.

'It was the last thing she ever…' Kiki turned and rested her hand on the stove to give herself strength. Alex stood up from the heirloom stool and placed a gentle hand on her friend's shoulder.

'If it's too difficult I can come back.'

'No, she would want this. Only…' Kiki turned her moist eyes to Alex, 'when you print recipe in your book…'

'That may not ever happen, I'm here for the love of cooking.'

Alex stopped there. They both knew they were wasting their considerable talents if it didn't happen.

'When you print recipe, name it *Marie-Nana's Dolmades Escargot*. That was her name.'

The hankie came out, followed by sobs and the last ingredients. Kiki moved towards the kitchen window and stifled another sob.

'We end now,' she said abruptly. 'As Marie-Nana said, "a week of tears in one day is too many".'

I was sorry to miss the scene, but Kiki acted it out word for word in the kitchen for us at the end of the day. For our rendition, however, the words were punctuated with shrieks of laughter, not tears.

The kitchen scene had not been Kiki's only challenge of the day. There was trouble in the village. Kiki's scam required total support from the whole of St-Anastasie-sur-Issole. She had persuaded them that they all stood to benefit from the gourmet tourist boom that would follow. Most were happy to play their part—a fête was a fête even without the flow-on benefits. All they had to do was mutter a few Greek words, slag off the Turks every now and again, and party with gusto on the day. Kiki had even shipped in some relatives from Greece to coach them on their Greek phrases—two nephews, Lennon and Ringo, and the granddaughter of her uncle's brother-in-law, Dusty. Clearly they had a thing about '60s' singers in Kiki's home town.

At that morning's final briefing and dialect coaching session, Lucien Valois, the boulanger, was making trouble.

'He always the troublemaker.' Kiki rolled her eyes at me. Ever since Lucien had taken over the boulangerie in the village six years ago, he had not fitted in. His brioche had never reached the dizzy heights of his predecessor and he refused to give the villagers the unofficial discount the old boulanger did.

The lure of tourist euros meant that Lucien had agreed to the Greque-en-Provence scheme and had gone so far as to produce a sweet form of pitta bread—his inferior brioche dough made without yeast.

That morning Alex had been with him while he baked the day's bread. Determined to experience fully his unique baking style, she threw herself into it with a passion, slapping the dough, tossing flour and wiping it through her hair. Lucien had not been impressed; he liked to keep a clean bakery.

'You have to be part of the dough, don't you?' she trilled at him through a cloud of flour. 'You have to love it, kiss it.' She kissed a croissant she had just made.

Lucien shrugged his shoulders. He normally mixed the dough in the big machine that Kiki had made him hide out the back.

It was early, he hadn't slept well and he wasn't used to having to talk to someone while baking, let alone do it all by hand. The woman was getting irritating, shoving her germs everywhere, pretending it was some form of authentic baking.

He sighed and wondered how much longer she would stay around as he watched her toss a sweet pitta in the air. Before he could snatch the dough back and bin it, she rushed forward and clasped him to her floury bosom. The pitta fell down and disappeared somewhere between them. Lucien didn't see where, his eyes were closed.

The woman was taking over his life, ruining his routine with her nonsense. It was too much for him and he blurted out, 'It's all rubbish. We're French, no one's Greek here. Get out, you foolish woman.'

He bundled her out of the door and slammed it behind him. His bakery was devastated, flour everywhere. Limp, yeast-free brioche dough lounged on every surface.

At the village coaching session with Kiki's nephews later that morning, Lucien told everyone what he had done. The session was being held at the indoor basketball court (built with EU money after a desperate plea from the whole community to do something about their non-existent youth drugs problem).

Panic ensued. Lennon was cut off in the middle of demonstrating the mouth shape for the perfect Greek *h*, as they debated what to do.

'We'll be arrested, all of us,' said Maurice, the senior village policeman.

'The scandal,' his junior moaned.

'Arrest Alex!' suggested Alphonse who ran the chemist.

'For what?' asked Maurice.

'You don't normally need an excuse,' retorted Alphonse.

'You can arrest her for ruining my bakery, and she stole a pitta down her dress,' Lucien complained.

'We should arrest you, you idiot. There's no backing out now.'

Edouard, the junior gendarme, suggested they fetch Kiki. 'She'll know what to do.'

Ringo sloped off to Kiki's house to warn her about Alex's discovery. They were about to enter round the back when he heard Alex in the kitchen. Hiding under the window, he witnessed the handover of the recipes. As Kiki moved to the window she had seen Ringo, hidden her startled cry in her hankie and quickly got rid of Alex.

By the time Kiki arrived at the basketball court half the village were ready to flee to the hills. She remained calm, but was confused. Alex had mentioned nothing about the incident to her, despite having arrived at Kiki's shortly after being thrown out by Lucien.

'My head, it was running nowhere for a solution,' she told me. 'I thought, Peter, he's clever, what would he do?' It was a dubious honour that within twenty-four hours of arriving I was an inspiration for a seasoned con artist like Kiki. The mood of despair was swirling around. Everyone was shouting. Alphonse blamed Lucien. Lucien blamed the police, the police blamed Kiki.

'What's happening?' The sound of a bad French accent silenced everyone as they all turned and stared. Thirty deer caught in the headlights of Alex's gaze.

'I know I don't belong here, but I thought I should come down and reassure you all.'

She moved to Lucien and put her arm around him.

'Dear Lucien, dear grumpy old Lucien. You don't like this at all, do you?' She wiggled his cheeks with her hands. He smelled a hint of the morning's sweet dough on her.

'I'm nothing to do with it. It was all her.' He pointed at Kiki.

'Dear sweet Kiki.' She moved over to her. The tortoise, I imagined, was shrinking as far into her shell as she could.

'After this morning I know how much trust Kiki has placed in me. And I want you to know that trust is not misplaced. Today…' She gulped and squeezed Kiki to her. 'Today Kiki allowed me to write down the recipes that her family have carried in their hearts for generations. I know what an honour that is.'

She turned to Lucien again. He stepped back, worried that pitta dough was fermenting in her bosom.

'Lucien is afraid that I will betray the trust the whole village is placing in me. He tried to deny everything this morning. Tried to pretend it was all a lie. We were making bread…' She paused, kneading imaginary dough in the air. 'There's a primordial honesty in that—a truth beyond words. I heard his soul, not his words.'

'You old roué, Lucien,' someone shouted. Lucien blushed, unused to being thought of as a seducer.

Alex continued, 'If you want to stop now, we will. Tell me to walk away today and forget I've ever heard of Greque-en-Provence and I will. Your secret will remain.'

She made an impassioned plea to let her share their magic with the rest of the world. Then it would be preserved and celebrated across the globe. 'Will you let me preserve your way of life?' she asked beseechingly.

The villagers grudgingly accepted her argument, allowing her words to allay their fears.

Alex sent up a volley of thank yous out so effusively that Lucien's missing pitta dough plopped out of the bottom of her skirt.

🌳

The Noirelle men's day was equally challenging. From the moment I woke, the bastard seemed to be in irritation overdrive.

He knocked on the bathroom door, asking why I was taking so long when I'd only been in the shower long enough to wet my hair. I was even more annoyed with myself for then rushing to be out as quickly as possible. He impatiently told us to hurry up then kept us waiting for ten minutes while he pottered around. He asked over and over again how we had slept, as if determined to get the truth out of us by sheer attrition.

We were going for a day out in the car, 'to explore our history and discover your legacy', without a word of exactly where we were heading.

'Trust me!' he said with a laugh.

Within fifteen minutes in the car, we learnt that the full tour of the roundabout he'd made as we left the airport the day before was not a mistake, but standard practice so he could be absolutely certain he was taking the right exit. Every time he did it, he would announce, 'How do you say it—better safe than sorry?'

'Tell me about your work in London, Didier,' he asked.

'I work for a charity which promotes safe sex and sexual health amongst gay men,' Didier announced in his usual forthright but non-confrontational manner. Marcel completely ignored his response. I'd watched his face, hoping for some flicker of shock, but there was none.

A few minutes later he started on me, as if striking up conversation for the first time.

'Tell me about your work in New York, Pierre, I am sorry, Peter.'

I didn't respond so he repeated the question very slowly and loudly.

'Tell me,' he pointed to his chest, 'about your work', he pointed at me, 'in New York', he pointed across the Atlantic.

'I'm a trendspotter and concept developer for an advertising and marketing firm.'

He lapsed into silence so I repeated my answer, louder in his ear.

'Not now, Pierre, I must concentrate, our exit is soon.'

He was obsessed with exits, as if he would be trapped for eternity on an autoroute if he missed one.

We drove up to the mountains of Chaine de la St Baume. There was a spectacular view, he said, some pretty villages and something that he needed to show us.

We did drive through pretty villages, full of remote farmhouses lovingly restored by English expats, all funding their glorious renovations by publishing Provençal memoirs. They stood out a mile—all rustic charm and gnarled olive groves, witnesses to history and Provençal charm. In St Anastasie, Alex had perhaps stumbled upon one genuine thing: it was the only village in Provence that hadn't had a memoir written about it. No wonder the villagers felt hard done by.

One village we passed was positioned on an impossibly steep hill and seemed even more neglected than St Anastasie. The 'for sale' signs on various buildings had been up so long they had historical interest. The main road through it was a series of hairpin bends. It was silent, as if no one lived there any more. I didn't bother noticing the name. As we drove out, Marcel casually announced it was where his father and grandfather had been born and raised.

'St Hubert?' asked Didier. 'Which was Claude's house? Can we stop?'

'No time.'

So much for history; it wasn't even worth a pit stop on the scenic tour.

'Our legs aren't strong enough for the slopes, eh?' I asked him.

He grunted and smiled.

'From what I remember, you both had the legs.'

It was the first reference he'd made to ever having been with us before. It was weird, the sort of thing a father would know.

We finally stopped in a village which, compared to the home of my ancestors, was a bustling metropolis. It had a town square with a variety of restaurants.

'Tourism,' Marcel said, 'we must be careful.'

This was the prelude to half an hour of shuttling between restaurants, examining menus and grilling head waiters. How they made each sauce, who supplied their meats, when and where the vegetables had been bought. At Le Provençal, there was a heated debate about which village produced the best goat's cheese. The bastard stormed away when the waiter would not concede.

When a venue was finally selected and we sat down at an outdoor table (the third table we were offered), a cheer went up from all the waiters around the square. Worse than the public embarrassment was the fact he was absolutely right in his choice. This lunch was no hasty sandwich and a can of cola, but the main meal of the day. Everything, from the lettuce in the salad to the goat's cheese from the best village in the area, burst with flavour. I never realised lettuce had a flavour, I always thought it was a means of putting salad dressing in your mouth.

There was no question of us selecting our own meals; he chose everything without even asking. He decided on a lamb cassoulet for me and a fish dish for Didier. It was frustratingly delicious. I tasted Didier's, hoping I would prefer his to mine. I didn't. Was there anything more infuriating than an arrogant bastard being right?

The superb rosé he chose reaffirmed my belief that it had to be the next big thing in wines. It was from a vineyard 'down there'—he pointed in the direction we had driven. I toyed with the idea of buying the vineyard, shipping the produce out to New York and making a packet. Almost seduced by the wine, but not quite, I could see how such a scheme would play out.

One disaster would follow another: I'd suffer harvest failure, struggle through a winter, bond with the mildly eccentric but ultimately wise locals, build things up slowly and unknowingly discover a sense of purpose. Then I'd get a chance to make a million back in New York, but at the last minute realise I'd learnt about a far better life making a poor but flavoursome living in Provence. Finally I'd reflect on my wholesome happiness as I stood with my new French wife enjoying the blissful scent of our herb garden wafting through the ancient courtyard drenched in a thousand years of golden evening sun.

Easier to import the rosé, mark it up and ship it on.

The wine, the food, the mood, the three of us relaxed together for the first time…I smiled. Didier laughed. Marcel said, *'Mes fils.'*

'So, this inheritance legacy thing,' I started.

'Later,' he interrupted, 'this afternoon. How is your mother?'

'Still alive,' Didier answered.

'She's fine, she said to say hello,' I added.

'Really?' He sounded interested. 'She does not hate me?'

'Why should she?' I countered.

He laughed, turning my comment into a gesture of friendship. 'Why indeed!'

Didier pursed his lips and looked down. I knew the look, he was searching for the right words.

'There are many reasons she might. Life was very hard for her after you left. I think it would be foolish for us to ignore what has happened. You wanted us to come here for reasons that you refuse to reveal. And there are many things we want to know. We have an opportunity to enrich our lives here, but we can't do it by ignoring the pain of the past.'

As Didier spoke, Marcel wiped breadcrumbs off the table onto the ground and watched as a sparrow leapt on them. He looked at the bird, nodding to himself.

'Forgive me,' he said quietly to the bird.

I didn't know what to say. I'd been playing flippant games with the bastard as we jovially goaded each other. Didier had sliced through that like cutting into an apple with a rotten core. Now I had formed an 'us' with the bastard, without even realising. We had been playing at dissembling. Didier had exposed it.

I tried to pat him on the shoulder but he shrugged it off.

'You've got a lot to answer for,' I said to Marcel, wanting to blame him.

'We all do, Peter,' Didier said to me.

Marcel was still looking at the sparrow.

'We will go now... you will understand, soon, very soon.'

In the car we drove back through St Hubert, but there still wasn't time to stop. The heat of lunchtime cooled in the thinner air. The dirty white rocks of Provence thrust out at us between the trees. Marcel didn't make any of the usual tuts, sighs, clicks and coughs that guided his driving.

It was possible I was feeling some pity for Marcel. Despite myself, I couldn't help thinking it must be hard being confronted with the sons you abandoned. This must have been what Mum meant about him being all charm. I didn't want to give in to the touching reunion and forgiveness thing. It was such a cliché, I might as well buy the bloody vineyard.

After slowing down to even more of a snail's pace and looking carefully at every turning, Marcel took the plunge, found his exit and pulled up in a gravel car park.

'We will walk now.'

The journey continued up a steep rocky path. No buildings, no other cars, just a path. The trees around us hinted at a great view. Marcel had difficulty gripping on the dry dirt and loose stones. He slipped and my arm went out automatically to help. He grabbed it, recovered and nodded.

After fifteen minutes we rested. A break in the trees allowed us to see the vast distance we had covered. It looked like days of travel. St Anastasie was too far away to see, but Marcel still pointed out where it was, wafting his arm around in several directions.

The path ran along the edge of a sharp incline. I looked downward. It wasn't a cliff, you could have got down all right, but one trip and you'd tumble a long way, bouncing off rocks as you went. If someone were out of breath and around seventy, the tumble would kill them.

'*Allons!*' he said after a pause to look at the view, and restarted up the path. He hummed and whistled a tune. He sang quietly under his breath and glanced at me to see if I would react. I recognised the tune but refused to show it.

Another fifteen minutes and we were at the top. The ground levelled off, stripped of trees. There was wind-mown grass and dirty white rocks, but it wasn't bare. There was a small church and a graveyard, only it wasn't really a yard because there was no wall. No need to mark out God's territory here.

Before we reached the first gravestone he stopped and held us back for a dramatic announcement.

'*Mes fils*, it is now time for you to meet the family. Claude, you already know.' He moved to a grave as if presenting people at court. The inscription read, *La Forza del Destino*.

'*La Force du Destin,* the Force of Destiny,' Marcel pronounced heavily, 'his favourite opera. Fitting, is it not?'

I tried to focus on connecting the man in the story, whose wives kept dying, with this gravestone. There was no actual grave marked out, just the stone on the rough grass.

Next Marcel took us to Alberto Noirelle (1903–1946). He was dead then, the young boy, our grandfather. Again I tried to connect. It must be significant somehow, meeting our ancestors like this. Didier crouched by the headstone and touched it gently.

Marcel posed in his grief, his hand on his mouth, his head turned to the wind so it ruffled his hair. He had a good head of hair for a seventy year old. At least I had that to look forward to.

I was avoiding the issue again. I focused on the name on the grave: Alberto. Somewhere between the story I had read and the grave, the name had found an O, or perhaps it had lost one between the reality and the story.

I tried, I really did, but Alberto had died before I'd even stepped onto the planet. We'd never even breathed the same air. Our only link was the man standing next to me, quietly beating his chest. My blood was a bit like his, which was a bit like Alberto's.

'These are our forefathers,' Marcel announced, 'from them we have a rich inheritance.'

I looked at Didier. The old man was going into pompous mode. I thought I could hear the voice from his letters.

'We have them to thank for strong legs, a full head of hair... and the wrath of fate. We must all pay the price for Claude's defiance against fate.'

'But I thought that was just the old bags in the shop gossiping?'

Marcel smiled. 'Fate's handmaidens are seldom pretty.'

'So what is the wrath of fate?' asked Didier.

'*Mes fils...* one of you will kill me!'

Too bloody right if you keep up with this crap! I thought.

'You think I am joking now,' Marcel replied, 'but when you learn the full story of the Noirelles, you will understand only too well that each of us is doomed to die at the hands of the fruit of our loins.'

I walked over to a vast slab of gravestone a few metres away and sat down. It was like a giant marble coffee table. Gravestone coffee tables were an interesting concept.

'Is that what we came all this way for?'

Didier glowered at me. 'Try to be in the moment, will you.'

'It's bullshit,' I whispered to him as he sat next to me.

'Of course,' he said, 'but that doesn't mean there isn't something extraordinary in our ancestry. There's something epic in every family history. Let Claude and Albert speak to us through him.'

'Fine!'

Marcel came and sat with us on my future coffee table.

'You are right to be cynical... no one would be happier than I to see the curse disproved. I am, as you say, next cab off the rank, am I not?'

He reached into his jacket pocket and pulled out more of the paper that the letter he'd sent to London had been written on.

'Perhaps here, with Claude and Alberto, we should continue their story. Permit me to read to my sons.'

Didier took to the moment with glee, nestling down as comfortably as he could on a marble slab. I lay back and watched the sky pass by as Marcel cleared his throat ready for an oratory performance.

ST HUBERT, 1914

St Hubert was a practical village when it came to matchmaking. It was mercifully short of fathers determined to hang onto their daughters as long as possible. The passion and recklessness of youth was something to be encouraged. As Claude's mother had known all too well, these were but lures for the trap of respectability.

Each year prior to the annual fête it was traditional for all the young single people to collect at one house for refreshments. They were chaperoned, but not too rigorously.

Hortense realised this was an opportunity to seduce the twins into the real world. The independent universe they played in as boys was in danger of becoming their real world. Beyond eating and sleeping with their family, they wandered off into their private world without caring where they were, sometimes having to concentrate even to see people standing in front of them. They ran down the steep streets laughing hysterically and then wondered why their knees suddenly hurt and they were flat on their backs. They would run into baskets of fruit outside and trip over. Looking around shocked, they thought they had been attacked by an invisible force. Talking to each other by tapping their fingers on their heads had been amusing when the twins were boys but in nineteen year olds it suggested a certain deficiency. They *were* beginning to talk again.

Hortense went to work to ensure that the Noirelles would host the young ones' refreshments this year. It was time, she decided, for Alphonse and Raymond to start courting. Physical pleasures might drag them into the real world and away from each other. Claude agreed.

'It must be done. They must find girls to court.'

Hortense looked at him sharply and pointed a knife that had been slicing beef.

'You stay clear, Claude Noirelle. The less you have to do with it, the better.'

Hortense argued their case before the fête committee meeting in the village hotel.

'The Noirelles are one of the oldest families in the village. It's only fair that Claude shoulders this burden at least once.'

There was a murmur of agreement. Claude could afford it all right. Hortense glanced around the room for dissenting faces. Only Madame de Beaumarchais looked at her. Everyone else examined their feet.

Hortense continued her argument. 'Claude has told me to spare no expense. He feels he owes it to the village.'

More mumblings.

'It still seems...shall we say, risky?' suggested Monsieur Beaumarchais. It was one of the peculiarities of St Hubert, that while Monsieur Beaumarchais had no 'de' in his name, his wife had miraculously found one.

'Don't be ridiculous,' Hortense retorted.

'We hardly need remind you of Claude's history,' Madame added to affirm the accuracy of her doom-laden prophecy. Hortense knew her game, so played her trump card.

'For heaven's sake,' she said directly to her rival. 'Claude won't be there, he's in Marseille for a month.'

Suddenly all eyes returned to her.

'Well, that's quite different,' said the patissier.

It was the best possible solution: Claude would foot the bill but keep well away.

'That's it then! The young ones will have their refreshments chez Noirelle,' the mayor announced once it was obvious the room was in agreement.

Madame de Beaumarchais still did not like it.

'They say the Noirelles are always trying to sidestep fate but one sidestep too many and fate bites you in the rear.'

Fate didn't bite any bottoms that year, but it did drown out the fête. For the first time in living memory it poured with rain. Living memory meant around eight-two years in St Hubert. It resided with old Rabais and he couldn't remember a drop of rain on the fête before.

The shop was the only cheery spot on the day.

'It's Fate's fête!' Madame de Beaumarchais delighted in her phrase.

'Still, it's the young ones I feel sorry for,' she added.

'They say it will rain every day until the twins marry and their wives die!' announced her daughter.

The kitchen table at the Noirelles' was crammed with food. Hortense had produced a range of delicacies including a special lavender béchamel sauce to go with the meats.

The torrential rain kept everybody away. The usual afternoon races and contests had to be abandoned. They hoped for a fine *evening for dancing, but the rain continued to cascade. Every time the intensity of the drumming on the roof relented, Hortense would rush to the window in the vain hope of seeing lighter clouds somewhere in the sky. The intense drumming resumed.*

The twins had been positioned in the rarely used front room, sitting in their best clothes. She had spent the day before coaching them in what fine manners she knew, but they were no gentlemen.

'Neither's the lot that's coming,' Raymond argued.

By nightfall, no one had arrived. They were all in the kitchen, ties undone, collars off, food stuffed in their mouths. The twins had wine. Albert had some mixed with his water. They had their own fête, dancing with Hortense in turns.

Albert, enjoying the fun, got up on his chair and impersonated his father singing to himself in his fields.

'I'm going to Marseille to lose myself in music. If I died listening to my son singing in the Opera Municipal...'

Everyone joined in the last line:

'... I would die a happy man.'

Hortense shrieked. He had his father to a T. She wished he could have enjoyed the merriment. There was not enough laughter in the house.

Their laughter was stopped by a knock at the back door. Nobody moved.

'Well, I'll get it then.' *Hortense bustled back to being a housekeeper.*

It was a drenched young woman, looking cold and miserable. Once she had got out of her wet clothes and was sitting wrapped in a blanket by their kitchen fire, they got down to the business of finding out who she was.

'Marie-France.'

'Very patriotic', Hortense replied, noting the girl was pretty even when wrapped in a blanket. 'What is it you want?'

'My father always said I should come here if anything happened to him. He said Monsieur Noirelle would look after me. I'm Jeanette's niece. My father has passed away, I've no other relatives.'

'Who's Jeanette?' Hortense asked.

'She married Monsieur Noirelle... after his first wife.'

Albert looked excited. 'You mean my mother?'

A brief vision of a relative all of his own flashed before him but was quickly extinguished.

'Heavens, I completely forgot about that one. No, Albert, not your mother, before your mother and after theirs. I remember talk of a wife who didn't last long. Well, I suppose that makes you family, of sorts. You can stay until Claude gets back, then he can decide what to do with you.'

When the blanket slipped from the girl's shoulder, Hortense caught the twins noticing her smooth white flesh. It would do well to have a young woman around the house, she decided. The girl was hardly a great match, but if one of the twins fell for her, that would free up the other one to get a decent wife.

'Have something to eat, girl,' she smiled broadly at the young woman, 'you must be half starved.'

The niceness was in vain. Within weeks it became clear that Marie-France was no crowbar to prise the twins apart. Instead of enticing them out of their world, she was lured into it. Instead of two people mooning around there were three.

'Which do you prefer?' Hortense asked her bluntly one day. She was sure nothing 'had happened' yet and wanted to make sure something did 'happen' before they started seeing her like a sister.

'They are both nice.'

'You can only marry one. I take it that's your plan, to marry into the family? Don't worry, I'll not stop you, but you can only have one.'

'But—'

'But my goat! You've got a month to decide, and not a word to either of them about this conversation or you'll be on the streets with neither.'

Hortense reported the conversation to Claude, who shrugged his shoulders and sat down by the kitchen fire with a glass of wine.

'You're right to hurry them. There's talk of war everywhere. They'll be looking for boys their age.' Then he added, as if he actually knew anything about it, 'War changes everything.'

Marie-France reported the conversation to the twins, who shrugged their shoulders and laughed.

'You must kiss us both with a blindfold on and see which one sets your heart alight,' announced Raymond.

They wrapped a cloth around her eyes and kissed her in turn.

The first took her in his arms. His lips were strong and he pressed his tongue into her mouth. There was a hint of serious passion. He was bold.

'Alphonse,' she declared.

The next kiss was more playful, more reticent, more determined to delight.

'Raymond.'

The third was strong and serious again.

'Raymond, pretending to be Alphonse,' she declared.

The next kiss came at her from both sides. She could feel four lips on hers, two tongues pushed to her mouth. Passionate and frivolous, intense and playful, it was overwhelming. She pulled back and removed the blindfold. They watched her in silence, smiling as if they knew the answer already.

'I can't choose. I might as well choose which leg to chop off.'

They cuddled her from front and back. It felt warm, wrapped in their world.

'You passed,' Raymond announced. 'This was our test: if you had chosen one you'd have had neither. We won't be separated.'

'But you must. I cannot marry two men!'

'Marriage is nothing,' declared Alphonse. 'We three are everything.'

They talked of a love triangle in the village. Hortense heard the talk and knew a decision had to be made soon. If she had to do the picking herself, she would.

She didn't have to. The war came. No one really knew why. It didn't matter. France was calling the youth of St Hubert, even the twins. Everyone said it wouldn't last long. They probably wouldn't even see any fighting.

Boys going off to war was a new experience for St Hubert. They tried to remember the last soldier who came from the village and failed. They were not a warlike people. War was bright costumes, brave adventures and Napoleon's hat. When the first drab green uniform appeared in the village, there was a general disappointment.

'You'd think they'd give them something a bit more cheery,' Hortense suggested, 'take their minds off the killing.' The world, in her view, was losing its magic.

The last day before the twins' departure was Albert's birthday. He was not happy. It was supposed to be his big day, but as usual they had snatched it from him. What annoyed him most was that Hortense was right.

'You can have a birthday every year, but they'll only be going off to war once.'

She felt sorry for him, because he was right too. The twins were always stealing his thunder. Somehow, for all their vagueness, they were more important than him.

Albert was dressed in his best, sitting in the rarely used front room with his father, Hortense and Marie-France. His father had bought him a suit (to wear to the opera probably) and let him choose which gramophone record he wanted to play.

Albert carefully chose what he thought Claude would like. Claude nodded when he heard the music and then walked to the window to see if the boys were coming.

They were parading up and down in the village in their uniforms, suddenly caring that people paid attention to them.

Albert was made to wait for them to come back before he could have his cake. Hortense watched the boy watching his father, while Marie-France worked herself up into a state twisting her handkerchief around her fingers. Poor boy, Hortense thought and decided he shouldn't have to wait any longer. She stole out of the room and into the kitchen where the cake was sitting. She'd divided it into two with the icing. On Albert's side it said 'Happy birthday'; on the twins' side it was 'Good luck'.

She walked back into the front room, proudly holding out the cake so Albert could see his side. He smiled when he saw it, but the joy was short-lived. The twins had decided to play a joke and jumped up at the open window in uniform with their rifles pointed.

'Bang!' they shouted in unison.

Hortense shrieked and the cake shot up in the air. Albert watched it fly towards him. He put out his hands, vainly trying to catch it. He caught half, which collapsed in his grasp. As it broke apart, in the midst of her shock, Hortense caught herself admiring how light her sponge must have been. The remainder of cake landed intact on Albert's feet, spreading out over them without disturbing the only remaining words: 'Good luck'.

Albert didn't feel lucky as Hortense took him off to the kitchen to clean him up. Everyone tried not to laugh, but the cake had splattered all over him. As she wiped him down, Hortense tried to discreetly taste a little of the cake. She had been right: the sponge was deliciously light. It would have been a lovely cake.

'Pity,' she said to herself. Albert caught her musing.

'I think,' she said, 'you deserve a big cake all of your own. Here, go the patissier, get whatever you want and it'll be just for you.'

'Should I bring it back so everyone can have some?'

'No, it'll be just for you, just for Albert.'

Hortense wished she could go with the boy, but she knew she would be needed to calm everything down. A wail went up from the front room: Marie-France was sobbing again over the twins' departure.

'Off you go, and make sure to tell the patissier I sent you.' Hortense suppressed a smile. 'He'll look after you.'

Albert brightened up at the thought of his cake. As he left, he looked back through the window the twins had popped up at to scare them all. He stood and watched as Claude patted Marie-France comfortingly and the twins smiled with embarrassment.

'Don't worry, we will come back!'

He stared in amazement. He had not thought for a second that the twins might not return. Now, suddenly, there was the prospect of having his father all to himself.

At their words, Claude turned his head to the window to hide his eyes becoming red. He didn't notice Albert watching him. In his father's sad, unobservant gaze the young boy saw where the twins had inherited their vague look.

He slipped away and scurried to the patissier with troubled thoughts. He couldn't forget the rush of glee he had felt as he realised that his brothers might not come back, but his father's look made him feel bad. He was selfish, very selfish, thinking only of himself. Perhaps he didn't deserve a cake.

In the patisserie he mumbled that Hortense had said he was to have any cake he wanted.

'Well, if Hortense sent you,' the patissier replied. 'Now, what do you like best?'

The patissier watched as the boy's eyes roamed over his cakes. They hovered over a meringue stuffed with apricot coulis and hazelnut cream and piled with chocolate shavings.

'You want the tête d'abricot?'

Albert stared at it. It looked delicious. He could feel the saliva rising in his mouth.

The patissier reached for the cake. He knew the twins were going off to the war and felt sorry for the boy.

'Don't worry, they'll be back soon enough.'

It seemed like no one expected them to come back.

'Here, keep your money,' said the patissier. 'Enjoy your cake and you'll soon see your brothers again. Tell Hortense I'm making her favourite next Tuesday.'

Albert sat on a kerb with the cake box open on his knee. He thought of Claude's face in the window and wondered if Claude would look like that for him.

'Far too many people spend their time thinking of themselves rather than others,' Hortense always used to say. Albert thought *he was one of them. He looked at the cake and thought that he probably didn't deserve to have it all to himself. But it did look delicious and the patissier would be upset if he didn't eat it. He would feel better if he could share it, but with whom?*

He was interrupted by a woman's voice.

'You could choke to death on that thing,' she said. Albert looked up. 'You're not going to sit on the kerb and eat like a common street urchin, are you?' she added.

Suddenly Albert came up with a solution to his dilemma.

'Would you like to share it with me, Madame de Beaumarchais?'

'Well, really!' She wanted to be offended but could actually find no cause, and it was a delicious-looking cake. She could smell the apricot coulis from where she stood.

'Don't you have to take it home to Hortense?'

'No, she says it's mine but…' He changed what he was going to say. 'Marie-France is saying goodbye to the twins.'

'Not a happy day for your family,' she said and added quietly, 'But when is?'

'Whatever do you mean, Madame de Beaumarchais?' Albert enquired innocently.

'Come with me. Let's see if Madame Dupont can't provide us with a fork. You never know, we might find something useful in that shop of hers.'

And so, for the first time, Albert was ushered into the place where they made all their predictions. The owner's eyes peered out between her piles of wares as her friend entered. They lit up when she saw Madame de Beaumarchais' young companion. The surprise did not cause a pause in the incessant motion of her knitting, however. Few things managed that.

'I found him sitting on the street like an urchin,' Madame de Beaumarchais informed her. 'The patissier was very generous to Hortense's little ward.'

Madame Dupont pursed her lips slightly and half raised an eyebrow.

'Poor boy, perhaps he might like a glass of wine to wash it down. He's practically a man now after all.'

'He's offered to share it with me!' Madame de Beaumarchais added.

'You can have some too,' Albert said to Madame Dupont.

They placed him on a stool by the counter and poured him some wine.

'What do you sell in here? Hortense says…' Albert stopped, deciding it was best not to repeat what she said: that God took every useless thing man had ever created and dumped it in Madame Dupont's shop.

'What are you knitting?' he asked instead, fascinated by her pulling the wool round the needles and looping the needles in and out. Her hands moved fast, independently from the rest of her body.

Madame de Beaumarchais found some forks for the cake, while her friend answered.

'A jumper for a boy about your age, but they say he'll die before the month's out.'

'Nobody's ever knitted me a jumper.'

'Well, it's something that a mother normally does, poor thing.' Madame Dupont glanced at her friend and then continued, 'What do you remember of her?'

'Nothing. Hortense says she was a free spirit.'

They cackled in agreement. Albert stuck his fork into the cake first and took a mouthful; he no longer felt guilt. The apricot coulis enveloped his tongue while the meringue gave a hint of chewy sweetness before dissolving completely. He grinned and laughed through his mouthful. Madame de Beaumarchais took a forkful. Her eyes widened in delighted surprise. She looked at the boy and they shared the moment's joy.

'Hmmm.' Madame Dupont cleared her throat as she noticed their obvious pleasure. In the middle of a row, there could be no pause in her knitting.

'Of course.' Her friend took a piece of cake on a fork and stretched over to Madame Dupont with one hand under the portion to stop any crumbs falling. The needles continued to move as the cake was lowered into her mouth. Her finger, which normally whipped the wool round the next stitch on the needle, paused in the air for a second's delight.

'For all his sins, he knows how to make a cake.'

'What was she like?' Albert asked about his mother.

'She was an instrument of fate, and that's the kindest thing that can be said,' replied Madame de Beaumarchais.

'Poor boy,' repeated Madame Dupont. 'I'm sure your father means well.'

'And Hortense has done a wonderful job...given the circumstances.'

'Your father cheated fate. He was never meant to marry and your family will pay the price. Have some more of your cake.'

'What price is that?' Albert asked with his mouth full.

'Ah, Fate alone knows,' replied Madame de Beaumarchais before popping another piece into Madame Dupont's open mouth.

Albert imagined Fate knocking at the door, demanding payment, and Hortense complaining about the cost of things while counting out her loose change into Fate's outstretched hand.

'Marie-France must be upset about the twins going. Tell us... which one, do you think, is she crying over?' asked Madame de Beaumarchais as she took the final piece of cake.

'She's upset about both of them.' Albert was puzzled by the question. 'We all like them equally.'

'So, she will be wishing farewell to both of them...'

'...at the same time...'

'...together.' The two women chuckled.

Albert was at a loss for words. He got a sense that his family was being maligned.

'My father is very kind,' he announced.

'He may well be, but Fate is not,' Madame Dupont sighed and purled another row.

Back at the Noirelle house, Marie-France had twisted her handkerchief into a sodden knot. She had no recourse but to run out of the house and sob further. It was a wise decision as Hortense was ready to give her something to really cry about.

The three Noirelle men remained in the front room, not sure what to do. Hortense waited for one of them to act. They didn't.

'Go after her, you dunderheads!' she fired off at the boys. Claude nodded, trying to look wise.

'And you're no better,' she turned on her employer. 'You've barely noticed Albert all day. He was looking at you through the window and you stared right through him.'

'Was he? Where is he now? Not much of a birthday for him. Poor boy.'

Claude expressed his sympathy as if he was talking about a neighbour's son.

Marie-France had run up to the lavender fields. The smell of the flowers always calmed her down. The twins found her there and took turns to kiss her tears away.

'Why must you go?' she asked. 'This war is nothing to do with us!'

'And your name is Marie-France, really!' said Raymond with a laugh. 'We must defend our country.'

'You don't give two sticks for your country.'

She was right, they were no patriots, but they were going away all the same.

'Hold me.'

They held her between them. Alphonse kissed the back of her neck. His kisses were soft and soothing. Raymond held her chin and lifted her face to his. 'We'll be back in no time,' he said and kissed her lips. Alphonse's kisses were getting more urgent on the back of her neck. She felt safe as they pressed their bodies against hers.

'What if you don't?' she asked, knowing what the question was leading to.

'Then we should...'

She stopped the answer with a kiss. She didn't want them to say it. If it just happened, that was one thing. If it happened because it had been said, that was quite different.

The twins took a hand each and led her to the barn where the lavender was hung to dry. The dirt floor was hard, but they made it comfortable with a bed of flowers. Four hands covered her body. Two mouths on her breasts, four lips on her neck. The scent of lavender invaded her skin and swarmed around her brain. She didn't know how, but they were both inside her, like an eddy whirling round and round.

Two became one.
One became two.

The twins didn't make it to the war. The steep hills of St Hubert took their toll first. There was quite some excitement when a motorised truck arrived to collect the boys and take them down to the station in Marseille. As tough as the army vehicle appeared, it was no match for the steep hills, the stony road and sharp bends. Cornering too fast and too steep, the truck tipped over. Most of the passengers managed to jump free, escaping with bruising and cuts. Not the twins: they rolled down the hill and exploded with the truck.

'It was like they didn't even notice. They were somewhere else,' said one of the passengers.

'They were smiling,' said another.

'They died with honour,' said the sergeant, attempting to disguise the embarrassment of them not even making it one kilometre from their home.

It had been a long time since there was a death in the Noirelle household, but Claude welcomed grief back into their home like an old friend. It took its customary place around the kitchen table.

Albert looked at the tears making a path down Claude's face and wished he could do something to comfort his father. He hadn't told him he'd eaten his cake in Madame Dupont's shop, or that he knew of Claude's struggle with fate.

A knock on the door soon revealed his new friends, however. A parcel was delivered for him. It was the jumper.

'It's the dead boy's jumper,' he announced gleefully, put it on and started dancing on a chair.

'I've got the jumper, the dead boy's jumper,' he chanted.

Hortense looked horrified that a child she had reared was dancing around gloating about wearing a dead child's clothes. She demanded an explanation. When he told his story she was even more appalled.

'Those vile witches! That shop is a cauldron of bile. Give me that!'

Forcing his arms up in the air, she pulled the jumper off and threw it in the fire. The wool smoke made the house stink.

'Albert, you must never go there. They are not nice women, my son,' said Claude.

It was the first time Albert had heard him say 'my son'. It was always 'my sons' and he would look at the twins or, more recently, their framed photograph.

At the word 'son' Marie-France burst into tears and began destroying a fresh handkerchief.

'For the love of us all,' Hortense snapped, unable to bear the miserable atmosphere any longer, 'stop snivelling and tell the old man your news.'

Claude's eyes fixed on her with a glimmer of hope. Marie-France nodded to him. It was true, she was pregnant. She dashed to the floor by his chair to sob some more tears onto his knees.

'If it's twin boys, she'll be a saint before she's a corpse,' Hortense commented to Albert as he sulked over his burning jumper.

It no longer seemed like some concocted story as we sat there looking at the graves in front of us. They were real people. I achieved the moment. There was a silence as Marcel folded his papers and put them back in his pocket. I didn't achieve more than a moment, though.

'Hang on…if Marie-France is pregnant and the twins are dead, how did the curse apply to them? They weren't killed by their son or daughter or twins or whatever she has.'

'Oh, she has a son all right,' Marcel rolled his eyes, 'but what do you think the twins were thinking about when the truck overturned? Their mind—for they probably had only the one between them—their mind was on their union with Marie-France and what their hearts knew they had created together. Had they not been lost in thoughts of their joint offspring, they would undoubtedly have leapt clear of the crash, as the others did, and survived!'

I threw my hands up. 'Of course, I should have thought of that!'

Clearly an answer for everything was part of our inheritance.

'Still unsure of our fate?' Marcel asked but did not wait for an answer. 'Then look at the grave upon which you are sitting.'

It was the grave of Fate's handmaiden herself, Madame de Beaumarchais. Didier and I leapt off it, the moment we saw her name. I felt like she had reached up out of her grave and pinched my bum. Marcel laughed, stood up on the stone and held his hands in the air.

'Come!' he said. 'This is the woman who has doomed us to patricide!'

He did a little jig and stretched out his hands to us. Didier's mouth was wide open.

'Come, let us dance for our fathers and grandfathers. The revenge of the Noirelle men.'

Didier looked at me as Marcel did another little flourish with his fine St Hubert legs.

'Well, I suppose it might just break the curse,' Didier said.

'Maybe, but it doesn't mean we've bonded or anything like that.'

We took his hands, stood up on the slab of the grave and danced a little jig between us, passing arm in arm, whooping like we were on some Scottish Hogmanay TV special. We took turns to dance solo while the other two clapped the silent tune.

As I twirled in the middle, I actually imagined Claude and Albert there, clapping along. My hands danced in the air, my feet moved swiftly and elegantly until my father suddenly shrieked, *'Merde!'*

He jumped off the grave and added, 'Run for it, *mes fils!*'

He was halfway across the graveyard when we heard a voice shouting. An old woman was hobbling towards us with alarming speed.

'That is the grave of my grandmother!' she shouted as Marcel disappeared as fast as his St Hubert legs could carry him. It was Madame de Beaumarchais' granddaughter.

'Shit!' I translated Marcel's comment as Didier and I sprinted after him. Our legs were put to the test as we skidded down the hill on the loose stones.

I had to stop for a rest. We stood there panting. Marcel was still ahead. He'd slowed down, but he wasn't stopping for anyone. There was no way he was going be confronted about what we'd been doing.

Didier was the first to be convulsed by guilt. 'That poor woman. She must be devastated.'

'Damn,' I said. 'She'd be a direct link to see if the bastard's telling us anything like the truth, and she caught us dancing on her grandmother's grave!'

'We can't do anything about it now. She'd kill us.'

It was too good an opportunity to miss. It was time to use my powers of persuasion for a good cause for once.

'You go after him. I'm going to talk to her.'

When I got back to the graveyard, she was sitting gingerly on the edge of her grandmother's slab. I staggered up to her, exhausted by the trips up and down the hill.

She looked at me hard and started shouting. I let her rant at me for a few minutes. It was standard call-centre procedure with irate customers: let them talk their anger out and eventually they'll calm down. When she did, I sat down next to her.

I pointed to Claude's grave.

'I'm Peter Noirelle—that's my great-grandfather.'

She nodded as if it made sense.

'Did you know my family?' I asked.

'Claude was still alive when I was born. He mated with the devil's spawn, according to her,' she indicated her grandmother below us. 'Didn't really believe her until now. You're all supposed to pay the price.'

'So we really are cursed?'

'You ought to be after that performance.'

The old lady stroked the grave and tears came to her eyes.

'You've insulted her resting place. I can't bear to think…'

'I'm sorry, I truly am. We met our father for the first time yesterday. We're not ourselves. This whole history thing's hard.'

She nodded.

'You never know what to believe. My grandmother was always predicting a terrible fate for everyone. It seldom came true. My mother was even worse. She said some people turned into animals. She saw them.'

I told her that perhaps she'd seen us turn into animals on the grave. That might have been what her mother had meant.

'No,' she contradicted me. 'It would be nice to think that, but no—she really meant animals. Grandmother was just strange. My mother was mad. My grandmother raised me after... after my mother was sent away. They ran the hotel in St Hubert.'

'How did you get up here on your own?' I changed the subject.

'Same way as you. This grave isn't a holy place any more. I cannot afford to have it replaced. I am a poor woman.'

I thought about it for a moment. I really was doing her a favour, I hadn't persuaded her into it. She'd virtually persuaded me.

'Perhaps I could pay to have it removed,' I said, 'and something new put up.'

'Well,' she sniffed, 'I suppose it's the least you could do.'

When I got back to Didier he was enjoying the view with a vague carefree smile on his face.

'She's fine. I handled it.'

'Handled what?' Didier fixed me with one of his looks.

'Nothing! We've reached an agreement. She's happy. We talked about the past a little. Seems the stories are pretty much true.'

I could tell from the minute we entered the car park that Marcel was anxious. He was sitting bolt upright in the car, waiting for us to appear.

We got in, Didier in the front this time.

'It's okay,' I said, tapping him patronisingly on the shoulder, 'we fixed it. No need to worry about her.'

'I have no fear!' he shrugged. We'd made him look foolish and weak. He'd run off and we'd stayed to face the music. He didn't like it.

'What did she say of our family?' he asked, as if worried about what the answer might be.

'Not much. She didn't seem too surprised when she learned it was the Noirelles dancing on the grave. I think she kind of knew her grandmother's predictions gave everyone a hard time.'

'She caused her share of misery… and the Beaumarchais family knew how to make money, that was for sure,' he added. 'You did not offer her money, did you?'

He looked at the rear-view mirror with the scam artist's terror of being ripped off.

I tried not to smile. 'We came to an agreement.'

Didier turned round to look at me.

'You're going to ship that gravestone to New York, aren't you? You're going to make money out of it. That's outrageous!'

'That is my son!' Marcel accidentally slammed his hand down on the horn in his excitement and we all leapt in unison. He even let out a squeal of shock. It was a ridiculous sight, three grown men scaring themselves in a parked car.

Marcel poised with his hand over the horn, pretending to be about to beep it again. When he finally did, we all let out whoops of mock terror.

'*Merde!* Run for it, *mes fils*!' Didier shouted, just like the bastard had done at the top of the hill, and we all laughed.

'Let us go home!' Marcel declared and moved the car slowly off. He beeped the horn once more.

'It has been a good day, has it not?' He looked at me in the rear-view mirror for a response. I felt a quiver of panic that I was being conned.

'Yeah,' said Didier, 'it's been a good day.'

'You're not bloody off the hook yet, you know.' I retreated to a snarl.

I knew I was doing it, knew I was spoiling everything, but I couldn't help it. Part of me couldn't stand the picture the three of us were creating. It was too nice; it wasn't supposed to be nice. Didier sighed and his shoulders slumped as if a day's hard work had been ruined. The bastard concentrated on the road and whistled quietly to himself.

Kiki took charge the next day. It was Friday and the fête was the following day. I was growing fond of her. I liked the enthusiasm she threw at her scam. I loved the way she had recruited an entire village into it. I was also grateful that all our errands did not involve Marcel. We needed the breathing space. We retreated into our caves. Apparently that's what men do: withdraw and sulk around in a dark room.

In Marcel's case it was literally true. He spent the day in his *cave*—that's French *cave* meaning wine cellar, not English cave meaning a hole in the hillside. His *cave* was under the house. All day long, as we carried out tasks for Kiki, I could feel him sulking down there. The foundations pouted under my every step.

In the evening, Kiki sent me down to check on him. She was smart. She didn't suggest that I might like to go; she told me to go and tell him dinner was ready. Her language skills might not have been brilliant but she knew how to handle moody men.

The *cave* was accessed from the garage. There was no door, just some bricks at ground level removed from the wall to make a big enough space to crawl through on your hands and knees. I called into the hole and was summoned by silence.

Through the tiny gap, the ground sloped up away from me. The two racks of wine stood on homemade brick legs by the entrance and then rested on the floor three metres away at the back. Between the two racks was a stool. He was sitting on it, pouring himself a glass of wine. As I looked up from my crawling position, he seemed to fill the whole of the back wall.

'What?' He was annoyed.

'Kiki wants you to come in. She's worried.'

'Kiki is always worried.' He shrugged his shoulders and slurped some wine. 'Perhaps she is right to be worried. You are so very angry you could kill me. I could be the first Noirelle to be killed in cold blood. Murdered by the hand of my firstborn.'

'Do you always have to be so melodramatic? Surely you wanted to kill your father sometimes?'

'Aah!' he said as if I'd hit an obvious nerve. 'We are not ordinary people. We dance on the graves of those who cursed our ancestors.'

I was getting uncomfortable on my hands and knees, and he was obviously in for a maudlin chat, so I sat down.

'Why do we do this to our sons?' He suddenly burst into tears. They weren't fresh ones, they rolled too easily down his cheeks.

'Perhaps it is not the sons who kill the fathers, but the other way round. I have ruined your lives, condemned you to the deserts of Australia. Destroyed myself too.'

He slurped some more wine but didn't offer me any, too busy with his dirge. 'I cannot even ask forgiveness. To ask is to demand too much—a final cruel blow heaped upon the blows already delivered. I cannot. I cannot.'

He drank again. There were a couple of empty wine bottles lying on their sides of his feet. Real wine bottles, not Pepsi ones filled from a vat. 'No, do not ask me to do it!'

I think in his head I must have said something. 'I'm not.'

'Good, that is as it should be. I will hold this guilt. This pain is my badge of honour, a tribute to the magnificence of my sons whose lives I crippled as surely as if I had thrown them before a speeding bus.'

'Stop it!' I said. 'For Christ's sake! We're not exactly leading shit lives. We did pretty well without you.'

More guttural groans.

'Yes, you are so wise. How could my cursed presence have helped your lives? The leaving of you was perhaps, unwittingly, the nearest I came to a noble, unselfish act. You are right!'

'Don't attribute your buggering off to unselfishness.'

'True, true, true.' He put his hands to lips as if thinking for a moment. 'Could you believe somewhere in your heart… I do not ask forgiveness…but that, in the end, it was for the best?'

'Okay,' I conceded. 'It was for the best.'

'Thank you,' he nodded. He wanted to hug me. I didn't move towards him.

Instead he sobbed some more, as if a vast burden had been lifted.

'Tell Kiki I will be out soon.'

I crawled out of the cave and sat in the garage for a moment, exhausted by his grand agony. It was bewildering: dancing on graves, sobbing in cellars, fake Greek festivals that might just solve my problems at work—all this was not what I had expected. He was like a kid who could only ever use the brightest, boldest colours in the paintbox to draw the picture of his life. I smiled to myself and succumbed briefly to the intensity of it all. The charm thing was working.

'Hello!'

Before I'd managed to stop myself thinking kind thoughts, his head stuck out of the hole like a dog in a kennel. I couldn't resist patting the dog's head. He pushed his tongue out and panted.

'It is time to eat, is it not? That is what you came to tell me, no?'

'Yes, that's right,' I answered and put a hand out to help him up.

After dinner Didier and I escaped into the garden for a few moments alone. We hadn't managed to speak to each other since the trip to the graveyard.

'I kind of ruined our trip yesterday, didn't I?'

'Yeah,' said Didier, 'but that's okay. It's hard. You resent him for everything one minute and then the next he orders a great meal, makes you laugh, makes you feel life's all fun and you want to be swept away by him but …'

'… but he's still the bastard, however much we get to know Marcel.'

'I feel it too, not as strongly as you do. I guess I'm just not as intense.'

'What d'you mean?' I challenged him, proving his point.

'Relax, it was a compliment. You're more passionate than me, you always have been.'

'Sorry,' I gave a mock scream. 'I'm going mad. The sooner we get out of here, the better. D'you think we can make a break for it before the fête?'

'No. I don't want to … and you are so loving the whole Greque-en-Provence thing. It's right up your street.'

'Maybe.'

'Maybe,' he mimicked me with a pout. In the dark it looked scarily like Marcel in the cave.

'Maybe not.'

'Granny knot.'

'Nose snot.'

'Poo pot.'

We laughed, just like the days when rhyming our way to bodily functions was the funniest thing in the world.

'What is this poo pot?' Kiki came out into the garden ending our brief moment.

'It's a plant that grows in the Australian desert,' I said. 'We were just thinking it might do well here too. We should get you some seeds or a cutting or something.'

An answer for everything.

🌳

Didier was right. I loved every bit of the fête. The next day, under the watchful eye of Kiki, we prepared the square. Every trestle table I set up she tested when she thought I wasn't looking. Nothing was left to chance in her vision of glory for the village. I'm not sure if anyone else quite understood it, but by sheer force of her will they strove towards it. Her determination was backed up by the two nephews who stood behind her like security guards until dispatched with a quiet word and a pointed finger.

Even Lucien the boulanger was cooperating. He staggered into the main square caked in flour carrying a vast tray of some sweet pastry. Alex followed just behind, coated in flour and with another tray that she slammed onto a trestle.

'Abrivar!' she announced proudly.

'Abrivar!' we repeated, despite the fact no one had heard the word before. Lucien dusted some flour off his apron. Alex had clearly effected some form of transformation in the boulangerie because he looked at her with a glowing pride. Twenty years of frowns seemed to have been wiped off his face.

'Nobody has baked abrivar since my grandfather died,' he said, 'but today is special. It is what he would have wanted.' This gift was the closest he would come to apologising for nearly ruining the whole event.

'It's bloody marvellous,' declared Alex. 'It's baklava made with fresh apricots.'

'Apricots,' everyone cried out in relief, even me.

'*Bien sur*, abrivar…it's such a long time…' Kiki became emotional. 'Your grandfather—he was a good man. This honours him.'

All the men present shook Lucien's hand in honour of his dear, departed non-existent grandfather.

'Look at us!' Alex shouted. She was incapable of saying, she only seemed to cry out. 'I think I've finally broken through with our crusty old baker. We discovered our passion in that dough, didn't we, Lucien?'

Lucien smiled and tried to look bashful.

'Marvellous, better than sex,' she cried out. Lucien gulped. I wondered just how much of themselves had gone into making the abrivar.

Alex dashed off to get ready for the fête. Lennon was dispatched to keep an eye on her. Kiki wanted to make sure she was out of the way for her final briefing of the villagers in the square.

First she congratulated Lucien. Abrivar was a stroke of genius. Greek phrases were rehearsed one last time and strict instructions on dress and behaviour were reiterated. There were to be no attempts at Greek national costume, no plate throwing and no Zorba the Greek dancing. She was quite convincing in her passionate belief, reinforced by her bizarre accent that could easily have come from Greeks living in France for two thousand years. The abrivar was removed to be kept cool and to enable Alex to make a grand entry with it at the fête.

There was one final hitch to be resolved. The ouzo/brandy hybrid drink that Kiki had planned to serve at the fête was not happening. Maurice, the senior gendarme, had been dispatched to Aix in the police van to get the ouzo. Unfortunately, as he was loading a case of bottles into the back of the van, the regional inspector appeared. Maurice had to give him half the bottles for everyone back at his station to stop him from turning up at St Anastasie that night 'just to see how thing were going'. Then the inspector remembered how fond his wife was of ouzo after their Greek island cruise. Another bottle was handed over. Then her sister would have her nose out of joint. Another bottle.

Maurice returned with just four bottles. Edouard, his junior broke one and then they knocked a second over while they were testing its quality. Two bottles alone couldn't deliver that authentic ouzo taste.

Kiki was not impressed. She cuffed them both behind the ear. She needed a way of getting that hard ouzo taste into the brandy. Everyone stood around thinking.

'What about Pernod?' suggested Didier. Everyone looked horrified; it was an appalling waste of good liquor.

'Aniseed balls,' suggested Maurice. 'I have some at the station. My grandmother sends them.'

A kilo of aniseed balls were duly crushed and stirred into the brandy barrel. The villagers tested the brew. A lot of puffing, shrugging of shoulders and flickering of hands indicated it wasn't right. The balls had made it too sweet.

'We need kick. Something for the throat.'

Everyone drew a blank, but if they wanted something to rip their throats out, the answer seemed obvious to me.

'Louis' gin,' I suggested, remembering the nasty taste of the gin Marcel had served on our first day.

'Louis' gin, but of course.' Louis himself was dispatched to top up the 'ouzac' with his authentic brew.

Ringo escorted us back to the house to help us get changed. It seemed we needed his guidance to look as authentically Greek as possible. He made us go through all our clothes and selected the loudest shirts we had. Seeing as we were from London and New York, that meant charcoal and navy blue. He made us turn the collars up and unbutton them way down.

'Where's my medallion?' I asked, peering down at my own navel. Ringo thought it would have been a good idea.

He made us rehearse 'Have a pleasant evening' in Greek with a French accent. We sounded like trainee assistant managers for the Athens' McDonald's.

'Finally!' Kiki was not pleased when we returned. 'I have to prepare. It take time for women. Look after everything until I return. Any Greek costumes, send away. And you,' she turned to the village band, 'no Zorba.' She went off with Dusty who was going to do her make-up.

I sat at a table. Didier grabbed a bottle of wine, placed it on the table and sat next to me. We watched the light change in the square as the sun began to head for the buildings behind us. If it hadn't been for the TV aerials on the roofs, satellite dishes on the outside of virtually every house and the advertising hording stuck onto the side of the chemist's, it would have been beautiful.

'It is a bit dodgy really, isn't it?' Didier had an attack of nerves.

'Don't go all moral now. Alex Beacham is no fool. She's the one who's going to profit most from this anyway.'

'Oh...not you then?'

I looked shocked and hurt.

'I'll drop the morality, if you drop the pretence that you aren't going to milk this for all it's worth when you get back to New York.'

'Deal.' I took my glass of ouzac and raised it high, so the last shard of sun caught the glass. Didier raised his.

'Go on, say it,' he growled. 'Say it!'

'To Dad,' I announced.

'To Dad.'

We drained our glasses until we choked—a matter of seconds. Straightaway a hand was clapping us both on the back.

'It is a bit rough, is it not?'

Marcel was there on cue. He put his arms around our shoulders.

'*Mes fils*,' I tried not to wince, 'we will make a good time tonight.'

I proposed another toast, but this time we switched to the safety of wine.

'*Aux hommes Noirelle.*' I toasted the men of our family in French so Didier would know I was serious.

'*Aux hommes Noirelle,*' they repeated.

'I have not yet told you of my brother, Hippolyte,' Marcel announced, 'he would have enjoyed this…although he might have provided a little more in the way of entertainment.' He laughed at his private joke. When he finally noticed that we were not in on it, he explained, 'Hippolyte was a pimp on the streets of Paris—the blackest sheep of the *black she*'s.'

He laughed again. I gave Didier a quizzical look; comedian Marcel wasn't very funny.

'Oh, come!' Marcel said in mock annoyance, 'Does our name not translate as *black she* in English, *Noir-elle*.'

I groaned, it was an English-as-a-second-language joke worthy of a Eurovision Song Contest host.

Regardless of that, Uncle Hippolyte was family history worth finding out about.

'A pimp on the streets of Paris,' I repeated. 'Perhaps I take after him—I work in advertising.'

'To pimps on the streets of New York.' Didier raised his glass.

'Ah,' Marcel lamented with a smile, 'you will be the death of me.'

We laughed, determined it would always be a joke.

The village gradually emerged into the square for the big night. Women smoothed down their dresses. Men pulled at their uncomfortable shirt collars. Mothers tutted at their children's selection of clothes and one girl was sent home to cover her navel. As they arrived, they all greeted us by name. It seemed everyone had been briefed as thoroughly on Didier and Pierre as they had been on Greque-en-Provence. I corrected the first six people who called me Pierre. They each looked worriedly at Marcel as if they'd made an error. He simply shrugged his shoulders and said, 'Children, what can one do?'

After that I gave up. I'd never see these people again, I could appear as Pierre for one night, even if the memory of having been Pierre before remained with me. It was easier this time round though: no one sniggered or said 'Ooh, Pierre is it?' and walked round on their tiptoes waving an imaginary handbag.

That night was a headlong journey down the path of least resistance, smoothed by plenty of wine. Kiki returned looking suitably made-up. Dusty had changed into an eye-catching and button-popping outfit. She was remarkably well endowed.

'Good grief,' said Didier. 'I'm gay and even I can't take my eyes off them.'

No one was allowed to touch the food until Alex arrived and saw the magnificent display. We all waited patiently, sitting at the tables around the outside facing the middle, with nothing to do other than stare at everybody else and glance occasionally at Ringo who stood at the corner of the chemist's waiting for Lennon to signal Alex was on her way. Kiki fussed over the food. Marcel sat with his legs spread in front of him staring at his feet.

Kiki permitted no music. She wanted the band fresh and in tune for Alex. They had been kept away from the wine. Everyone was getting restless waiting for her to arrive. There was food to be eaten and partying to be done, but not yet.

I looked at everyone sitting around the tables. There had to be over one hundred and fifty people and I was amazed to see so many young people. In the little time we had spent there, it seemed like everyone was over fifty. There were children, teenagers and some very attractive women. I wasn't the only one to notice. There were just as many young men capturing Didier's attention.

'You steal the women, I'll console the boyfriends,' he whispered in my ear.

As the village teetered on the brink of rebellion and a few distinctly non-Greek expletives were coughed out, Ringo finally gave the signal. Alex was on her way. Everyone stood up and started chatting politely. A string of children ran laughing across the square. Marcel ran easily and gracefully to the chemist's corner, ready to escort the guest of honour. The wheezy old man who had made his way from armchair to dinner table was now a lithe escort. I must have been pissed already because he looked quite debonair—smartly dressed with a devilish glint in his eye. I could see him seducing rich matrons at the baccarat tables of Monte Carlo.

He looked entranced as he kissed Alex's hand and paraded her into the square. Alex was also transformed. She appeared to have twice the amount of hair piled high up on her head. She wore a flowing white pleated dress. It was the full Greek goddess look. Kiki might have banned the villagers from Greek clichés, but Alex had no such qualms. She was an all-conquering Helen of Troy.

A second gaggle of children ran over to present her with a bunch of flowers. Alex squealed with delight as Kiki welcomed her to the food tables. Stopping at one particular dish, Alex turned to Kiki and pressed her arm. 'Thank you,' she whispered.

Kiki smiled through her tears as Alex chose to kick off the festivities off with *Marie-Nana's Dolmades Escargot.*

'Let the fête begin!' she announced and bit into the savoury.

It was the call the ravenous crowd had been waiting for. The band struck up and the village charged at the food. Kiki had to fend them off to ensure that Alex filled her plate first. Dishes were stripped bare and replenished. There was enough for all to have their fill. Especially of the lavender moussaka—there was plenty of that. Having tasted it, I knew why. I spat out what I had in my mouth under the table.

'That's our heritage you're spitting out,' Didier reminded me. 'The blood of our forefathers went into that lavender. It could be descended from the very field the twins seduced Marie-France in.'

I flicked some of the flavour of our ancestors at him.

Alex ate in rapture at our table.

'Aren't we lucky?' she grinned. 'But then this is your culture, isn't it. You have a blood connection to all of this. Marvellous; bloody marvellous.' Her hand swept out, indicating the square, the village, the hills and beyond to Claude's lavender fields.

'It just shows,' she articulated through a mouthful of moussaka, 'how important our inheritance is. You're so lucky to have this as your legacy.'

'Yes, and you really don't think about it until one day it just pops up when you least expect it,' I said.

'How true.' She pressed my arm sympathetically. 'Now, what is it that you do in New York?'

It was a polite question. She paid no attention to the answer, distracted by the last scraping of lavender béchamel on her dish, until I mentioned my agency. The béchamel was forgotten.

'Oh,' she used her casual tone, 'don't they have the G&K account? Do you work on that account?'

'Yes,' answered Didier gallantly between sips of wine. 'It was Pierre who came up with frozen sandwiches for them.'

She pointed her smile at me and told it to fetch.

'Oh, clever you. You must be terribly influential. My dear boy,' her arm joined the smile on the mission and lassoed my elbow, 'we are going to have to talk.'

After what she thought was a suitable pause, her arm rose to indicate the glories of Greque-en-Provence before us. I had counted to eight. I thought she would have at least made ten before coming up with the suggestion.

'Wouldn't it be marvellous if the whole world could share just a little taste of this magic?'

Alex placed one end of a *Marie-Nana Dolmades Escargot* in her mouth and leaned toward my mouth with the other end. Her lips bore down, gurgling noises emanating from behind the stuffed vine leaf. It could have been the snail trying to escape.

Alex's eyes became vast as they approached. The dark kohl eyeliner grew textured and lumpy and seemed to break into piles rather than a line. On her cheeks I could see the brush strokes of foundation. I could tell she had swept outwards on each side from her nose. The tiny facial hairs at the top of her cheeks had clung onto the powder. It all blurred as the dolmades loomed even larger.

'Alex!' A voice made her draw back.

'Leave my boy alone. Come launch your dessert.'

Marcel had rescued me from the seductress. She tried to stand up, dolmades still in her mouth like a saggy party blower. I had to steady her with one hand. With a finger of the other, I pushed the delicacy safely inside her mouth. She flicked her head back and swallowed it whole.

For all the vivacious love of food and horrible seduction, Alex was no fool and she knew a good food concept when she saw it. One that could communicate boutique style in a mass market. She knew it. I knew it. She knew I knew it. We had an understanding.

Alex and Lucien the boulanger entered the square carrying the vast tray of the apricot dessert between them. Lucien blushed in advance of the lewd remarks he knew he'd get, but I could see a sliver of pride in playing an integral role in the fête. A fanfare from the band brought on a hushed silence. Everyone remained still, waiting for something.

Alex looked around with glee at all the eyes on her. She raised her hands. Her white 'Greek goddess' dress was sleeveless. Her shaved armpits were prepared for such a gesture, but the sweat rings on the dress beneath them were not. I tried to ignore them and concentrate on her hands. They didn't move. She turned her head from side to side looking to each corner of the square. The teeth of Aphrodite gleamed in her open mouth but still there were no words. Her tongue sat poised on the tip of her incisors, waiting for the hands to move, waiting for some precise second. She took a deep breath. We all did the same. She glanced around the square again.

'Ab—ri—var!' she screamed at the top of her voice, finally bringing her arms crashing down as if starting a race.

'Ab-ri-var!' everyone chorused and began slamming their glasses and plates down on the tables in a slow rhythm. Alex held up a slice of abrivar in one hand, grabbed Lucien's hand with the other and began a Zorba-style dance as the villagers chanted 'ab-ri-var' to the tune of 'Here We Go'. It was like a food-obsessed football crowd. The chant got louder and faster as villagers joined Alex's dancing line. Faster and faster, Alex dragged the villagers around, leading them with the slice of abrivar held up. She kept pace with the ever-increasing rhythm of the chant until it was impossible to sustain. We broke into spontaneous cheering and shouting.

I was standing by my table slamming two plates down at the same time, cheering without a second of self-conscious thought. The cake, the history, the whole event might have been fake, but the sheer spontaneous joy was real. That night she might have been the one being conned, but Alex helped weave some genuine magic.

For all the massaged history, it was a glorious food experience. Admittedly the lavender moussaka was only passable, but the bouillabaisse with a side-order of souvlaki worked brilliantly. Marinated fish, superbly grilled vegetables, the heady smell of the Provençal herbs that impregnated the hummus served on Lucien's brioche-based pitta—I was swept away by them all. Greque-en-Provence worked. If you could drink enough wine to forget it was a snail wrapped in a leaf, even *Marie-Nana's Dolmades Escargot* was a garlic-infused delight. I was too busy enjoying the experience to work out exactly why, but if it could be bottled and sold it would be my biggest idea yet. This was just a blurry note at the back of my mind. That night I was enjoying, not observing, and perhaps, right there in the confused creation of a new culture, I actually belonged to something.

As everyone cheered, Marcel went up to Alex, removed the abrivar from her hand and held it to her mouth. She plunged her lips over the end and tore some off. Juice ran down her chin. Marcel wiped it with his thumb and licked it.

Half the people in the square went to the large tray and took a slice of abrivar and presented it to someone else's mouth.

I watched Didier clamp his teeth into a piece offered by one of the young men he'd identified earlier. Dark curly hair, tanned skin—I knew Didier could not resist. Their smiles said it all. Didier grabbed the slice and held it above the man's head, making him stretch upwards. He jumped and...my view was blocked by a piece of abrivar held by a young woman I had not seen when I did my sweep of the square earlier. There was no way I would have passed over her. It was the eyes. Her irises were such a dark brown they almost disappeared into her pupils, saved only by the flecks of amber. I was transfixed by the amber.

'Abrivar,' she said.

'Abrivar,' I replied and tried to bite.

She pulled the piece away and I clamped on air. She offered it again, teasingly waving the piece back and forth in front of me. I lunged but she moved away again. I did a fake lunge, she moved, I grabbed her waist and bit into the cake. Moist, sweet and delicious, it tasted like two thousand years of joy. I closed my eyes, loving every dissolved drip as it trickled down my throat. My mouth melted but I could feel someone was licking my lips, stealing my crumbs. My tongue shot out on a rescue mission. It was her turn. I held the abrivar between our faces, daring her to bite without my lips getting there first. Her lips darted forward and seized some of the sweet but not without having to touch my lips too. She giggled, grabbed the rest of the slice and ran away.

I felt the familiar slap on my back. I smiled. His slaps had become a joke that was all the funnier for being familiar. We watched the girl disappear.

'I hope Kiki didn't mind your little show with Alex,' I said.

Marcel laughed his laugh and said Kiki knew how important it was to keep the guest happy. We sat down together, his arm resting on the back of my chair. The sun had set but the night air was warm. I could feel his fingers brush against my shirt as he gesticulated. He was so French: even when his arm was out of sight, it still had to do the talking. Kiki waved to us from the food table. Alex was trying to drag her into the middle of square to join the dancing.

'About yesterday...' he began.

'Forget it. I have,' I said and I had. It was washed away by the sweetness of the abrivar.

He nodded.

'Your girl is dancing on her own.' She was swaying in the middle of the square, holding onto her skirt, casting glances at us and then turning her back the second she caught my eye.

'She is called Claudine, works at the abattoir in Brignoles. Strong hands. Supposed to be seeing Jean-Marc, but look at the way she moves. She is not happy, not satisfied, you can tell. Her mother was a beauty too, and trouble. The parents want Jean-Marc and Claudine to marry. It will happen, but there will be trouble. She wants more than he can give.' He was whispering close. The words brushed the fine hairs in my ear as they passed, making me smile.

'She needs desire, not love, not respect. Look at her hair. It is pretty but it does not shine. It needs lust. Jean-Marc has none, not for her anyway. Go...dance.'

I walked over, unsure what had just happened. She turned to me as I approached.

'Claudine.'

'You know my name?'

'I have friends...' I put my hand on her hip, feeling her skin beneath the thin cotton fabric of her skirt and swayed to her rhythm.

We danced, we moved, we laughed. Occasionally I twirled her around. It was polite, a precursor to something not so polite, something I didn't want to plunge into and should probably not have gone into at all. I became obsessed with her hair. Marcel was right. I decided I could give her that sparkle.

Marcel moved on to Didier, whispering in his ear. Didier laughed, looked shocked and then grinned again. Lots of happy grinning. I lost sight as Claudine and I gently turned around. When they came back into view, Marcel had his arm around Didier's shoulders. He'd only dared rest his arm on the back of my chair. Didier got the full body contact. Marcel's other hand kept touching him, slapping his thigh, squeezing his bicep, testing him out like a side of beef. Didier looked like he was enjoying it. I almost felt jealous. Was Marcel more comfortable, more relaxed with Didier? Of course he was, I reassured myself, that was Didier's talent. Everyone was more comfortable with him.

Claudine stopped moving suddenly. I wasn't paying her enough attention. She rolled her eyes, weary of guys who looked over her shoulder. I pulled her closer, kissed her just behind her ear. Her body squirmed at the attention she had been hoping for. She looked younger than me, probably early to mid-twenties. She was no girl, but she didn't look worn down by life.

The next time Didier and the old man turned into view, Didier was nodding in a certain direction and whispering into Marcel's ear. He was indicating the guy who had fed him the abrivar. The guy's friends were too busy watching Claudine and me to notice. He glanced at us briefly and then looked at Didier. Marcel was now whispering back, laughing, squeezing Didier's shoulder harder, rubbing his hair.

Claudine and I worked our way slowly round. Too slowly. Distracted from my own seduction, I wanted to observe Didier's.

Claudine resisted my movement, trying to slow our rotation to a halt. I persisted, but it was too late: by the time I could see them again, Didier had gone. Marcel was still there. I smiled at him and he waved me away. He was telling me to stop observing. I nodded and stroked Claudine's hair. As I did that, she began kissing my neck to demand all my attention. She got it.

The band was making their best attempt at a samba-type song. It sounded like a Ricky Martin wannabe doing a gig in a lift. Claudine took it as a cue to move in even closer. Her rhythm was perfect, even if the band's wasn't. She made the dull notes sexy, pressing her thighs around my leg and squeezing hard. Her face had a happy, carefree smile as she gently rested her head on my shoulder. Below, her wicked legs were insistent, unstoppable and arousing. I wanted to move her over to the food table, throw her onto the vast tray and have sex in the remnants of the abrivar. She did too. She looked at me with pure lust. I thought I'd melt like a slice of abrivar in her mouth. It was irresistible.

'Oh, Claudine,' was all I could say. The tension was unbearable yet I was terrified that it might peak and fade away before I'd managed to say or do anything. I couldn't invite her to Marcel's house; she probably still lived with her parents, or even with the supposed boyfriend.

Where was he? I suddenly remembered the rest of the world. I looked around the square: everyone was engrossed—in another person, a bottle, an argument. We were alone.

The only person who noticed us was Marcel as he waltzed Alex past. The earthy father flirting with son had been replaced by a suave European charmer sweeping an Australian heiress off her feet. Alex's eyes were closed and her head rested on his arm as she wafted by. Marcel's hand moved down the small of her back to her bottom. She did not resist. He raised his eyebrow at me and flicked his head to say 'Go on, get lost' and floated past us. He was a smooth dancer.

I gripped Claudine hard and felt a shudder. I couldn't let the moment pass. 'Is there somewhere we can go?'

She smiled, gave my thigh one last clench and then led me off. The relief brought laughter. The tension would be fulfilled, we could relax. Now everything was funny. The moon peeking out from behind a satellite dish on a building, the old poster for Uniprix supermarket, the paving stones, the windows. It was all hilarious as Claudine plunged me into the night village. We made a left turn down a narrow lane and then into another alley. In one doorway was a couple, the next doorway was also occupied. We weren't the only ones to disappear for a while. We took another turn and found an unoccupied spot.

The moon shone down on us but now it wasn't funny. I leaned in to kiss her and tasted the abrivar on her lips. We kissed longer and my hand reached straight up inside her tight midriff T-shirt, under the bra to the soft flesh of her breasts. They were hot. She grasped my arse as I pushed her against the wall. Suddenly our hands were everywhere. We had to explore our entire bodies in seconds. It was urgent—the delight of each patch of flesh was only a precursor to the next. Her hand moved to the front of my trousers. I was hard and uncomfortable, trapped by trousers and underwear. She sighed, almost with relief, and with one expert hand undid my fly. I stepped back to drop my trousers. She lifted her skirt and removed her underwear. My hand reached to the thighs that had trapped my leg before. They were moist, deliciously moist.

We slid together, grunting, pushing at each other, trying to get deeper. There was no caressing, no tender moment of intimacy before the passion started, no deep eye contact, just pure, driving sex. Hands were no longer for gentle stroking but used to get better leverage, everything was about the pounding, grunting out breaths as we thrust at each other. Soon her grunts became cries, her hands gripped my back, and then I lost all sense of where she was and who was what.

I slowed down, prolonging her orgasm until she pushed me off, satiated.

She leaned back against the wall, panting. Her hands went up to her hair and she pulled her fingers down over her face, dragging her lips with it. The moon lit up her hands and I saw her thumbnail with terrible clarity. It was indented. I took her hands and held them up to the moonlight to make sure. Both her thumbnails were indented, just like Marcel's, just like mine. I remembered when I had first noticed his nails at the market in Aix. It seemed like months ago. His words about Claudine's mother being a beauty came to me. I felt a wave of nausea. I'd not only betrayed Peony and screwed a complete stranger without a condom in a back alley, I'd fucked my half-sister too. And he knew. He'd made me do it, whispering about her hair in my ear. I stepped back quickly, banging my head on the wall behind.

The bump made me catch myself. I was going mad, swinging from finally appreciating some good qualities in Marcel to the extreme of accusing him of setting me up with my sibling. She looked nothing like me.

'What's the matter?' Claudine whispered.

'You really don't want to know. I'm going crazy.'

I pulled her to me and examined her hair in the moonlight, deciding that it definitely had a new sheen.

'Lots of people have indented fingernails.'

She gave me a bemused smile and nodded, putting my comment down to some faulty translation work.

'It's complicated,' I said, 'but nothing for you to worry about.' I tried to make a mental note that my judgment was flying all over the place, but I knew I was too drunk to remember it in the morning.

'What's complicated?' she said. 'You have a girlfriend, I have a boyfriend. We had fun, nobody will know. She's lucky to have someone like you, so upset over a little bit of fun.'

Peony, she reminded me again. At least now I could put all my anguish down to guilt.

Claudine pouted and swivelled her hips like a little girl. I kissed her.

She walked me back to the square but said her goodbye around the corner, so as not to arouse suspicion. As I entered the square I felt all eyes were on me, accusing me of depraved acts. They did look at me, but they looked at everyone returning to the square at that time. It was the late-night sport, working out who had disappeared with whom. The crowd had thinned considerably. I figured half were dispersed around the backstreets of St Anastasie. The rest were at home complaining about the grunting coming from their back wall.

I was relieved to see Didier sitting alone at a table. He grinned knowingly as I approached.

'Don't. I'm a loony. I've just sailed myself way past the two-chop point and back again.'

Didier's smile suggested things were looking pretty good for him. He had enjoyed an interesting time with Jean-Marc, he said, which explained Marcel's comments about Jean-Marc not giving Claudine what she wanted. I drained Didier's wine, fetched another bottle and poured out two glasses.

'Jean-Marc,' I said, 'talk about keeping it in the family.'
'What?'
'You know who Jean-Marc's girlfriend is? It's Claudine... the one I was dancing with. We went for a stroll.'
'Shit, we're home-wreckers!'
'Did you notice Claudine's thumbs?'

The minute the question came out, I knew it sounded stupid. Why would someone who'd spent the last hour with his mouth pressed against another man's body notice some girl's thumbnails? I carried on.

'They're indented. Her thumbnails are indented.'

'And that means...?'

I held my hand out and Didier's too.

'I managed to persuade myself that, because we have them and Marcel does too, Claudine is our half-sister.'

'Oh, my God, you think you've fucked your sister?' Didier's head tossed back as he laughed. '*Flowers in the Attic* here we come...ooh, did you think this before or after?'

'For God's sake, after!' I began to laugh hysterically.

Didier stopped laughing. He gave me a look I didn't understand, like he was trying to peer inside me.

'Peter,' he said in his counselling voice, 'are you sure you're OK with all of this?'

'Of course!' I slurped some more wine. 'It's been fantastic...and I, well, I actually liked him tonight. There's something almost magnificent about him, you know, if you ignore the past—which generally we can't, but we can tonight. If you do that, well, he's sort of...fun.'

I was drunk and babbling, but Didier understood me.

'Bloody hell, you don't pour out half measures, do you?'

'So I'm drunk, so what?'

'It's been a great night, Peter, but let's not get carried away.'

'I feel bad about Peony,' I announced. We weren't officially going out, but when you don't talk about it fidelity is kind of assumed. Didier had it easy. Gay men it seemed, didn't assume anything until it was stated and agreed on.

'Workshop!' Didier declared and pulled a marker pen out from nowhere. Obviously he never travelled without one. I expected Caryn to emerge from behind the chemist's wheeling the whiteboard across the square. He wrote 'Pierre—sister fucker' on my forehead in lieu of a nametag. I wrote 'Didier—gay home-wrecker' on his.

'That's not fair!' he moaned when I told him what it said.

'Please save your value judgments for the post-workshop evaluation,' I said in my best, but slurred, Caryn voice.

'I take your point on board. So let's explore sexuality and Greque-en-Provence. Brainstorm, let's rip.'

Soon we were plastering the tablecloth with all our excuses for back-alley sex. At the time they seemed to make lots of sense:

Everyone was at it.
He was a full-on member of the Clan McQueer anyway.
Her thighs insisted.
It was the abrivar.
Dad shagged Alex and when I grow up I want to be just like him.

Soon we were both lying on our backs on the table. I vaguely remember something about having to establish ownership of our words. There may possibly have been some pant-dropping and drawing around our arses on the table as a signature, but I couldn't be too sure.

We were supposed to be watching the stars, but the lights around the square were very bright and our eyesight was hazy. Suddenly the lights went out. We noticed the change but weren't sure what it was. We looked around. The square was completely deserted. We thought perhaps we should go back to the house, but the table was extremely comfortable. We'd make too much noise if we blundered in now.

'The walls are thin, as well we know,' said Didier.

'Paper thin!'

The next sound I was conscious of was a familiar cry.

'Mes fils!'

I leapt up, knocking the table over and sending Didier crashing to the ground. 'Shit, what?' He peered at me. It was daylight already. It felt like we hadn't even finished talking.

'Pierre, Didier, you must give me your help! Quick!'

Marcel was shaking us in turn, trying to jolt some sense into us.

'Quickly now, to the house!'

He took each of us by the hand and dragged us to the house. Didier kept his eyes closed, allowing himself to be dragged blind. I squinted into the bright morning light, opening my eyes more when the cool shade of the narrow St Anastasie streets hit my face.

Marcel looked like he hadn't slept much either. He'd managed a change of clothes from the night before, but that was about all. As my mind gradually began to function I figured some disaster had occurred. Lucien had probably had a fit of pique and revealed all to Alex, again.

Once inside, we were allowed to collapse into the high-armed chairs. What had seemed badly designed and uncomfortable previously were suddenly the height of luxury compared to the table we'd just slept on.

'It's Kiki!' Marcel announced. He was beginning to look frantic. His red eyes might not have been from lack of sleep.

Didier went into carer mode. His concerned look was undermined by the words 'gay home-wrecker' on his forehead. I tried to rub my forehead discreetly.

'Marcel, tell us what's happened.'

'Kiki has vanished, kidnapped, run away!'

'Don't be stupid!' I didn't have the carer gene that Didier had inherited from somewhere other than our father, probably via osmosis from Frank.

'What do you mean? What has happened to her?'

'I do not know. Kidnapped... possibly run away!'

It seemed strange that a woman of over sixty would run away like a peeved school kid. Perhaps she was at the end of the street with a cardboard suitcase and her teddy.

'Peter, make some coffee.' Didier banished me to the kitchen. I wasn't much use in the living room. It was the easier job, even if it did involve moving.

I hung about in the kitchen waiting for the percolator to hiss hysterically at me, trying to wash my forehead with dishwashing liquid. The whole percolating process seemed very slow. It must have been, because Didier came in to see how I was progressing and to report on what he had discovered.

'Kiki's not been here all night. He says he doesn't know why, but there's something he's not saying. Without a whiteboard and play-dough, I don't think I can get it out of him. You give it a go. I'll do the coffee.'

'You might try washing your forehead while you're in here,' I offered.

When I walked into the living room Marcel started getting agitated.

'So Kiki's not come home.'

He nodded.

'Because of something you've done?'

He put his hands out, palms up, and pouted slightly, admitting for the first time the possibility that it might be his fault.

'Something you did last night?'

He shrugged his shoulders.

'With Alex?'

He threw his hands up, and then sank back into his chair. 'I am an old fool. Every time I build a life, I tear it apart again.'

Didier returned with the coffee. Marcel looked awkward, as if about to get in trouble with the teacher.

'Kiki's scarpered because she caught him porking Alex.' I précised the situation.

Marcel sniffed and nodded, looking pleadingly at Didier.

'It is true, I am a monster. It was the night, the mood, the abrivar—you felt it yourselves.'

It seemed like the entire village had been unfaithful last night, but Marcel was the only one who'd got caught.

'So she just took off?' Didier questioned.

'She is a very passionate woman... possessive.'

Didier handed the coffees around. Marcel sat in his chair staring out of the window, silent except for coffee-slurping noises and lip-smacking.

I figured that must be what he did when he was nervous and uncomfortable: retreat into silence. I watched as he nodded to himself occasionally, as though a timeworn dialogue was being played out in his head. Beneath the melodrama, the sighs and self-flagellation, I think I saw some genuine regret.

'So what are you going to do?' Didier asked. His sympathy had diminished as mine had increased.

'What can I do? It is finished!'

'Do you want her back?' I asked.

'I would lay down my life for her return, but...'

He didn't look like the magnificent seducer any more. I wondered if I'd taught him he couldn't correct his mistakes. For him, our visit might have been an attempt to right a wrong and therefore prove to himself it was possible. I'd fought his will all the way, proved it wasn't possible to change the past. I was probably still drunk, but I felt a need to show him that he could make amends. I needed to know myself that mistakes *were* redeemable, anyone's mistakes.

'That's it!' I jumped to my feet. 'We're going to find her. We'll have you at the doorstep with flowers, contrition...no, that's too obvious. Dids and I can go in first, commiserate, let her know what a bastard you are...she'll see an ally in me, then we can gently bring her round, as if we're all forgiving you. Then we bring you in—'

'You can leave me out of this,' Didier objected.

'But this is your thing!' I was amazed. 'Workshopping, relationship-building all that crap!'

'You're running a marketing campaign!'

'What?'

'Excuse us a moment.' Didier marched me into our bedroom and began whispering. 'Two days ago you were all set to throttle him. Now you're his best friend in the whole world, scamming Kiki into forgiving his infidelity!'

'I can't win with you!' I blurted out. It's not fair, I almost added. The one time I thought I was doing the right thing.

'He's been unfaithful to his wife—she might be better off without him. Maybe, maybe not, but that's for them to sort out. She's not even his wife. He's still legally married to Mum.'

'I thought we were supposed to give him a chance!'

'We did, and he blew it by fucking Alex.'

'We all did some fucking last night.'

'Yeah, but we weren't all being unfaithful!'

I sensed a judgment in his words—Marcel and me, we were the unfaithful ones. Not like pure sweet Didier. I teetered on the brink of saying something nasty, something hurtful. I teetered and I fell.

'Well, it's easy being faithful when you're too scared to commit to a relationship.'

We both breathed hard. It was a long time since we'd had a stand-up 'want to say things to hurt you' row. We'd only ever had them in bedrooms we shared.

'And when have you ever committed to anything other than yourself? You hated Marcel because he's just like you—'

'Fuck off—'

'…but now I guess you're in love with the pair of you.'

'And I suppose you're the commitment master—one dead boyfriend and a lesbian flatmate for a wife. You should get married, to show just how committed you are.'

'And exactly who have you ever had a relationship with?'

'You sanctimonious prick!' I shoved him down onto the bed. He pushed me away.

'Two minutes' silence!' he growled at me.

We stood breathing heavily and staring at each other for two minutes. It was one of Didier's techniques. It was either that or punch it out. For the first minute, I burned to try the other option. For the second, I could see how horrible the things I had said were, and that he had a point.

'I'm sorry,' I said when the time was up.

'Me too.'

'I still want to help him… I guess I need to know that mistakes can be rectified.'

'That's your decision. I respect it, but I don't agree with it. I know I asked you to give him a chance, but Mum was right. He *is* all charm. It's fun and exciting, but go beyond the charm and well… I don't want you to get hurt.'

'Puh! I'll be fine.'

We drove Didier to the airport. Marcel let me do the driving, but insisted we take every exit after the one for Aix-en-Provence to be better safe than sorry. The airport looked different. Sure, it was still the same old '60s' block and cavernous hall, but it felt like an age since we'd last been there.

'I'll see you in London real soon,' I said to Didier and gave him a hug.

'Take care,' he said.

While we talked, Marcel wandered into the florist to persuade the assistants to sell him some flowers at cost price for Kiki. He told a charming story of needing to woo his wife back and eventually one of them caved in. With all his flannel, it never occurred to the assistant to ask him why he wouldn't pay full price if he loved her so much.

'Here,' he said on his return, 'some reading for the plane.'

He handed Didier more history. Didier insisted on having it copied there and then so we could both read it.

As I buckled up my seatbelt in the car to drive home, a wave of panic came over me. For all my new warm feelings, I'd never actually spent a long period of time alone with Marcel. I'd never even attempted normal conversation. The panic passed as we got moving. I felt weirdly comfortable in the car with him, for a brief moment.

The comfort was soon broken when he began singing one of his old songs.

'*Non, non, non,*
je n'me marie pas,
ni avec un prince,
ni avec un roi' he sang in a little falsetto voice.

'Do you remember that one, the girl who would not marry a prince or a king?'

I shrugged my shoulders. One of the objects that didn't disappear into the box of lost things was an old vinyl record. It had a picture of a girl holding a bunch of flowers on the cover and contained traditional French nursery songs. I remembered looking at it. I'd wanted to play it, but I knew it was soft. Tough lads didn't play records with little girls on the cover. It would still be at Mum's.

'You're hardly one to sing about not marrying,' I commented. He nodded and pointed out that the next exit was only two kilometres away.

'So what's going to happen with Greque-en-Provence?' I asked.

It looked as if the Noirelle family crisis had blown that scheme up. Its success depended on careful cooperation between Kiki and Alex which, thanks to my father, was now impossible. Marcel nodded, heaping this new guilt on his head like a fresh batch of ashes.

'That dream is ruined too, but compared to losing Kiki, what does it matter?' He turned his head to the window and added, almost to himself, 'There will be bills to pay... St Anastasie has invested so much, the food, the ouzac...'

He began whistling again.

On our return, Marcel headed down to the village square to stand there with the flowers he had bought at the airport. He had figured that with some family members still in St Anastasie Kiki would not have left the village. He looked like a nervous young boy waiting for his first date. Apparently it was how he had first wooed Kiki.

I went down too, hoping I could rescue our workshop tablecloth, but it had gone. The entire square had been stripped of any hints of Greque-en-Provence.

I left him to it. Back at the house I felt especially alone. I hadn't been there on my own before. It wasn't my home, that was for sure. I pulled out the story, relieved to have something to distract me from such empty-inside thoughts. Besides, I'd tried working the plasma screen TV and couldn't get any channels.

ST HUBERT, 1919

The end of the war only brought extra discomfort for St Hubert. While the war raged elsewhere it had been something to follow, little flags stuck on the map on the hotel wall. The end of war brought home the boys they'd learned to live without. Injured men who had lost their fine St Hubert legs and struggled to keep their balance walking down the steep hills. Screams in the night set everyone on edge. They weren't unsympathetic, but no one had expected the soldiers to actually bring the war home with them, like ugly souvenirs that sat on the sideboard. No one dared say they didn't like them.

Rodolphe, Marie-France's baby, was four years old. He had immediately inherited all Claude's love for his fathers, the twins. At sixteen, Albert knew he had to stake his claim for his father's love or be sidelined forever. Claude was a good father. He provided for his family well. Hortense thought he indulged them too much, not in a doting sort of way, but in the way he shrugged his shoulders, looked at her and said, 'Why not?'

Unlike the gurgling toddler, Rodolphe, Albert could not rely on grief for the dead to support his claim for paternal love, so he chose to win his father's attention through his other great love and joined the church choir. Claude was quietly confident when his son was not thrown out of the choir immediately and secretly allowed himself a moment's hope that perhaps some good might have come from his union with the singer, Giselle. In church he strained to hear Albert's voice in the choir, but could never quite make it out. Albert was deliberately hiding his voice.

Father Binot asked Albert why he sang so much more gently during services than in practice.

'You have the finest voice in church. It's a gift. Your father would be delighted to hear you.'

'I want to surprise him,' Albert announced. 'On his next birthday I'd like to sing something from one of his favourite operas. I don't want him to know anything until then.'

'That's a beautiful present. Other young men might be more inclined to gain public praise rather than keep their talent a secret. You are a good son. Do you know what to sing?'

Albert confessed he did not and asked for help. Father Binot readily agreed. Albert was not a bad-looking boy with a great singing voice; spending some additional time with him would be pleasant. He selected something from La Forza del Destino, *the first opera he had taken Claude to see and still the old farmer's favourite.*

Albert's speed in learning amazed the priest.

'It is truly a gift from above, made greater by your determination to use it for a good cause.' He heaped praise on the boy's shoulders with a gentle hand. The gentle hand itself

was a powerful motivator. Albert wished to be finished before it slipped elsewhere.

Binot suggested that after Claude's birthday, Albert might continue his lessons. 'I have no doubt you will soon become lead singer,' he beamed at his protégé.

Albert winced to himself, sure of what the rest of the choir would say if he was suddenly made the star after private lessons.

'I'd have to ask my father's permission,' he said, deftly delaying his response.

Albert had never returned to Madame Dupont's dark shop. He had learned the true value of their predictions during the war. They had encouraged with a gentle persistence the rumour that the patissier was a German spy. Their main evidence was the existence of apple strudel in his range of pastries. Hortense had been forthright in his defence, marching to the shop and demanding to know exactly what crucial information the Germans could garner from St Hubert.

'If anyone's aiding the Germans it's you and your accursed socks!' she thundered. It was true: every soldier who pulled on a pair of the socks knitted by Madame Dupont did seem to die within days.

Despite Hortense's blistering defence of the patissier, the rumours got as far as Marseille and a junior police detective was sent to investigate. After thoroughly examining the suspect, and some detailed sampling of his baking, it was decided the patissier was in fact a true patriot. However, in the interests of the war effort, he used pears instead of apples (a far less Germanic fruit) in the strudel and renamed it Tarte de Marne, in honour of the boys who had fought so bravely in that battle. It became one of his most popular items.

On Claude's birthday, Albert enlisted Hortense to persuade Claude to sit blindfolded in the front room. Claude sat with fatherly good humour in his chair, expecting Rodolphe to appear before him to sing happy birthday. There was some shuffling, a cough and then out of nowhere a sublime voice began to sing. The most sublime voice Claude had ever heard. It must be Caruso right there in his own living room, singing to him in person. He listened in awe, unable to believe that the great Caruso would come to his village to sing to him. He thought he might remain blindfolded and soar away with the music, but he couldn't, he had to see the great man and witness the tide of joy flooding his front room. He removed the blindfold and received an even greater surprise when he saw it was Albert singing.

At first he thought it must be a trick. He looked behind his chair, expecting to see Caruso hiding and singing while Albert mouthed the words in front of him. He wasn't there.

Claude turned back, perplexed. The voice seemed to be coming from Albert. He slowly realised: Albert had a far greater gift than a visit from Caruso. Hortense nodded to him. His most fervent wish had come true.

No one could consider him cursed now, Claude thought, not with this blessing. Hortense watched him carefully. She didn't want him dying of happiness right there. Too intense a joy could kill a man. She knew that. She didn't know anyone who had actually died of happiness, but that didn't make it untrue. If there was anyone for whom joy could be a challenging experience, it was Claude.

'Thank you, God!' Claude mouthed to the ceiling as the recital came to an end.

'Albert!' burst out Claude, 'Albert.' He fell on his son and hugged him intently. It was the first time the boy had heard his name called out in joy. As he felt his father's arms around him, he knew his plan had worked perfectly. This then, he thought as he breathed deeply, is a father's love. Never before had he felt that his father was his, and his alone. Now he experienced a love that was not portioned out. No twins, no nephew; just a father and his son.

Albert held on as long as he could. Claude enjoyed the moment too. The taint of Giselle had hampered his love for Albert. Now it had been released and it soared. Here was something wonderful from his ill-fated marriage. Perhaps destiny was playing with an even hand after all.

That pure moment ended and life returned, bringing with it thoughts of Rodolphe, the twins and the memory of Giselle. The pure love was still there, but the real world beyond the hug tainted it, like white sauce stirred with a dirty spoon.

Claude grilled Albert about how he had pulled off the deception. 'I didn't suspect a thing. It's incredible,' Claude repeated.

Even more incredible was how short-lived Albert's joy was to be. Within a week, his father produced a surprise of his own.

'Pack your bag, Albert, we're going to Marseille, to the Opera Municipal!'

This was not unexpected. A trip to the hallowed hall was inevitable. But Albert was expecting to return as well. He didn't.

'You're to have an audition with the choirmaster at the Opera. If he accepts you, you'll be taken on for training. I shall pay your board and keep and you will work at the Opera until you are ready to go on stage. You will be a brilliant singer, my son. Brilliant.'

This had not been part of Albert's plan. Fulfilling his father's dream was not supposed to result in being banished to Marseille. He was trapped. If he sang badly in the audition to fail it, his father would be furious. If he sang well, he'd be left alone in the city and Rodolphe would have a clear run at home. Claude's faith in destiny might have been restored, but Albert's was being challenged hard. He thought of Madame Dupont's shop. This was what they meant about fate biting you in the behind.

The choirmaster at the Opera Municipal only needed to hear a minute of singing. Albert was in. Claude stayed one night with his son to see him settled. When he left, Albert sought a hug, hoping that it might be filled with the same warmth as before. But Claude seemed almost eager to leave him. He was in a hurry to get back to St Hubert and boast of his son the opera singer. Albert watched his father's truck bouncing away over the cobbles of the Marseille street. Claude's head jigged up and down, as if it were on a spring.

Although he had most afternoons free, Albert had lessons and practice every morning and each evening he had to help at the theatre with the performance. For the first week he did nothing except get pushed out of the way. He couldn't believe how shabby it all was: dusty canvas backdrops, ropes everywhere, torn and tattered costumes. Old women smoothed over the cracks on their faces, pretending to be nubile virgins. Fat drunks pretended to be virile. How could this fool anyone, he thought, as he watched the guards in the chorus scratching their balls on stage while a cracked-face woman trilled.

As he left the theatre after the performance on his first Friday, a small envelope was pushed into his hand. He shoved it into his pocket and trudged back to his lodging on rue Haxo, thinking about what would be happening back home. Hortense would be getting in a huff; Marie-France would be being less than useless; and Rodolphe would be banished outside, walking between the rows of beans like Albert used to as a child.

His reverie was interrupted as he was about to cross rue Paradis. A hand clapped on his shoulder pulling him back. It was his roommate, Jacques. Several years older than him, Jacques was already performing in the chorus with the occasional featured part.

'Where do you think you're going?'

Albert shrugged his shoulders.

'It's Friday, we've been paid and La Jolie is calling.'

'You've been paid. I'm going back to our room.'

'Didn't you get your envelope?'

Albert pulled it out of his pocket and opened the corner. It was full of money.

'Is this all for me? Just for hanging out at that stupid Opera?'

'Yes, you've got to pay for your board of course, but keep that aside and the rest is yours.'

'There must be some mistake. My father pays for my board.'

'Some mistake!' Jacques' eyes lit up. 'That's no mistake, that's divine intervention. What are you waiting for? Hurry!'

'So what's La Jolie?'

In a city that prided itself on being down to earth, La Jolie was as earthy as it got. It was packed out with sailors, factory workers and half the chorus from the Opera. There were shows, there was food, there were a few fights, but, most importantly, there were drink and women.

At the door the smoky stench of Albert's future washed over him. It was delicious.

'Wow!' he said, looking at the scene in front of him. It looked like there was a shortage of chairs. Everyone had someone else on their knee. One of the ball-scratching chorus singers was lying on a table having wine poured into his mouth from a height. The wine filled his mouth, cascaded down his cheeks and onto the table. At the edge of the table, young women were sitting on the floor, heads turned up to catch the dribbles of wine in their mouths as it spilled over the edge. Not a drop hit the floor.

'Let's get some wine,' Jacques suggested.

Half a bottle later, Albert was on a table protesting his love of La Jolie, Marseille and the greatest institution in France, the Opera Municipal.

'I stake my claim to this wonderful world,' he announced and burst into the song they'd been making him learn that week. Jacques and the other lesser lights of the Opera glanced at each other. Albert was a live wire, but he was also a talent.

Another half bottle of wine and he was asleep under the table. When he woke, it was daylight. La Jolie and the stragglers left there were looking pretty miserable. Albert staggered home under the weight of his first hangover. At the door, he fumbled, tripped over a pair of boots and fell into the room. A girl screamed and Jacques sat up in his bed.

'The boots! You don't come in when the boots are outside. Where's your respect for the ladies? Poor Thérèse!'

'It's Margot,' she tossed wearily at him as she dressed.

Albert was still ill on Monday morning. His teacher was not impressed.

'You could have a great voice, but not if La Jolie is going to be your rehearsal space. I hear you gave quite a performance.'

Albert smiled.

'If you want to end up like Jacques with the occasional ten-line walk-on, go ahead. If you want to star in the Opera you need to work. And if you don't want to star, you're wasting my time and your father's money. You can go back to St Hubert.'

For the first time, the thought of going back to St Hubert didn't fill Albert with longing. Perhaps he was meant to be in Marseille. Perhaps this was the life he was meant to be living.

Albert thought Jacques lived a pretty good life. The stars of the opera had the hardest lives of all. They were always fussing about 'the voice', or dust in the air, or the exhaustion of rehearsals. Still, he wanted to please the choirmaster. If he worked hard at his lessons, he might still be able to make the occasional visit to La Jolie.

Once a week was very occasional, he decided. Twice wasn't excessive and three times was justified if it had been a hard week.

He learned fast. Learned that his voice was good, not just by Father Binot's biased standards, but by Marseille standards. He learned to drink a bottle of wine without passing out and he learned that girls loved it when he sang to them as if they were the only person sitting in a vast auditorium. Michelle, in particular, loved it when he sang to her.

Michelle was the reason Albert left his boots on the landing for the first time.

'Work, money and now this...' Albert leaned back in bed and looked down at the naked body with him. He was impressed with how quickly he had passed from boy to man. Michelle was less impressed with the speed of his passing, but he was young, she thought she could teach him a thing or two.

Albert thought things could not get better, but they did. He was sent on stage as part of the chorus. He roughly knew what he had to do and the words he didn't know he could mouth. It meant more money and he didn't have to do anything else around the theatre all evening. He could play cards with the rest of the boys. He wasn't nervous. All he had to do was follow the group and not sing before anyone else.

'It's a test to see if you get stage fright,' said Jacques. He actually had a part in this production. 'They're grooming you—watch out. Shit, I'm on!' He threw down his cigarette and strode on.

Albert had a momentary panic. He was enjoying life as it was. Life was good. Moreover, life was easy. If he became a star of the Opera then there would be more work. The stars seldom appeared at La Jolie. Jacques clearly wasn't impressed with any of them, or their lives. Perhaps he should not pass the test.

But then, it was his father's most fervent wish to hear him sing solo on the stage. Albert's nerves increased as the rest of the chorus surged around him ready to enter. The faces of Jacques, the choirmaster, his father and, for one scary second, Father Binot seemed to be in the chorus with him. Perhaps it would all be irrelevant, perhaps he was experiencing such terrible stage fright his career would end that night.

Before his stomach could get its churning underway, a sharp push in his back moved him onto the stage and the heat of the lights hit him.

Suddenly, under the lights, the tatty costumes became splendid and the woman with the cracked face turned into a nubile virgin when she sang. It was real. All the dust, ropes and rubbish backstage produced magic. Any thoughts of making mistakes or who to please shot out of Albert's head. All he could think of was being part of this new world forever. He didn't want just any part, he wanted the lead roles. He wanted to hear the crowd silenced for his solo, just like they were now for an old guy with a barrel chest who was singing with all the subtlety of a drunk sailor.

Albert buzzed with excitement and ambition. He would be the greatest dramatic baritone the world had ever seen. But first he had to celebrate his new-found passion at La Jolie by instigating a singing and drinking game. He led a group of singers leaping from table to table. At each table they had to sing the same note as he did and follow it with a gulp of wine, getting faster and faster until they were running around the tables, throwing wine at their faces and letting out wild whooping noises. Finally Jacques tripped on the edge of a table and skidded across it, causing four tenors and a baritone to crash down on top of him.

In the midst of the laughter, Jacques noted to his friend, 'You're hooked. I'm going to lose you to study and stardom, I can tell.'

'Never!' declared Albert. 'Never.' He knew Jacques was partly right—he was going for the lead roles—but he'd never abandon his friend and he'd never give up La Jolie.

Jacques took it upon himself to rescue Albert from a life of boring voice work. When La Jolie began to lose its allure, he found another bar, another club, another café. There was always another place. Michelle came along for the ride. Albert told her he was in love. She laughed and said she was too.

Within a year he was playing support roles—one of the Opera's youngest featured singers ever. Jacques called him Mozart, the prodigy. Claude came to Marseille especially to see his son, delighted at his progress. His voice had grown remarkably but it was still immature.

'You must work harder on it,' Claude told him.

Albert felt he could do nothing to please this man. 'You left me here alone. I had no one to look after me, but I got through it, got through all those miserable months on my own. I've done better than anyone else and yet all you do is criticise. What do you know anyway, you're...'

He stopped short of saying 'just a yokel'. The shock on Claude's face was enough to silence him.

'I'm sorry, Father,' he muttered. Claude accepted his apology.

'I can't sleep properly because my roommate isn't serious about his singing. He's out all night and comes home drunk. I need my own place. I'd pay for it out of the little I earn, but I'd have to give up my Italian lessons. I suppose I could do without them for a while.'

This was a part lie or, as Albert told himself, an 'unfinished picture'. His father readily agreed to pay for a better room and even stayed in Marseille an extra night to help him find somewhere. They found a place with its own stove and sink. Claude was not so eager to depart this time, wanting to linger and savour the life of an opera singer.

Albert did not want his father experiencing his life, however, especially not the part that involved his wife, a very pregnant Michelle. On hearing the news of her pregnancy, Albert had done the honourable thing and felt himself extremely mature, going against the advice of his friend.

'She's not really the type you have to marry,' Jacques said. 'There are ways you know and, besides, you're hardly the first footprint in the snow.'

Albert challenged him, defending his fiancée's honour.

'Have it your way,' Jacques replied, and decided against making Albert ask how his future wife used to make her living.

Despite his increasing exhaustion, Albert was impressed with himself—a rising dramatic baritone with a wife and family. At eighteen he had what most men spent a lifetime trying to achieve. Everyone was happy. The Opera was pleased with his progress, his father enjoyed boring St Hubert silly with stories of his son, Michelle was a mother, and Albert had a son named, in a fit of classical good taste, Hippolyte. Even Jacques, despite the occasional whinge, did not feel abandoned.

The flush of success did not last long. The excitement of going on stage soon gave way to the drudgery of traipsing on night after night to sing the same words, while the same fat old men still got all the adulation. The thrill of parenthood dissolved into the screech of the baby and Michelle's constant demands for food and clothes for the child. He felt like a swallow desperately hunting for food all day long to toss into the massive mouth of its infant before going off to find more. Michelle also wanted things for herself: clothes, crockery, ornaments. She complained he was never at home, always studying or performing or drinking with Jacques. She wanted to go out.

Wherever he went, hands were being slammed on tables: his teachers demanding greater focus, his wife demanding money or Jacques demanding another drink. Demands and secrets went round and round. He couldn't tell the Opera about Michelle, he couldn't tell Michelle when he was out with Jacques, and he couldn't tell Jacques that the Opera Municipal said they had high hopes for him.

If this was adult life, he wasn't ready for it. He could barely stand another week, let alone another twenty years. He was too young. He should be enjoying life he told himself, like he used to.

Then his teacher added to his woes with 'great news'. On his recommendation, one of the best teachers in Italy had agreed to take Albert on as a pupil.

'It is a remarkable opportunity,' his teacher told him. 'An honour. A virtual guarantee of success.'

'And an impossibility,' Albert thought, tortured by an opportunity which he could not take being dangled in front of him.

'All you have to do is pay for your own keep. Your father will no doubt help.'

That night Albert dreamed he was outside St Hubert on the steep road. He could hear the slaves' chorus from Nabucco being sung in the village. It sounded so perfect it filled him with a joy he could not describe. He tried to walk up to the village to join in, but continually tripped over. Each time he fell, the road grew steeper and steeper. He looked back and saw Michelle and Jacques pulling at his feet, tripping him up, while Hippolyte clapped and smiled every time he fell over. The blissful singing lost key and turned into screeching. Albert woke to the sound of Hippolyte crying.

'I am accepting the offer to train in Italy,' he told his teacher quietly. 'It's too good an offer to pass up. But please, I would rather keep it quiet. Singers can get jealous.'

The teacher smiled knowingly.

Albert knew it was the most terrible and wonderful thing he had done in his life. It was his destiny, but he was well aware that every destiny had its price. He left two months' rent and living expenses on the table, along with a promise to send more money from Italy. The money Claude sent to him, he would forward to Michelle. He'd have to find some other means of supporting himself in Italy.

Going quietly, not telling anyone, was the best way Albert told himself. This time, there would be no screaming, no fists on tables. He was too young for the life that had overtaken him in Marseille. Going away was for the best. Eventually everyone would see that they were all better off without him. It was, he almost persuaded himself as he sat on the train rattling eastward, as much for them as for himself.

Marcel returned from the square after two hours, without the flowers.

'It is good,' he announced. Dusty had collected them from him without a word.

'Does it mean Kiki will talk to us?' I asked.

'No, it means her family are willing to allow communication. They are a very traditional family. Descended from Spartans. Fierce warriors.'

Apparently there was nothing to do but wait. With Kiki gone, it was down to me to find some food in the house. The fridge was stacked with uneaten lavender moussaka. I looked around for the microwave. There wasn't one. Kiki had hidden it to make her kitchen look more authentic for Alex. I slopped some out into bowls and carried it through to the living room.

Lavender moussaka is not a dish best served cold. We barely touched it. Marcel stared gloomily out of the window as if his life was making off for the hills and he was determined to watch it go. I tried to distract him.

'So did Albert really become a great opera singer?' I asked.

'That remains to be seen.'

'You must know.'

'Indeed I must, for soon our family story will cease to be history and become living memory.' He broke off, looking up suddenly. 'Someone is coming.'

He shot up out of his chair. I was expecting him to run for the door, crying 'Kiki!' Instead he ran into their bedroom and shut the door, leaving me to attend to the guest.

It was Dusty. I've never really been a 'talk to the jugs because the face don't count' kind of guy, but with Dusty it was hard. She was wearing a blouse that opened in a way that defied gravity. The natural fabric weave revealed the curve of her breasts perfectly. However much I tried not to look, there they were.

I didn't think I'd stared that long, but before a word was said, the flowers Marcel had been holding hours earlier were slapped across my face, some Greek (without a trace of a French accent) was hurled at me and Dusty stormed back to the gate. From there, she turned and said in a sing-song manner that suggested she'd rehearsed the line without a clue what it meant, 'You come tomorrow at three of the afternoon to the basketball stadium. Just you. Not him.'

She understood the last two words, as she tossed them towards the house and sent them flying faster with big flick of her hand. The breasts looked like they were going to fly off through the window too, but she stopped them and walked off.

Marcel saw this as a good development, but he wasn't the one with gerbera petals up his nostrils.

At the appointed hour the next day I made my solitary way through the village. I left Marcel lying on his bed, forearm draped over his eyes protesting he didn't deserve such a son or such a wife.

Even the home theatre system and plasma screen TV were more luxury than he deserved. I'd suggested he watch something to take his mind off his misery. It was my attempt to find out how to get the damn thing to work because I didn't fancy another evening of the drama queen sobbing into his cold moussaka, but I was foiled. He could not distract himself from his remorse, he claimed.

No matter what flowers and insults might be tossed at me in the basketball stadium, nothing could be worse than Marcel's grand misery.

The village was quiet as I walked through. The few people around nodded knowingly, scowled or shrugged their shoulders. I presumed everyone knew what was going on. I had a brief moment of concern for Alex. If she had any sense she'd have fled before being chased off the edge of a cliff by a posse of pitchfork-wielding villagers.

In the basketball stadium there were five chairs set out in a small circle, exactly in the middle of the ring at the centre of the court. There was a perfectionist in our midst. Ringo greeted me with his a flick of the head and manipulation of the toothpick in his mouth. He closed his mouth over the entire upright toothpick then pushed it out again.

I took my seat in the negotiating ring and discovered what had happened to the tablecloth Didier and I had done our impromptu workshop on. It was spread out on the floor along with all the drunken excuses we had written.

Dad shagged Alex and when I grow up I want to be just like him was placed right in front of me. I was also able to confirm we had drawn round our bums and signed them too.

The tablecloth forced me to jettison the 'do we really know that's what they were doing?' argument. Round one to Kiki.

Once I was sitting in position and it was clear that I'd seen the damning evidence, Kiki was led out by Lennon and Dusty. She looked slightly taken aback when she saw me. That was good, I thought; my main pitch would resonate with her if she was surprised it was me, and not Didier, who had stayed behind. Point to Peter for surprise character witness.

'My Peter, you are good to me!' She held out her arms, ready to be kissed. I leaned forward and kissed both cheeks. They were dry.

'You come to keep me from him. That is good.'

We sat down, Kiki next to me.

'Perhaps we could talk alone?' I suggested. Kiki looked shocked, triggering a chain reaction from Dusty, Ringo and Lennon.

'What did he say?' Lennon asked angrily.

Kiki dismissed it as unimportant.

Putting one hand to her mouth, she held mine with the other, nodding quietly to herself. 'Monster...you know that.' She gestured to the cloth of guilt beneath us.

The time had finally come for me to do what I did best and what I was there for. Time for the pitch—and the first rule was, always agree with the client's initial analysis before you completely contradict it.

'Yes, nobody knows better than me.' I nodded in unison with her.

Ringo was splayed out on his chair with his hands behind his head. Lennon leaned forward as if listening intently. Dusty tried to stay upright, resting her strained spine on the chair back. I flashed the guys a furious look and they started nodding sympathetically too.

'Monster,' Kiki uttered again.

'Monster,' I repeated and glared at the nephews.

'Monster,' they echoed.

'I gather you did not expect to see me?' I asked.

'No, I did not!' Kiki replied.

'Are you not wondering why I, the one who hated Marcel most, am here with him?'

Kiki thought for a moment then nodded.

That was my cue. I launched into my personal journey with Marcel the magnificence of his style, the taste of apricots in the market, the grandeur of his history in the graveyard. His love of life and his charm. She sat impervious to my pause after each of his virtues until, finally, she nodded and conceded one of them. That was my cue, I could begin to reel her in.

'Does he not always find the best restaurant?'

'He does,' she agreed.

Ringo, Lennon and Dusty stared at her and nodded when she seemed to agree to something.

'Does he not have a passion for life greater than any other man?'

They waited for her response and nodded in agreement when she finally accepted my words.

'He is swept away by the passion of his life, the intensity of moments, as I know only too well.'

Her hand grasped mine in sympathy. Ringo, carried away, grasped Lennon's hand.

'The fête was such a moment.'

Kiki's hand snapped back from mine. Ringo did likewise. I was determined not be distracted. They were all entranced: a moment's pause and the spell could be broken. You had to carry the whole room, not just the key people, I knew that. One single dissenter could poison an entire basketball court.

'A man cursed by the mistakes of his life, hounded not just by the force of destiny but by the furies of his own guilt.'

They all nodded.

'Didier and I are victims of those errors.'

Kiki returned her hand to mine. 'My poor Peter!'

Sympathetic groans from the audience.

I grasped her hand in both of mine and went for the big line.

'Kiki, the reason I am here today is to tell you that I forgive him.'

I gazed deep into her eyes, ignoring the stifled sob from Ringo. I held her dry little turtle hand in mine as her head shrunk back slightly into its shell and her eyes widened with the implication of what I had said.

'Yes, I forgive him. He is a man of huge character, a man of many wonders and many flaws. He is cursed by those flaws, even more than you and I. I have learned to forgive those flaws and, if you truly love him, you must too. You must accept that he is doomed to make tragic mistakes and his life is a perpetual struggle to correct them.'

She gasped.

'Forgive him, as I have done.'

Ringo and Lennon were on the edges of their chairs. Dusty leaned forward, resting her breasts on her knees to stop herself toppling over.

'Oh,' Kiki let out a quick breath as if in sudden realisation, '*mon pauvre Marcel!*'

I'd done it.

As Kiki and I walked back through the village, I wondered just who had persuaded who. It was a safe bet that this wasn't the first time Marcel had transgressed, but now there was a little glint in Kiki's eye and a bit more power to her elbow. She knew who had the upper hand in the relationship now. If he wasn't already, Marcel would soon be as pliable as pitta brioche dough.

When the gate creaked open at the house, Marcel ran out and laid himself low on the ground at Kiki's feet. He refused to move.

'Puh!' she said and walked into the house, 'tell him, when he is finished, I will be waiting in the bedroom.'

His head came up sharply while his body remained respectfully prostrate.

'*Mon fils*, you are brilliant.'

I nodded and did a 'puh' and shoulder shrug of my own.

Marcel stood up and suggested I take a walk around the village.

'You did what you are good at,' a saucy grin crept across his face, 'now it is my turn.'

He ran into the house, but appeared again quite suddenly with more Noirelle history in his hand. He thrust it at me.

'Here, do not come back too quickly!' He gave me an earthy groan and a wink.

I shuddered as I walked out the gate and heard a girlish shriek from Kiki. You're never too old to be repulsed by your parents having sex.

MARSEILLE, 1931

Destiny fulfilled or a fervent wish come true—it amounted to the same thing. To Claude, it was destiny. The hum of expectation at the Opera Municipal was a deafening buzz in his ears. To his eyes, everyone looked more excited than he'd seen at any previous visit to the opera. They were here to see his son, Alberto Noirelle, perform his first lead role in La Forza Del Destino.

It had taken ten years of intense training in Italy for Alberto Noirelle to reach this point. Ten years of dedication to the craft under the finest teachers in the world. It had not come cheaply. Time and again Alberto had written to Claude asking for more money. There was voice coaching, acting classes, Italian lessons, accommodation, not to mention a wife and son back in Marseille demanding more and more money. Michelle never failed to mention his desertion, how hard life had become and how deprived poor little Hippolyte was.

Luckily Claude accepted the exorbitant costs of everything in Italy without question. His son's career in opera should not be stifled by lack of funds, no matter what economies had to be made at home. Here was proof that a Noirelle could transcend his fate and Alberto carried the hopes of the whole family.

Claude took his seat in the almost full auditorium, chafing under the collar of his new shirt and hoping the almonds he had nervously devoured earlier would not repeat on him. Sitting next to him was Rodolphe, a handsome young man of sixteen. Claude had decided this would be the perfect occasion to introduce his grandson to the glories of opera. A moment for the Noirelle men to be united in sublime art. Hortense and Marie-France had expressed as much disappointment as they thought seemed genuine and stayed in St Hubert.

It was Rodolphe's first time in a theatre. Everyone looked so rich, and so comfortable in the opulent setting. Were Claude himself less nervous he would have been able to reassure the boy and point out the dust on top of the gold painted adornments. He did manage to point up to the back of the theatre to the seat where he had sat on his first visit to the Opera. This was true progress, Claude thought, as he measured how much nearer the stage they were.

Claude had refused to go back stage to meet his son before the performance. He didn't want to see the machinery behind the magic.

'I want the first time I see you to be as a proper opera singer, as if I were just another member of the public. We will meet afterwards,' he had shouted on the telephone. As much as he enjoyed new technology, Claude always assumed it needed a helping hand, or in the case of the phone, extra volume to help his words on their long journey.

When Alberto first appeared, it took a moment for Claude to recognise him. He had added a few kilos to his waist while in Italy, along with the O to his name. He seemed so much older, more than ten years older.

Once he was sure it was his son, sublime bliss set in. This was the moment he had lived for. His son, singing one of his favourite roles better than anyone else before him. He could die happy, right now he thought to himself.

And he did.

It could have been the sheer beauty of Alberto's singing, but it was more probably the almond that popped up and blocked his windpipe coupled with Claude's determination not to cough during his son's performance.

Under strict instructions not to move or make a noise, Rodolphe studiously stared at the stage, refusing to look round even when his grandfather gripped his hand tight on the armrest and refused to let go. He assumed that getting carried away by emotion was usual for his grandfather at the Opera.

The ushers carried Claude away during the first interval, after having waited for the auditorium to empty.

'It's my grandfather,' Rodolphe stuttered to the house manager, his hand still in the ball that had been gripped so tightly. 'Claude Noirelle, Albert's father.'

The house manager flew into a panic and debated with the ushers whether Alberto should be informed. They stood for a moment with their hands over their mouths, unable to find the right course of action.

'You must decide,' one usher suddenly announced to Rodolphe, 'you are the next of kin.'

Relief swept over the house manager's face. 'Yes, you decide!'

They all stood and waited for a decision. Rodolphe stared at the body of his grandfather. All he could think about was how Hortense would scold him, as if it were her runner beans that had been killed. He wanted to say the right thing, to honour his grandfather.

'The patrons are returning!' an usher whispered quickly. Rodolphe thought of the hundreds of important people and the respect and adoration his grandfather had for the Opera Municipal.

'What would your grandfather have wanted?' the manager asked.

'Tell Alberto after the performance,' Rodolphe decided.

'Good,' said the manager before he could change his mind, 'Would you like to see the second act?'

Rodolphe was led back to his place. He kept his hand off the armrest for fear of feeling Claude's hand again.

Alberto barely recognised him after the performance.

'You've grown, quite a handsome man. Too handsome for the girls of St Hubert, eh? Where is my father?'

It was left to Rodolphe to take his uncle to the prop room where Claude's body had been laid. He was resting on the ground under two palms trees from the Aida set.

'He died,' said Rodolphe as they looked at the body. It seemed to Rodolphe that he must make Claude's passing as noble as possible. 'He was overcome with joy. It was the happiest moment of his life and he just…'

Rodolphe omitted the almonds.

'"If I could die hearing my son sing in the Opera Municipal…"' Alberto began to quote his father.

' "… I would die a happy man."' His nephew finished the line they had both heard so often.

'Destiny finally smiled upon him.' Alberto smiled down at his father's body as kohl eyeliner ran down his face.

Hortense and Marie-France came to Marseille for the reading of the will. St Hubert had been shocked to learn of the death of one of its leading citizens, although they *did say that fate had finally caught up with him.*

'I wonder if the remaining Noirelles will hold out as long,' Madame Dupont had questioned.

'They say Albert caught tuberculosis in Italy. He may well have sung his last.' Madame de Beaumarchais sighed for the little boy who had shared his cake with them.

'You look like a real opera singer!' Hortense declared when she saw Alberto and prodded him in the waist. 'You didn't starve in Italy then, Albert.'

'"O", it's Alberto,' he corrected her.

'Oh.' She raised her eyebrows.

Hortense was the only one to receive good news from the will. Claude had left her a cottage in the village and a small amount of money. He had always promised to look after her and had been as good as his word. Alberto and Rodolphe were to have the house and farm jointly, but with Alberto's expensive tutelage in Italy there were many debts to be paid off. They would both have to be sold.

'You must all come and live in Marseille. I will provide for the family now.' Alberto was stung with guilt. 'It's what he would have wanted.'

He wasn't sure how he would manage, but having shirked family responsibility once, he was not going to do it again.

'Not me!' announced Hortense. 'I'm done with housekeeping, and I wouldn't last a day here in Marseille. Besides, someone's got to stay in St Hubert to keep those old witches in Madame Dupont's shop in check.'

They could all see Hortense, released from the burden of housekeeping, dedicating her life to plaguing the old gossips.

'And what about the patissier?' Marie-France asked slyly.

'That old fool! I suppose he needs me to keep him from going mad too.'

Rodolphe was not too distressed at moving to the city. He had dreaded the thought of taking over the lavender farm and Marseille had so many attractions: cinemas, theatre, people, excitement. He could go to the movies every day of the week if he wanted.

So the Noirelles changed from being a country family of farmers to a city family of performers. However, Alberto's family was not yet complete. He still had not found the courage to visit Michelle and Hippolyte. His own son would be eleven years old.

At the Opera, Alberto had renewed his acquaintance with Jacques. Years in Italy and a lead role still hadn't changed him completely. La Jolie might have closed down but there were other bars to be introduced to. It took a couple of bottles of wine before Alberto could raise the subject of his family.

'Have you seen Michelle?'

Jacques looked awkward.

'Best to let things lie... you did the right thing going to Italy.'

'Do you know where they are?'

'Forget them.'

'Tell me!'

'Very well, she went back to her old trade. I suppose she had to get money somehow.'

'What do you mean?' He thought of the stream of money that had flown from St Hubert to Milan back to Marseille, all for her. And besides, what 'trade'?

'I tried to tell you before you married her, but you were too infatuated. She was a whore before you met her and she's one again now.'

'But Hippolyte!'

'Best little pimp in the business from what I hear.'

Alberto had not been above the occasional visit to an 'establishment' in Italy, but being an occasional customer was a world away from your wife and son working in the industry.

Ten years of guilt, which he had carefully wrapped in money and posted off to Michelle, erupted into anger. How much easier his life would have been, how much less debt Claude would have amassed, if only Alberto had known the truth all those years ago. Michelle must have cackled as she wrote those badly spelt letters demanding money.

Hopes of reuniting his family were torn up and he thought of how naïve a boy he had been. His anger did not extend to Hippolyte. His son had faired worst of all. He must be rescued.

Jacques tracked down Michelle's address. They had moved closer to where most of their business lay, nearer the old port. It smelled of fish heads, boat oil and a thousand years of business. Their apartment was on the fourth floor of a run-down building, the floorboards trodden into the same colour as the walls. At the top of the stairs, the wall was virtually black where panting customers had paused and grabbed the corner for support. Hundreds of filthy, grabbing hands heading towards his son. Alberto shivered, repulsed.

He knocked on the door. A boy answered. He looked older than Hippolyte would have been.

'You're early,' he said without looking, 'come back in...'

He finally looked up and realised it wasn't his expected visitor.

'What do you want?'

Albert was shocked into silence. This business-like boy was Hippolyte.

'First time? I can fit you in in about an hour. Give me the money now and I won't give your spot to anyone else.'

The boy smiled. Nervous first-timers were easy. If you got them to pay and go away, they seldom came back. If they did, he denied everything and shouted for the police.

'I haven't come for a...woman.'

'Oh!' The boy bit his lip. 'I can probably find you someone but it'll take time. What are you after? A sailor, bit of rough?'

Alberto stared in horror as his son talked like a fifty-year-old madam.

'No, I've come for you.'

Hippolyte rolled his eyes.

'Sorry, I only take the bookings. The youngest I can get you is fourteen.'

'No, I'm your father.'

'I don't do that stuff. OK?'

Alberto felt a small surge of relief, grabbing at the only blessing in this nightmare.

'I don't want that, Hippolyte. I am your father—Alberto Noirelle.'

'Oh, shit!' The boy looked shocked for the first time then quickly recovered. 'We were starving, we needed the money.'

Alberto glanced over the boy's shoulder, the building might have been squalid but the apartment was red and plush.

'Come here...' He moved forward to touch his son, but Hippolyte went to close the door on him.

'No, wait!' Alberto stopped the door. Used to getting rid of unwanted customers, the boy punched Alberto hard in the stomach. The father resisted, grabbed the boy's hand as it flew towards him for a second blow and pulled him out into the corridor.

Within seconds, the boy was under his arm being carried off down the stairs. Hippolyte bit into the hand clasped over his mouth, but the harder he bit, the harder Alberto pressed his hand.

It was not the triumphant return to Marseille Alberto had planned. He had hoped for glory: his father's joy, his wife's forgiveness and his son's adoration. Instead he got his father's corpse, his wife's depravity, his son's hatred and the dead twins' family as his responsibility.

Every moment of the day there was a crisis. Marie-France, used to having Hortense running the house, struggled to produce a meal. Hippolyte ran off to the nearest prostitute at every opportunity. At the Opera, Alberto barely had time to rehearse his roles before he was on stage performing. His voice suffered. Reviews were lukewarm. The Opera Municipal was beginning to doubt the wisdom of bringing him back.

At least there was Jacques, and a couple of bottles of wine after the show. It was his only relaxation. The wild excitement of La Jolie had gone; the whole city seemed quieter, better behaved. Nobody sang or danced on tables any more. When he tried once, he was told to sit down and shut up. The younger singers were shocked at his behaviour.

'Bah!' said Jacques. 'Those young ones might know how to sing, but they still need to learn how to live!'

He shouted the last half of this across the bar. Alberto nodded and slammed his glass down on the table, smashing it. They were thrown out.

They sat on the edge of the pavement in rue Haxo on the spot where Jacques had stopped him with his first wage packet. The cars trundled past them.

'So this is my fate then!' Alberto said ruefully to his friend.

'At least you have progressed. You've been to Italy and come back a star!'

'But we're both sitting on the same street,' replied Alberto.

Life eventually settled into some sort of routine. Rodolphe got a job in a movie theatre. Alberto was not impressed. He said live entertainment was the real art, but the job brought in money.

Hippolyte stopped running away. He'd made it back to his old apartment only to find his mother had vanished. 'She took off the week after you went,' a neighbour told him. 'Said it was your father's turn.'

He still liked to walk the streets around the old port where he'd catch that smell of fish and oil. It meant comfort for him, especially when it was wrapped in the scent of the girls who used to work for him. He was a kid again now; they cuddled him, kissed his head and sent him on his way. He went back to his father's house without being dragged there, but resignation to his situation did not remove the burning anger from every glance he gave his father.

With a calmer home life, Alberto's singing was improving. It was a struggle to win his reviewers over, but slowly he was doing it. The world was not alight for him, but it was warming up.

Marie-France, after Hortense had visited for a fortnight and given her some intensive coaching, managed the house fairly well. Sometimes Alberto wouldn't go out after the performance. He would come home and sit with Marie-France. They'd talk of St Hubert, Raymond and Alphonse. Somehow it was safe to *talk about them now. Even for Marie-France, they were the past now. Exiles from a different world, they enjoyed their memories.*

It was strange viewing her through a man's eyes. She was older than he was, but somehow she didn't seem much older than she had in the village. Alberto felt much older, as if he had overtaken her. He saw what the twins had seen.

Marie-France had only made love once in her life, in 1914. The chances of her ever finding someone else receded with every year, especially living with Alberto as a husband in every other sense.

As they sat there alone in the night, it was too convenient. It was easiest for them both to give in, and when they did they finally laid the twins to rest.

Nobody was too surprised when Marie-France revealed she was pregnant once again with the next addition to the Noirelle family.

I read through the story sitting on some steps leading down to the main road through the village. I figured that wasn't really enough time for Marcel to complete the reconciliation so I wandered through the village itself. It looked quiet but large sections of the population lurked behind corners ready to jump out at me, like cut-out figures in an army shooting range.

First off it was Jean-Marc. As I walked past a laneway, he grabbed my arm and pulled me quickly out of view.

'Wrong one!' I said, worried he was going to leap in with a pash.

'Where is Didier? What has happened? Your whole family is disappearing. He didn't say goodbye.'

I tried to work out if he knew I'd had sex with his girlfriend or whether he actually cared. I thought it best not to mention it.

'He flew back to London. I'm sure if you need to talk, he would be happy for you to call him.'

'Really?' Jean-Marc sounded delighted. I think I was having a tender moment because I felt perhaps this one might be quite good for Didier.

'Sure. I know he'd want to hear from you.'

Jean-Marc grabbed my head and kissed me hard on the lips—no tongue fortunately.

'Give that to him from me!'

That wasn't going to happen, but before I could tell him, he'd run off. Someone was walking up the steps at the end of the laneway.

It was just as well he ran off because it was Claudine of the strong hands and insistent thighs.

'What did Jean-Marc want? Does he know about us?'

'No… I don't think he'd care if he did.'

She nodded. 'Your brother?'

I winced, trying to remember what Didier's current policy on outing other people was. I felt she deserved to know.

'Yes.'

She wasn't surprised and took it as a cue to push me up against the wall and kiss me again. Without the alcohol and abrivar, there was no being swept away. I gently removed her from my mouth.

'The girlfriend?' she tutted. I nodded as sympathetically as I could.

'Never mind—here!' She grabbed my head and kissed me hard.

'Give that to her from me!'

With that she ran away, taking her amber-flecked eyes and, even in the sober light of day, magnificently sheeny hair with her.

I barely got another ten metres when I was stopped again, by Maurice, the senior gendarme. He wanted to know what was supposed to happen with the leftover ouzac.

'The regional inspector might enjoy it. It pays to keep him happy.'

He grumped up when I told him it wasn't a good idea to spread too many details about Greque-en-Provence.

'Pah… Alex is gone. There will be no tourists, only the bills for your family to pay.'

I didn't like the idea of being partly responsible for the costs of the fête. Before I could respond, Lucien approached, demanding to know what we had done with Alex. They were supposed to bake together that morning and she had not turned up.

'You old roué!' The gendarme nudged Lucien's shoulder and got a swift cuff around the head. Maurice cuffed him back. Lucien started pushing.

'She's an old tart! Marcel had his way with her, did you not know?' the gendarme shouted. 'Down there, in the alley, like a cat!'

'She is not! She is a woman with a passion only for food!'

A punch was thrown and it was on. This drew out Alphonse, the chemist, who was keen to watch the scrap. They fell to the ground and began rolling across the main road.

The chemist suggested now might be a good time to make my escape.

'What do I need to escape for?'

He laughed and pointed to the street corner. A posse of angry villagers was marching down the street.

'There he is!'

The mob surged forward but was momentarily distracted by the two fighting seniors who, after a brief tussle with Maurice's handcuffs, had managed to lock their hands together. Lucien taunted Maurice with the key, threatening to throw it away.

'Throw it,' the gendarme shouted. 'Somebody, quick, kill me now! I would rather die than spend an hour in this old fool's company.'

'See what your precious regional inspector thinks of you when he sees you've been harassing one of the village's leading citizens!'

'Pah! He'll give me a medal for arresting the mastermind behind the criminally bad croissants that have been flooding the village.'

The key was tossed and one-handed combat resumed.

The chemist was right: I should have scarpered. The band was insisting that someone pay for their services. The butcher was out of pocket, as were the vegetable supplier and the fruit merchant. The whole fête had been organised on credit. Now that the scheme had fallen apart and the tourists would not be flooding in, they wanted payment.

'Speak to Kiki and Marcel!' I took a step backwards. Why was I the object of their anger?

'We cannot, they have run off!' the accordion-player said.

'But they're at home together, I left them there.'

There was an uproar of disagreement. They thought I was lying. The Noirelles had ripped everyone off. The celebrity chef had vanished. Someone had to pay.

I worked out amid the babbling wrath that, far from spending hours in reunion lovemaking, Marcel and Kiki had done a runner.

'Maurice, arrest Pierre!' someone shouted.

'My name's Peter,' I mumbled automatically and caused even more outbursts for denying my French heritage. Fortunately Maurice paid them no attention. He was too busy aiming his pistol at the handcuff chain and threatening to shoot himself free. If he had to spend one more minute in the company of the boulanger he'd shoot himself, he declared. 'Or I could eat your brioche, that would kill me as quickly.'

Lucien started at him.

'Better still, I could just shoot you!'

There was nothing I could do. I had my credit card, but that was up at the house. I contemplated sprinting back to the house and shouting that I could charge the whole fête to Visa but I sensed they were looking for a cash settlement. Words were failing me. There was no persuading them out of this one.

It felt like they were gradually stepping in closer and I had visions of myself being carried off to a guillotine. There was nothing for it: I turned and legged it as fast as I could. A shout went up, the crowd ran after me and the hunt was on. I swore that when I looked over my shoulder I could see a flaming torch.

A new noise was added to the sound of the mob: a car horn. Someone was forcing their way through the crowd at pretty high speed. The car slowed down a little as it approached me and the passenger door flew open. Without even looking who was driving, I ran alongside and leapt in.

'Thanks!'

'No worries!' said the driver in a heavy French accent. It was Jean-Marc. After our brief meeting, he'd written a letter for Didier, having decided the kiss wasn't enough, and had gone up to Marcel's house to give it to me. The house was empty, locked up and my suitcase had been standing by the gate with an envelope attached.

'I realised you would be in trouble as the only Noirelle left in town, so I took the bag and got the car.'

In the back seat of the car were *two* bags.

'I'm coming with you!' Jean-Marc whooped. He leaned out of his window and shouted 'I'm gay!' at the St Anastasie town sign as we tore past it.

I took the letter off my case and opened it.

My dear Pierre,
We need to celebrate our love for a few days. I trust you will be able to manage everything. Give my love to Didier.
Your father,
Marcel

That was it. My father, my bastard father. Abandoned again, only this time to a mob of angry villagers and a recently liberated gay man who was coming out to every car we passed on the road to Marseille airport. I tossed the letter out of the car window to blow away with the contents of Jean-Marc's sexual closet.

I think Didier liked the present I brought him from Provence. Most people get a water jug with some rustic grape design; he got a live-in lover. And it *was* a present from me. At Marseille airport I ended up forking out for both airfares on the next flight to London. Given that he'd just rescued me from a lynching, I felt obliged.

Jean-Marc had been horribly excited at the airport and kept asking me how he could be 'more gay'. I told him he was doing a pretty good job of shouting it from the highest high and, other than getting sued by Tom Cruise, there wasn't much else he could do. He looked devastated, so I went to the music store, bought him a Kylie CD and told him to learn the lyrics. The CD Walkman went on and I had peace for the rest of the flight.

Sadly, that peace left me with my thoughts. Not a good idea. I tried to focus on something else as I stared out of the window, but it was useless. Jean-Marc's incessant self-confessing must have been catching because I had a bit of admitting to do as well. Experiencing Marcel buggering off again meant I couldn't pretend any more that I didn't remember him.

I did. I dusted off the memory tapes that I'd tried to leave behind in the box of lost things and played them again.

He was great fun, my dad. With him it was all games. I remembered walking along the street with him swinging me by the arms. It was always Mum who told me off. He'd let me do anything I wanted, even once told me what to say to Mum to get me out of trouble.

He'd go away a lot 'with work', whatever his work was. I never really found out. I'd ask when he would be coming back and Mum would show me on the calendar how many days it would be. One time my father didn't come back. There was a call and Mum said he had been 'delayed'.

I didn't know what 'delayed' meant. I knew what laying down was. I thought he'd been strapped to a bed and couldn't get up. He got strapped to more and more beds after that. When I asked Mum when he was coming back, she'd say, 'Soon, as soon as he can'.

Then, one time when he had been away for weeks, Mum said, 'He's not coming back this time. It's not anyone's fault, he's been delayed indefinitely.'

'Definitely' was obviously a prison somewhere. My father had been strapped to a bed in there and they wouldn't let him out. Now I realised I probably hadn't been too far off with the bed interpretation.

I wouldn't be confessing all this, but Didier and Caryn workshopped it out of me. When Jean-Marc and I turned up, it was straight out with nametags and into some psycho-mask play. We all had to take a persona out of a hat at random, draw their face on a paper mask (Caryn had a ready supply of blank templates) and then play them. I drew *five-year-old boy* and next thing I knew I was sitting on the bottom of our stairs in Croydon waiting for Dad, telling Didier to be quiet and wait too. Turned out Caryn had ambushed me. All the personas in the hat were five-year-old boys and she made me pick first.

The touchy-feely stuff didn't end there. Under the pretence of Caryn and Jean-Marc needing some bonding time, Didier took me out of the apartment and suddenly we were in Clissold Park next to Richard's tree.

It was bigger than I'd thought it would be. I could have easily killed it off if I'd visited when it was first planted; now it was big and strong. Clissold Park, where it lived, was tucked away on Green Lanes north of Newington Green. It was one of those great British summer evenings when the sun shines like it's going to be five o'clock forever. You don't really appreciate them until you've lived elsewhere.

I 'fessed up to Didier about my feelings. I'd figured resistance was useless, I might as well give in. Part of me wanted to. I felt the need for a bit of family support.

'I hated Richard for what he put you through—that's why I never came here. I knew it was wrong and I was worried I wouldn't be able to hide it. I thought you'd hate me if you knew I wanted to piss on this tree.'

Didier smiled. 'I did once.'

It had been an innovative grieving process that he and Caryn had come up with. He'd hated Richard sometimes too for his illness.

'Caryn took me to see this kinesiologist who listened to my body and said it was holding all this anger that had to be expelled. I had to think of an outrageous act to get rid of it, so I came and pissed on the tree. It worked.'

'What about the poor tree? It was innocent,' I said wryly. I should have known better.

'I was worried about that too, but the kinesiologist had this patient, a cab driver, who could hear trees talk, so he came and sat with the tree for an hour. It was amazing. We hadn't told him anything about why it was planted or what I'd done, but the tree told him everything—said it was happy I'd expelled my resentment and it was now growing better because my anger wasn't holding it back. We're connected because I planted it.'

He kissed one of the leaves and had a bonding moment with his child.

I watched and smiled nervously. I wasn't sure if I should communicate or just 'be in the moment' silently.

'You know you've never told me you love me,' Didier announced. I didn't respond, assuming the comment was addressed to the tree. He turned and looked at me. He wasn't doing a Prince Charles; he was talking to me.

'Get out of here. Of course I have!'

'Then do it again now.'

I pouted and shrugged my shoulders. He crossed his arms. I rolled my eyes. He lay on the grass, rested on his elbow and stared at me intently. I cleared my throat. He blew some air out of his lips up into his hair.

'I love you.'

He was right; I hadn't said it before.

'Right, now say it to the tree.'

'I don't think it would be honest to tell a tree I've just met that I love it.'

'No, tell the tree you love me.'

I leaned in and pretended to whisper to the tree.

'Trees are quite deaf, you have to speak loudly.'

I scowled at Didier; he was never this stubborn as a kid. I blamed Caryn.

'Fine. Tree I want you to know that I love my brother Didier. Now can we please go home?'

There's no point pretending that when I got back to New York that was it: father incident over, normal life could now be resumed. For one thing, there were bills to pay. I didn't like the idea of a posse of angry villagers hunting me down from Europe so I coughed up for the bills. I might have tried to put it down to an attack of conscience, but it was as well to keep the villagers on side. The tourist boom might be off, but I didn't see why, with a bit of careful massaging, Greque-en-Provence couldn't be worked up into my big idea for this year. The less the village had to do with it the better, so I didn't want any loose ends flapping about attracting media attention.

I contacted Maurice at the gendarmerie, got him to collect a list of bills and wired the money over. I knew half the claims were about as legit as the EU funds the villagers had procured for the basketball court, but I managed to squeeze most of it out of my research budget from work, who billed it as 'concept development' to G&K, who probably passed it on to their customers through a price hike on their bestselling range of muffin mixes.

Peace was restored to St Anastasie. I was no longer hated and Maurice had made up with Lucien. Marcel and Kiki still hadn't returned from their emergency honeymoon. Even Lennon, Ringo and Dusty didn't know where they were. Maurice had 'let' them into Marcel's house. Feeling at one with the culture, they had decided to stay there.

Despite the conflict-resolution work, things weren't all neat and tidy with me. I cursed Didier and Caryn and their persistent workshopping as I lay in my bed and found it was suddenly very empty. The dirty foreigner in me that had made me such a good trendspotter now made me a rootless drifter. I felt as if I'd absconded from my own life and didn't belong anywhere.

On top of that, I knew that if I stopped enjoying being an outside observer I might lose my professional edge. Then I panicked that I was having doubts, because the doubts themselves would ruin my judgment, and it all careened downhill from there.

I had gone to France a confident, trendspotting genius and returned a nervous self-doubting has-been who couldn't spot a trend if he was snorting it.

The too-hard basket had finally coughed up its contents right onto my lap. There was that ill-defined sense of 'something missing'. It felt like I'd put together all the pieces of a jigsaw puzzle but the picture I'd got wasn't quite the magnificent snow-capped vista on the box. There were still snow and mountains and trees and a lake, but my picture was smaller, less magnificent than I thought it was supposed to be. Yet I couldn't find any missing pieces.

Perhaps it was experiencing Marcel's way of living life on a grand—even if dubious—scale that made me feel my life was lacking something. I didn't feel very 'epic' in New York. I sensed there was supposed to be something behind the snow-capped scene, something that didn't come in easy-to-fit pieces. Something you had to add for yourself.

I told Peony everything. It must have been a dramatic tale because she stayed awake throughout. Admittedly I had made sure of her attention by talking over dinner and keeping the coffee flowing. She was a good listener.

'You feel bad about having sex with that girl?'

I did a bit, but I thought perhaps I ought to feel worse. Peony didn't help: she shrugged off that part of the confession. According to her, we had not established any parameters so I could hardly have stepped outside them. She was cool about it—too cool.

'I haven't slept with anyone else. You want to ask, but don't dare, so I'm telling you. Like I have time. Like I have the energy… I haven't slept so well since you went off.'

It sounded like her way of saying there was something more to *us* than sleeping together.

'Guess this puts us on a new level,' I said.

'So—monogamy, no sharing of assets and we don't have to meet the parents for at least three months.'

That was it. I was in an official relationship with a verbal agreement. With Peony's skill in law it felt as binding as a written contract, but in all my uncertainty at least this seemed like a positive step.

Mum's only comment when I finally got round to calling her and telling her about the trip (I lost the toss with Didier) was 'typical men'. She didn't elaborate.

I asked why she didn't have any photos of him.

'He took them. I didn't realise until after he went. He was going off more and more. Then I realised we wouldn't see him again. There was always the vague hope that he hadn't run off, that he'd been kidnapped or murdered or something, but when I went to pull out a photo so you wouldn't forget what he looked like, they were gone, all of them—negatives, the lot. I knew then that he'd planned it. Like he wanted you to forget.'

'Why?'

She laughed. 'Oh, Peter, I told you before. If you try and understand why he does anything, you'll drive yourself crazy. It's just not possible. He's him, he's your father.'

'So not Frank then. He's our dad, not Frank.'

She sighed a transglobal weary sigh. Obviously we boys never grew up.

'Frank did the hard part. Any man can tell a four-year-old kid he loves him and make him feel special. Try expressing love to a hormone-ravaged fifteen year old, bigger than you are and burning with violent emotions. That's tough, that's real love. But Marcel is your father. What that actually means and why you think it's so important is beyond me.'

She must have felt she was being a bit hard because she added, 'It must have been quite confronting for Marcel, you look just like him.'

'I look like him? You never told me.'

'Well, sometimes I glance in the mirror and think I look like Dame Judi Dench but that doesn't mean I'm going to hunt the woman down and tell her.' Marcel wasn't the only one who defied logic sometimes.

The news that excited Mum most was that we'd met Alex Beacham.

'Is she the same in real life? She's marvellous.'

I was surprised. I didn't think cooking shows were Mum's thing.

'But it's so obvious that she goes around having it off with all these sexy men in wonderful locations. She's an inspiration to us all. Even Mrs Blenkinsaw thinks she's great.'

I knew Alex had appeal but I had no idea it was this impressive.

'Is she coming to Alice, d'you know? Can I meet her?'

At work, Hugo provided the only proof that other worlds had changed as dramatically as mine in the last few days. His office was transformed. 'Welcome back!' he shouted at me from between piles of paper.

I had phoned Bethnee-Chantelle, his assistant, to make a ten-minute appointment somewhere in his competitive quotient only to hear that he didn't do appointments any more.

'Just to make my life even freakin' harder, everyone's just gotta show up and hope he's in the mood. I am so hating this!' BC, as we called her to avoid cracking up over her name every time, was not in a good mood.

Hugo told me the paperless office was a thing of the past. 'It's all about organics.'

'Bit '90s, isn't it?'

'Not food, meaningful live contact with people. The organic process of work. Feeling things other than a keyboard in your hands. Real things!' He gripped two fistfuls of paper with relish. The immaculate desk and two computers were gone. Instead there was mess—piles of papers, folders and objects.

'It's what everyone's doing!'

It was, in fact, what he told everyone they should be doing. Most people just said 'yes' and then ignored the idea, which he took as evidence that it was taking off like wild fire.

'So the quotient is no more?' I formed the all-important triangle with my hands.

'It was the right thing at the right time but 9/11 changed all that. Now it's about people, it's about contact, it's about real things.'

He took my hand and pressed it to the old oak desk he'd had brought in.

'It's made out of wood from an old hospital up river. I don't make appointments any more.'

His thoughts were leaping freely from one point of interest to the next.

'See what the day brings. If clients want to see me, they turn up. That's it. Simplicity, connection. Touching real things…connecting with the past again. The past—it's important.'

'The past is the new future!'

'Exactly—now, your exciting new food concept for G&K, I'm ready for it, and believe me they are too. I've seen the expenses, it better be good.'

'It is,' I lied. With no Alex, Kiki missing and the villagers liable to pick up their pitchforks at the sound of my name I had a lot of work to do on it. I had to bluster and so swept organically through the opening Hugo's new office gave me.

'Look, I've got a great food concept for G&K, but this conversation is leading somewhere else so I'd like to run with it.'

'Great. I knew you'd get it.'

'It's a little side venture I stumbled on in France and I think it would make the perfect coffee table in here. It's all about the past, about connecting. I'll let you have the first import for here, if I can use it for publicity.'

'Any conflict of interest with our clients?'

'No.'

'Will it take up much of your time?'

'No.'

'Let's go for it! What about the food idea?' Hugo asked.

'In good time. Just got to talk to some people, make sure it sits right.'

'Has it got history?'

'About two thousand years of it.'

'Fantastic.'

I'd already received an email from Madame de Beaumarchais' granddaughter, demanding I hold up my end of the bargain concerning her grandmother's grave. She'd been busy online and found an American company that produced video-graves that played footage of the dear departed for all eternity. For the right price, the gravestone that we'd desecrated would be shipped to New York and I'd arrange for a new video-grave to be sent back. For the dears who had departed before the video age, photomontages could be created with a soothing Mantovani soundtrack.

'There are others who are worried you have danced on their ancestors' graves,' she added.

Madame de Beaumarchais' granddaughter was a pleasure to do business with. She'd obviously seen all those TV ads about cute peasant businesses exporting all over the world thanks to the internet, because I had a contract emailed to me within a day. A week later I had photos of every grave that we had allegedly desecrated. Some were not even in the hilltop cemetery. It seemed a lot of people were keen to update their dearly beloveds' resting places.

I thought for a second whether grave renovation in general could be a goer—why spend eternity with the same old headstone? It was something to slip into the file of potential concepts.

In return for the gravestones of Madame de Beaumarchais' granddaughter's friends I negotiated a bulk discount with the video-grave company. Everyone was happy. The grieving relatives got cash and hi-tech graves. The granddaughter made a tidy sum, the video-grave company got a big order, and I got to do a classic 'mark 'em up and ship 'em on' exercise.

Madame de Beaumarchais' stone was airfreighted over while the rest were sent by sea. Hugo adored his new coffee table. He made me tell him stories of Madame de Beaumarchais. I told him what I could remember from Marcel's tales and made up how she'd died, determinedly fulfilling her prophecy of her own doom.

It was a good confidence-booster and proved I could still work it, but it wasn't the big idea. I was convinced Greque-en-Provence was. That night had been magical—the mood, the energy, the sexuality of it all. It was intoxicating. The concept of culturally rich food that gave you a sense of really living with every bite *had* to be a goer. But my work was cut out. I needed proof that people would like it and I needed the right person to front the whole campaign, a food expert with a passion for living. I needed Alex. Besides being the perfect salesperson, she was the only one who'd actually written down the recipes for the first time in two-hundred generations.

In the end, I didn't need to find Alex, she found me. I'd been out for a lunchtime meeting with the web designer for my gravestones, website. Walking into reception I heard a distinctive voice.

'Abrivar!' she screamed with her hands thrust in the air. For a moment I could feel the sweet juice trickling down my throat and saw Claudine's amber-flecked eyes.

'Hello, Alex. What an expected surprise. Come through to the boardroom.'

We both knew we were there to negotiate, and that a mutually satisfactory outcome was within reach, but I still needed the upper hand.

'So, Alex, did you fuck my father?'

She laughed.

'You don't muck around. What happened to the charming Provençal—'

'Did you?'

'Yes, and you've got quite a job on your hands if you're going to follow in his footsteps.' Alex made her own bid for ascendancy. It was a good return.

I told her about Lucien furiously defending her honour with Maurice.

'How sweet,' she smiled.

'I nearly got lynched for still being there after you all scarpered—'

'I didn't scarper. I had to go the Algarve to run a sardine-cooking course for a group of Toorak tourists seeking time out from their high-powered lives. It was an absolute pain, but those fishermen! Oh, the forearms! Bliss!'

She shuddered with pleasure at the memory. If she could do that on camera we were halfway there.

'So, business?' I got serious. I wasn't going to give her the biggest deal of her life on a plate.

She pitched *Alex Beacham Discovers… Greque-en-Provence*. The name was smart: it left her open to diversify into other food ranges when the first fad died. She wanted G&K to launch a range of gourmet foods based on Kiki's recipes to coincide with her new book and potential TV show. The potential for a TV show would be dramatically enhanced if she got the G&K deal.

Alex would be to European cuisine what the Crocodile Hunter was to Australian wildlife. I pictured her wrestling a giant *Marie-Nana's Dolmades Escargot* to the ground.

We did have one problem before we could pitch it to G&K.

'You do know the whole concept's complete bollocks, don't you? Kiki made the whole thing up.'

Alex looked shocked. Before I could continue she had recovered.

'Nothing,' the shock solidified to steel, 'nothing will take away the magic of discovering such a unique and delicious food culture. It's every foodie's dream. *Nothing* will stop me from sharing this discovery with the world and *nothing* could ever make me break my commitment to protect that culture from outside influence—that's a non-negotiable.'

'I'm sure G&K can accommodate your wishes. But there is a slight hitch: Marcel and Kiki have gone AWOL.'

'What?' Alex wasn't pleased with that development.

'It's your fault. If you hadn't been caught shagging my dad, they wouldn't be off mending their relationship God knows where.'

'Bugger.' Alex bit her bottom lip and left some lipstick on her tooth. At that point Bethnee-Chantelle stuck her head through the door.

'Oh, sorry, didn't realise anyone was in here.'

'Does Hugo need me?'

'Who'd know?' she said. 'He's given up the phone completely. When people call I shout through to him, he shouts through to me, I shout down the phone. I am so, like, over it!'

Two minutes later we could hear her hollering out, 'It's Mike from G&K, they want a meeting on the big new idea.'

'Tell them to pop in.'

'They want to know when.'

'Pardon?'

Bethnee-Chantelle screamed, 'WHEN?' then, 'This is so totally lame!' at the top of her powerful voice.

We decided to adjourn for a drink elsewhere. I didn't want Hugo knowing anything about our problems. We went to the bar in the Hudson Hotel. It was all stag horns, illuminated floor and unusual seats. I perched on a log and Alex reclined on a perspex throne.

'Look,' I said, 'I can start doing some market research on the side. We'll have to fund it ourselves. Hopefully Kiki and Marcel will turn up before long and we can pin them down with some sort of contract.'

'Could be a bit dodgy having them involved.'

'Christ! The less I have to do with them the better, but I don't like loose ends and I don't want them doing some exposé just as we're about to hit the market.'

I stopped. I'd lost Alex's attention. Some hulking great over-fifty year old had wandered in, acting like the bar was his private hunting lodge.

'Sorry, dear boy... can we finish things up for now?'

🌳

Seeing as Peony and I now officially had a relationship we decided we ought to try doing 'relationship' things. We didn't do too well. First off we tried meeting our respective work colleagues. She came to our Friday night drinks. It probably wasn't a good occasion to choose as I rarely went to post-work drinks myself.

The first person I tried to introduce her to had already met her. One of the accounts executives had been booked for running a red light, pleaded not guilty and ended up in court facing a ruthless cross-examination from Peony.

'I'm surprised you didn't go for the death penalty,' he scowled.

'We don't have the death penalty in this state,' she answered dryly. I burst out laughing, but neither of them thought it a joke.

As it was a Friday after a hard week, Peony then managed to doze off and knocked a drink into someone's lap. I caught someone mouthing the word 'drugs'.

I reciprocated the effect at a dinner party for some of her friends. Instead of talking law, like the rest of them, I drank. When the conversation finally got round to what I did, I made them all go to our host's computer and log on to www.honourthepast.com. I showed them the test website for the gravestone coffee tables and regaled them with made-up stories about how the various people died. Perhaps I shouldn't have used the word 'regaled'; 'appalled' is probably more accurate.

Peony's friends said I was obsessed with death and had no conscience.

'You have been kinda focused since you came back,' she commented. 'The graves, the food thing, what are you trying to prove?'

'I'm not proving, I'm trying to find. Am I obsessed?' I asked Peony. She threw her hands up.

'You wanna talk obsession? I spent five hours in the middle of the night going over six years of credit-card statements to prove some guy had been on the intersection between 6th Avenue and West Houston before and so had prior knowledge of the traffic lights he charged through on red, and all to get a lousy hundred bucks added to the fine. Jeez, there's gotta be a better life than this.'

'You're right! There's got to be something better.'

'But what?'

Neither of us knew, but we had sex to celebrate the fact we'd found something in common.

Despite the concerns of Peony's friends honourthepast.com was going well. Hugo loved his new coffee table so much he got rid of the hospital wood desk. All his meetings were now held at Madame de Beaumarchais' graveside.

I arranged for a writer and photographer from *NY Style* magazine to come and do a shoot. At first the reporter couldn't see past the mess of paper in the room, but after Hugo gave his 'organic' speech she began to see possibilities.

'Give me half an hour to work the room?' she asked and proceeded to make high neat pillars out of the paper piles, giving the room a more structured chaos. Hugo was photographed sitting cross-legged on the table, playing with the clockwork train he'd brought in from his old toy box at home.

'I don't want to see these for sale at less than five thou,' the writer told me. 'It'll devalue our publication if they're any cheaper. What promotion are you doing?'

'We're not,' I announced, suddenly realising the best way of pushing them. 'That wouldn't be respectful. The website address is being listed exclusively in your article. People can bid online for the stone they want.'

It would be a not so silent auction. The list of bidder names would appear with their bid, squeezing out the maximum from the competitive New York home style scene.

'Oh my God!' the journalist exclaimed. 'I am so loving that right now!'

♣

Two months passed and still no Marcel and Kiki. It was typical of the old bastard to be irritating by his absence. It wasn't like I wanted anything from him other than a signature on a piece of paper, and then I'd be happy for him to vanish forever.

Not only was he ruining my plans for future wealth, but he was blocking the past too. Without him there were no more stories of Alberto and Hippolyte. Didier and I had got hooked and wanted to know what happened to them.

Marcel and Kiki's mysterious disappearance wasn't the only hurdle that Greque-en-Provence struck. I was pretty excited when the results of the taste tests based on Alex's recipes arrived. I was expecting at least a few score tens (nought being 'yuck, I'd rather drink engine oil'; ten being 'I'd kill my children to taste this delicacy again') but was confused by the sea of ones and twos waving before my eyes. Lavender moussaka had even managed a minus score (two of the test subjects had vomited).

Abrivar scored positively but certainly not anything that would set the hearts of G&K alight. I was stunned. My midnight paranoia about losing my touch kicked on into a daytime reality. I had been wrong before, but I'd never been wrong when I'd had that overwhelming gut instinct that said 'YES!'

I'd felt that with this. I knew Greque-en-Provence had something about it. I knew it was my big idea, but somehow nobody else did. I racked my brains for what was missing, pored over the less than enthusiastic taster feedback. There had to be some clue. My eyes landed on one comment, 'Who the hell thought up this crap?' and I thought I had my answer. Alex was missing.

I breathed easier. I wasn't wrong, I'd just got the wrong stuff tested. It was Alex's personality that was going to drive these products; it was worthless testing them without her.

'What was I thinking?' I asked her on the phone as I explained we'd have to do more testing. 'Fancy believing it was all about taste, not image. I must be crazy!'

Bethnee-Chantelle phoned me.

'Hugo's got an organic pile of doggie-do to dump on you if you don't have something to present soon.'

I could hear him shouting 'No pressure!' in the background.

'Yes, all right,' she screamed back at him. 'Give me a goddamn moment. I can't stand this any more. I'd rather climb up a rhino's ass and strike matches than do this job. No pressure!'

The last two words were shrieked down the phone at me and she hung up.

I hastily cobbled together an idea. Power-pudding for the gym-bunny market. It was just normal custard made with sugar substitute and a tonne of protein powder. Toss in a bit of L-carnitine, L-lysine and L-wankenine and there you had it: low fat, low carb, high protein—'a moment on the lips, a lifetime on the biceps'. It wasn't my best work but it was enough to keep Hugo, via Bethnee-Chantelle, from screaming down the phone.

Peony's comets were my solace that evening. I spent ages tracing my fingers across her skin. My mind drifted from one thing to the next: Marcel, Kiki, positive results for Greque-en-Provence, a sense of fulfilment, a sense of belonging.

'Hello?' Peony brought me back to the present. My fingers had stopped.

'Sorry, it's just…' I couldn't finish the sentence.

She tried to speak for me.

'You started learning about the past, you got all those stories, you found your father and suddenly you've lost it all again. I've had defendants get off with much weaker excuses than that. It can't be easy.'

I shrugged it off, but perhaps she was right. Perhaps what I needed was to get back in touch with the past that had been dangled so briefly before me.

I soon got my chance. The next day there was an airmail envelope at work. The weight saved by the envelope was offset by the wad of normal paper crammed inside. There was no name, no return address and no letter, just another chapter in the story.

I peered at the envelope and saw it had been posted in Greece, but I couldn't narrow it down beyond the stamp. The story itself was not on old stiff paper put through a typewriter—it was new paper, from a laser printer. This chapter of the story had been written recently. I faxed it off to Didier. Settling down to read, I realised how eager I was to learn more. Peony was proving very perceptive.

MARSEILLE, 1946

A boy abandoned by gentleness, deserted by hope, alone at sea and clinging to the shipwreck that was once his father. That was Marcel Noirelle at fourteen years old. On the edge of manhood without having experienced childhood. He did not know of the family that used to be, just of the drunken body he often found slumped across the kitchen table downstairs.

Marcel lay in his bed not wanting to wake up. He heard the gulls of Vallon des Auffes. Their very cries raised the alarm, betraying the presence of those who sought to hide from the world in the little fishing village, accessible only by sea or a dangerous footpath over the rocks.

Beneath their raucous cacophony he could hear the gentle cheeping of Bibi, his one comfort, his only friend. His father had brought home the little budgerigar one day in a gentler mood. It was only the call of Bibi that made him move from his bed each day.

He had few memories of what once had been. Marie-France had died a slow and painful death, sacrificing herself to give him life, as he was often reminded. It was his father's cruellest reproach. Rodolphe did not stay much longer. Without his mother, there was little to keep him in Marseille. As soon as the opportunity presented itself he stole away to America, taking as much money from the house as possible. Hippolyte did not remain either. Instead of half-hearted escapes to the old port area, he made it to Paris and never returned.

Even Alberto's voice had deserted them. Ruined by the woes of life, drunken shouting and smoking, it began to crack. The promise which his return from Italy was supposed to fulfil dissolved like a summer mist in the dawn, leaving a harsh day.

Dazzling the young Alberto with the promise of glory, Fate, that fickle mistress, had snatched everything away and taken his heart too for good measure.

And so father and son made their way in their world, alone. There had been some good times. Marcel remembered when they would lie in their beds at night, singing old songs to each other. His father would sing a line and he would repeat it, over and again until the song was learned. He would fall asleep with a note on his lips and his father's cracked voice singing soulfully into the darkness.

That did not happen any more. Now Alberto went out drinking, or worse, drank alone in the kitchen. Marcel had tried to stop him once, taking the bottle away from his father's lips, only to earn a sharp blow to the head for his trouble.

He gave up and sought only to avoid his father, but sometimes even that was not enough. One night he woke up to find himself being vigorously shaken.

'Marcel, go and clean the kitchen.'

He went downstairs in his pyjamas to find the kitchen floor covered in broken bottles and smashed glasses.

'I'm too far gone to clean the mess...it's dangerous,' his father slurred.

As Marcel attempted to sweep up the glass, his hands and feet brushed over the shards which stabbed his unseasoned skin. Blood issued forth and trickled over the dustpan and brush.

'You're just making more mess! Hurry up!' his father roared with another blow.

The faster Marcel tried to clean, the more stains he made with his own blood. He passed the night mopping and bleeding, mopping and bleeding, until Alberto finally passed out and the boy dropped, weak with exhaustion, onto the kitchen floor.

That was before they had fled to Vallon des Auffes, hiding from Alberto's creditors. Marcel felt so weak, so pathetic, that each day was a struggle. He was lucky, he said to himself, that he had Bibi. Many people would not have such a blessing.

Somehow he found the will to get out of bed. Through his window he could see the jagged rocks on the shore. They were his playground now and sometimes his sanctuary. Some fishermen had left their nets out to dry on them. The gulls shrieked their shrill alarm.

Normally Alberto would be asleep at the kitchen table when Marcel came down in the morning. Marcel would wake him, help him to his bed—a stinking nest of sheets—and then return to attend to his beloved little yellow and green bird.

This morning Alberto was still awake and still drinking. He stared at the boy as he crept to the stove.

'What are you doing up? Go to bed!'

'It is morning, Papa. I shall make you some coffee.'

'Nah.'

'Please, Papa, I think it would do you good.'

The boy had tears in his eyes. This was worse than ever. His father looked like a pig bladder full of liquid, swaying and ready to burst. He slipped off the chair. Marcel moved to help him up.

'Get off.'

Alberto swung his hand and focused enough to hit his target, the boy's head.

'No!'

'Yes!'

More blows rained down on the boy. Marcel knew it was time to escape. He dashed out of the cottage and down to the rocks.

He scrambled up one large rock, leaped from the top onto the slope of the next and climbed over. Down on the other side there was a small crevice he could crawl into and press himself up at the back. There he could hide from the monster that had taken his father's form.

Alberto blundered after him, shouting invectives. Marcel remained silent, hugging his knees, waiting for his father to give up, go home and fall asleep. He waited and listened, straining to hear any sound above the crashing of the waves and the urgent shrieking of the seagulls.

Eventually he felt it was safe to emerge. Trembling with fear, he slowly climbed up the large rock and looked over the top.

'Hello, Marcel!' Alberto was there, poised on the other rock. He was smiling, ready to leap across at his son.

He jumped but landed badly. His arms flailed in the air as he lost his balance. Panic forced its way into his drunken red eyes.

'Help!'

Marcel stared at his father, frozen. If he did not help, Alberto would fall backwards onto the sharp rocks below. Something *stopped the boy from moving. The hand of fate pressed hard upon his chest and Alberto cried out, 'No!'*

Alberto's hand made a desperate final lunge and then he fell. His head bounced on the rock he had leapt from and landed hard against the jagged rocks below, smashing his skull. He lay still as blood flowed out of the wound and made its way to the frothing sea.

Marcel stared at the body, knowing that his inaction had killed his father. He had wanted to help him. He had tried desperately to move, but something had not let him. He looked out to sea. To the left he could see the famous Château d'If. He stared at the prison as if at his future—a future burdened with the knowledge that fate had rendered him a patricide.

There was only one thing left to do now. Marcel knew not why, but he leapt back across the rocks, made his way to the cottage and brought Bibi's cage outside. He opened the little door. With a moment's hesitation, as if unsure what freedom would hold, the bird took to the air and vanished in a green and yellow streak.

'It's floridly horrid.'

That was the only response I could come up with when Didier asked me what I thought. He called me after reading the story and was equally stumped.

'I don't know what to say. I mean, it's an awful thing to happen, but the way he writes about it...'

'It's like Barbara Cartland's his ghostwriter. His writing style has changed over the years.'

Right as ever, Didier decided we should look beyond the delivery to the message and what light it actually shed on Marcel's character.

'I suppose anyone with that sort of childhood would have a few issues,' I offered.

'It would explain why he was so concerned with proving all the Noirelles killed their father. If it was fate he might feel less guilty, but even so...'

The doubt clanged like a rusty church bell. It didn't make sense.

'Why's everyone so horrible all of a sudden?' Didier asked. 'I liked Alberto before. Rodolphe was nice enough.'

'Something's missing. Something must have happened between the stories to make them all change.'

'Perhaps it's Marcel who changed.'

'He's softening us up again. He wants us to pity him. I can see him flailing around at his laptop, tears drenching the keys.'

'Pausing only to prostrate himself on the floor and beg forgiveness of the dust mites he's treated so badly.'

I talked it through with Peony who applied her legal mind.

'If it was a witness account, I'd be looking for something or, even better, someone to corroborate.'

Brilliant! She was becoming more invaluable by the second.

There was only one person who could do that, and I didn't even know if he was alive—Rodolphe. I was fired with enthusiasm. I would track him down.

Marcel had said Rodolphe had to gone to New York. It was a slim clue but our only one. I tried a whitepages.com search for the city but came up blank. Broadening it to the whole of the US, I expected a thousand potential Rodolphe Noirelles but there wasn't a single one. A Google search came up with nothing. Perhaps he'd changed his name.

It was only at the height of my frustration that I realised I had a fabulous resource at my fingertips—Peony.

'You don't need me to do dodgy things at DANY,' she told me. 'There's a perfectly legal website that will probably tell you everything. It really shouldn't be legal but this is the good old US of A, so it is.'

She was talking about US Search.com, the scariest website there is. For a mere sixty dollars I got an entire profile: name changes, criminal record and location. It was that easy. A Rodolphe Noirelle born in 1914 had changed his name to Rudolph West, been done for public indecency in 1965 and had moved to Fort Lauderdale in Florida over ten years ago. There was even a phone number.

When I called and asked if he was Rodolphe Noirelle, he hung up immediately. It was him. The next day I called and got the message bank. I left a message saying I was Marcel's son and a brief explanation of why I wanted to speak to him.

I left it another day so curiosity could sink in. I didn't want to put him off with harassment. This time he answered the phone and didn't hang up.

'He gave us all these stories about his grandfather and his father and you. We wanted to know more,' I explained.

'Oh, he gave you those, did he?'

'You've read them? Are they true?'

'Of course they are.'

'Can I come down and see you? There's—'

'Sorry, I don't do family.'

'Oh.' I loaded disappointment into the one syllable and then stayed silent and hurt. If I waited long enough, he'd feel the need to fill the gap, make some gesture of conciliation. Eventually it came.

'I see you've inherited his persuasive skills,' Rodolphe finally said. His French accent had been wiped clean. The American accent was studied but non-specific. He could have been from anywhere in the US.

'I really would like to talk to you. Perhaps we could meet somewhere?'

'Oh, well, I suppose I've only myself to blame.'

'What?'

'Nothing. I haven't been to New York in a long time. Meet me in the Palm Court at the Plaza Hotel next Tuesday at 1.00 p.m. You'll buy me lunch.'

Obviously information on our family didn't come cheap.

The *NY Style* double-page spread on Hugo's coffee table and honourthepast.com worked brilliantly. Within two days of the article appearing I'd received five hundred bids on the various graves and there was still a month before the stones arrived in New York. Without a cent paid in advertising they were the hottest items on Manhattan.

The journalist from *NY Style* phoned me to say she'd been swamped with calls from people wanting to make private knockout bids. I refused.

'Everyone wants to know who the genius is behind honourthepast.com. We could do a bit of a feature. You visit your favourite graveyard, mourn over a lost loved one. Blah, blah, blah. Very tasteful.'

'I think it would be better if we kept my identity secret…but possibly when the bids are complete we could run the winners in the magazine.'

'Ooh,' she squealed with a cover story in her eyes. 'Exclusive?'

'Mmmm, tricky, this story is bigger than both of us. You know someone's flown a helicopter out to check on the ship's progress?'

It was actually true but I didn't know it at the time.

She winced audibly. I could see her standing at the other end of the phone, hopping from one foot to the other, pleading for the new toy she really really wanted.

'I might be able to manage something if you can do me a favour. There's this sensational Australian chef and I promise she's going to be the next big thing. Tours around Europe unearthing hidden culinary treasures. Massive with the over-fifties. You know: men want her, women want to be her.'

'Deal!' she snapped quickly before I changed my mind on the coffee-table feature.

Oh yes, I thought, I definitely still had it.

The second set of Greque-en-Provence focus tests which featured Alex were an improvement. Apparently the food tasted better when Alex presented it. Abrivar averaged eight (very good but not sensational) and the lavender moussaka at least made it into positive figures. *Marie-Nana's Dolmades Escargot* rated well as long as no one knew it was a snail wrapped in a leaf.

As much as I wanted to run to G&K and say we had a hit, in all honesty I couldn't. Based on this it wasn't a sure-fire winner. I thumped the table in frustration. It was like the key ingredient was missing, as if we'd forgotten the sugar or the snails or something.

Time for more fobbing. I tossed jelly syringes at Hugo. Kids' food for adults. Mock fat syringes full of jelly that people could squirt in their mouths, over body parts, up orifices. It would be a huge hit for all of five minutes. Ten minutes if we could get a Republican senator to claim it was promoting drug use.

Tacky, but I was safe till the end of the year.

The Palm Court at the Plaza was a vision of gold and mirrors with a few potted palms tossed in to tone down the opulence. It had an atmosphere of nonchalant intimidation that came from knowing it didn't have to try. The waiters were genuinely friendly and helpful, making them all the more imposing.

I was nervous anyway. Rodolphe was living history, he'd actually known the original owner of the coffee table in Hugo's office. He was the first relative of my father I'd ever met and both my uncle and a cousin—two for the price of one, or, given the fact that I was paying for an exorbitant lunch at the Palm Court, two for the price of six.

I couldn't see Rodolphe immediately. There was no one obviously looking out for me or even peeking cautiously from behind a palm. Once I announced myself to a waiter, I was steered towards the rear of the Court. I spotted him sitting with his back to the room, monitoring me in the mirrored wall in front of him. His shocked face betrayed him as he quickly began perusing the menu.

He was immaculately dressed: starched collar, tie, waistcoat and suit, with a small sprig of lavender in his buttonhole. His hair, mostly grey but partially white, was locked into place and parted with a ruthless straight line. The smart appearance only accentuated how well preserved he was. It was hard to believe he was over eighty and had just flown up from Florida. How he coped with the heat there in such clothes I had no idea. He looked scrubbed clean. White flawless skin, freshly shaven. I could see him soaping furiously under a cold shower, repeating phrases to bleach his accent away.

'Well, aren't you a chip off the old block. Any others?'

'Only my brother, Didier... as far as we know.'

'Tell me more about your visit with him.'

He listened attentively, pausing me briefly with a hand gesture as he ordered the braised lobster. I opted for the chef's salad.

He nodded to himself and murmured agreement as I completed the tale of the trip.

'He never was one to face the music. So, what do you want? I'm meeting you because I feel a little sorry for you, but we're not going to be pals. Make the most of this... a glass of champagne, the Pommery Rosé,' he added to the waiter. He, at least, was making the most of the free lunch.

'You seem very wary. I thought Marcel was just little when you left.'

'He was about eight. Even then he had this ability to get people to do whatever he wanted. Alberto spoiled him horribly. We all did. He was the little one. You thought you were being strict with him and then you found yourself pressing fifty francs in his hand and patting his head. Saw him again when Alberto died. Just the same: older, more aware, and then...'

He paused to drink his champagne and looked at me as if waiting for the next question.

'And then?' I repeated.

'And then what?'

'You saw him again after that. People aren't as cautious as you are over someone they only knew as a child.'

Rodolphe raised his eyebrow. 'Perceptive too. He came to visit me in New York. It was the summer of '64—stinking hot as usual. I lived in Greenwich Village. He was a charming man, full of life. He managed to find fruit that tasted like real fruit even in this city. Apricots, as if he'd brought them from home.'

'Apricots!'

'Yes, apricots.'

We each paused for a moment remembering the apricots. Rodolphe snapped out of it.

'He stayed with me, enjoyed the sights of New York, utterly charming as ever. My...well, I suppose it's okay to say now...my gay friends all adored him, too much. He seemed to be working his way through them. They came rounds lots, he'd be very friendly, then suddenly I wouldn't hear from them again.'

'He wasn't sleeping with them, was he?' I was aghast.

'No. He'd get them all worked up, they'd make a move, he'd be shocked but understanding. They'd be so terrified of him saying anything to anyone, they'd pay him off.'

'Blackmail?'

'Not really. He never threatened a thing, just let their imaginations run riot. It was a tough time back then. We could get sacked, abused, imprisoned.'

'What did you do?'

'I packed him off quick-smart before he got himself or me into serious trouble.

'I see.'

'In the end I managed it on my own. Did what is now referred to as a "George Michael"—toilet, policeman, the usual.'

'Hence the move and name change.'

'Your research is a little too thorough.'

He drained his glass of champagne and ordered another. I told the waiter to leave the bottle. I needed him well oiled for the next part.

'What's with the whole sons killing their fathers thing? Did he make that up?'

'No... it's true, in a manner of speaking. My fathers died because they were too distracted thinking of me to leap from the truck. Claude could have died out of sheer happiness from Alberto's singing rather than the almond...'

'...and Marcel let Alberto fall onto the rocks?'

'What?'

'The last story... Alberto chasing Marcel in an alcoholic rage.'

'What *are* you talking about? I never wrote anything like that.'

I displayed a mouthful of chef's salad to the entire Palm Court as my jaw swung open.

'*You* wrote the stories?'

'Of course. Did Marcel pass them off as his? Typical!'

The sound of pieces clattering into place drowned out the genteel tinkling of the piano. It was Rodolphe who had written all the stories, not Marcel. Our father had just claimed he'd written them and it never occurred to us to question that. The last florid instalment was clearly Marcel's work. I told Rodolphe his version of Alberto's death. He laughed.

'He always was a drama queen. It's complete rubbish! Alberto never raised his hand against anyone and he didn't drink his career away. He had a brilliant career performing all round Europe. There were even records made—I have them. Yes, he liked his wine—he was French for God's sake—and he wasn't very good with money, but he was a wonderful man and did everything he could for us. I did come to the US, but with his blessing. Hippolyte did run away to Paris at a young age, but they were reconciled in time.'

He laughed and shook his head at long-buried memories.

'You know, all these years I've tried to wash away the past—because of the policeman, your father, my fears. France was a completely different world. It's hard to believe any of it ever existed... Ah, Alberto, it's good to see you again.'

The floodgates of nostalgia had opened. I wanted information from him quickly, before he was completely lost in age-old memories.

'So how did Alberto die?'

'Alberto? Dead?' He paused for a moment as he returned to the present. 'Ah yes. I'm sorry, you'll not know yet what bliss rarely recalled memories can be. Alberto's death, yes. I don't think that's really a suitable conversation for the Plaza.'

I must have looked crestfallen because he reached across the table and patted my hand.

'*Ne t'enquiete pas!*' He told me not to worry in French, laden with a Marseille accent. 'You poor boy, you fell for the charm, I can tell. Everybody does. Here...' He pulled a folder from a bag under his chair.

'I brought a set of the stories for you—a complete set. I had dreams of a play once. God help me, even of a musical back in the '50s. Can you imagine! I had visions of Mario Lanza as Alberto!'

The lunch was over. I paid the bill. Just as we were about to get up to leave he spoke again.

'One more thing.' He pulled out a home-recorded CD. 'I thought perhaps you might like to have this. The sound quality isn't wonderful, but it's your grandfather singing. Just so you know that he really was quite wonderful.'

It had been one of the most remarkable conversations of my life. So good I actually wanted it to be over before anything could spoil it. I wanted Didier to be there too.

'Can we just wait here for a moment? I'd love you to speak to Didier.'

He would be on his way home from work so I called his mobile. He was on his bike, cycling through traffic.

'Pull over, Didier, I've got someone who wants to speak to you.'

'Hello, Didier, this is Rudol… this is your uncle, Rodolphe.'

He said his true French name with relish. It rolled wonderfully off his tongue. Didier was in tears within a minute; there'd be some serious debriefing back at the apartment.

Outside the hotel, the stink of the manure from the Central Park horse-and-carriage rides hit us.

'I do love that about the Plaza,' Rodolphe commented. 'Doesn't matter how rich you are in there, you still come out and smell shit! I know I said I didn't do family, but it might be nice if we kept in touch. If you're ever in Florida…'

He spoke nervously, not used to making familial gestures.

'That would be great. Thank you for talking to Didier.'

'Seems like a nice boy.'

'Yes,' I laughed, 'takes after you, I think.'

'Really? It's amazing what's passed on in the genes… *Au revoir*, Pierre!'

He lowered himself into a cab.

'*Au revoir.*'

PARIS, 1941

'The Oberstleutnant is complaining he ordered a redhead with big breasts. He says if he wanted a flat-chested blonde he'd send for his wife. Michel wants the guns we're storing for a raid tonight and we've run out of champagne. Happy Birthday.'

Nicolette knew how to turn up the drama to please Hippolyte. Another day at the infamous Hippo's, made special because it was the owner's twenty-first birthday. Free champagne for all clients ensured it was their busiest day of the year.

'Send him Juliette. Tell her to have him done by 10 p.m.— a finger up the bum by 9.50 if necessary. Once he's left the building, let Michel into the same room—the guns are beneath the floorboards under the bed. Send out to Maurice for more champagne. Pay him double.' For Hippolyte, it was all too easy.

'Juliette's still got the clap.' Nicolette reminded him.

'It's our new wartime policy. Girls with the clap are allowed to work, but only with Germans.'

'The resistance will be thrilled: we'll infect our way to liberation. Maria's coming down with flu. Any good?' Nicolette suggested.

'Great, send her in to kiss him, but nothing else. I don't want her with a dose of the clap.'

'Jeanne's little boy's got measles. We could wipe some scabs on the Oberstleutnant's handkerchief.'

'Perfect, the war will be over in no time!'

Nicolette kissed him and left the office to carry out his instructions.

The greatest pimp in Paris—that was the claim of those who worked for Hippolyte. He had a natural talent for prostitution. He was drawn to it and he was good at it. Not the act itself, but organising it for everyone else. 'What can I say,' he used to argue, 'it's in my blood.'

When he had run away from Marseille he'd thought he was escaping his father. He'd hated him because he'd always hated him. He hadn't wanted to be rescued from his mother; he'd been quite happy where he was. Now, years later, he realised there hadn't been anything to be resentful about. When he thought of what his father had done, he conceded he would have done exactly the same. It had taken a long time to admit it.

Now, when travelling around France was difficult, Hippolyte felt a need to see his father, Marcel and Rodolphe again. He tried writing to their old address, but nobody could be sure of getting anything through.

'I was so angry with him for taking me away from a life of pimping,' he smiled to Nicolette.

'What a monster!' she replied, playing along with him.

'How could he!' Hippolyte enhanced his fake outrage.

'Don't worry, you will see him again. I'm sure of that.'

When he'd arrived in Paris at the age of fifteen, knowing nothing about the city, Hippolyte's nose took him to Place Pigalle. It didn't smell of fish heads but he knew the area instinctively. The air had an illicit breeze that made him feel at home.

He found Nicolette and Thérèse, just a few years older than him. They found him adorable, and took him to the rooms they shared. He gave them what money he had and they let him sleep on the floor of their sitting room. He watched how they worked, bringing men back to the rooms. They were good, he decided, but they could be better. They weren't very businesslike: they did not look after their money and didn't invest in their business. They were vulnerable too, he thought. Sooner or later, some customer might get nasty. If they were on their own in the apartment, it would mean serious trouble.

Hippolyte saw a role for himself and suggested he should look after them, for a fee.

'You... our pimp! You must be joking,' Thérèse laughed. 'There's enough mean bastards out there trying to muscle in on us without you starting. Men, you're all the same!'

'Sorry,' said Nicolette. She wasn't even sure if he knew what a pimp was.

It was when one of those other bastards suggested they work for him in return for not getting their faces slashed that Nicolette announced they already had someone looking after them.

Hippolyte played the tough guy role and saw the man off. It wasn't hard, he was from Marseille. He could handle anything a Parisian threw at him. That night they paid him in kind to celebrate their new business arrangement. They agreed to let him 'manage' them, as he termed it. He looked after them, they looked after him.

Within two months he was looking after ten girls. Within a year, he had taken over a whole building. The deal was simple: he took thirty per cent of their earnings. Ten per cent for himself, ten per cent for their own savings and ten per cent for business investment. He used the money for business investment to pay for doctors to check them out and treat them, to deal with pregnancies and buy them new clothes. His girls discovered they could charge more if they wore expensive clothes.

The brothel came about two years later. Off the streets, there were fewer dangers, fewer threats and better customers. And more money.

At Hippo's everyone was happy. The girls were treated better than anywhere else. The clients knew there'd be no trouble. The police liked their kickback and the fact he kept his business off the streets. His rivals liked the fact that he didn't try to take over their territories. The greatest pimp in Paris.

Hippolyte was fond of all the girls, but Nicolette and Thérèse were his favourites—until Thérèse found a man who wanted to marry her. She wanted to be respectable.

'There's no shame in what we do,' Hippolyte reminded her. 'Everyone else might think so, but we know different, don't we?'

He waited for her and Nicolette to agree. They looked at each other. 'We do, Hippo, we do.'

Thérèse asked him to give her away at the wedding. At the age of eighteen, he took the role seriously and paid for the entire wedding.

'To the world's youngest daddy,' Nicolette proposed a toast on the night before the wedding. The three of them were having a final dinner together. For all their vows of undying friendship and determination that the wedding wouldn't change a thing,

Nicolette knew Thérèse would not be back. Her future husband could tolerate her past, as long as it remained there.

Hippolyte pushed an envelope across the table to Thérèse. 'It's your savings.'

It was a bank book in her name and the account held a lot of money. She was stunned.

'When you said you were putting money aside for us, I didn't think for a moment you really meant it. I assumed you spent it. I would have. Shit! Hippo, if I wasn't getting married I'd give you the fuck of your life!'

'Now that would make for a spectacular wedding day,' said Nicolette. 'The bride and the father of the bride caught in the act.'

The wedding was a triumph considering the bride's guests were trying to hide the fact they worked in the sex industry, and three of the groom's guests had slept with the bride. Imbibing the spirit of romantic bliss, Nicolette and Hippolyte became more tender than ever before.

'I couldn't cope if you left me too,' he whispered to her.

'I wouldn't.'

'Marry me?' he asked.

'Marry me?' she asked back and smiled. It was what they always said.

'I asked first.' He stood up and took her hand.

'I asked second.' She stood and they took to the dance floor.

'I mean it this time.'

They paused for a moment, each looking at the other, trying to work out if the other really was serious. The word 'yes' sat on Nicolette's tongue, trying to jump out, but she held it back.

'So you weren't serious the other times?' she asked instead.

'I'm the most serious man I know. Look at me, not even twenty-one and a respectable business man.'

'Oh, very respectable!'

'You haven't answered my question.'

'One day, you'll ask me and mean it. Then I'll...'

'...say yes?'

'Answer you. Now, move your foot back. You may be the greatest pimp in all Paris, but you're a dreadful dancer.'

She withstood the battering of her toes as long as she could and then sat down again. She kissed Hippolyte's hand.

'I need some money. Something to get rid of again.' She patted her stomach.

'You don't have to.'

'Yes, I do. Christ, you'd think my tubes would be knackered by now, wouldn't you, but no, they just keep going. And all those women desperate for babies.'

Hippolyte looked at the happy bride.

'D'you think we'll ever see her again?'

'No,' said Nicolette. 'It's just us now.'

The war didn't change much. They milked the krauts for money and helped the resistance where they could. It was a two-way bet. Whoever won in the end, they would be on the winning side. As Nicolette said, 'It doesn't matter which side you're on, you always get fucked at Hippos.' That was their official line. They didn't tell anyone how much money they gave to the resistance, nor how much they took from the Germans.

Hippolyte put his success down to his attitude. There was no shame in prostitution. For him, it wasn't the sex work that the girls needed saving from, but the lives that put them there. Prostitution was the escape, not the trap.

Whatever his girls wanted, he helped them achieve it—education, training, husbands. One of his girls had become a medical student. Another had got into movies, after paying for acting classes with her savings.

All this before he was of age. And now today was his twenty-first birthday. At midnight, Nicolette returned to his office. The Oberstleutnant had come and gone and been, infected with gonorrhoea, influenza and measles. The resistance had their guns and the champagne once again flowed like water.

Hippolyte was holding a glass of champagne up to the light, watching the bubbles intently as if he could see something inside them.

For all his success, he was still a boy, Nicolette thought and loved him even more. That, to her, was the secret of his success. He was an innocent. It simply did not occur to him that there might be anything immoral in what they were doing. It was all good and pure. She wished she could believe like he did, wished she'd never been impregnated with that dirty feeling from her very first trick. Hippolyte had almost wiped it out. He'd made her believe she was good...almost.

She had got too rid of too many problems to ever believe it completely. Perhaps Hippolyte was just naïve. One day, it might all come crashing down and he'd see their filthy business as though for the first time. At twenty-eight she felt old, too old for him. Too old for this.

He watched his bubbles.

'It's like they'll go on forever,' he said.

'They don't,' she answered.

The bubbles kept rising right through to the end of the war. With the profits that he made Hippolyte refurbished his establishment, making it bigger and better than ever.

His letter to Alberto had managed to get through. He even got a response with news. Rodolphe had gone to America before the war had even started. Marcel was the same as ever, only older and smarter. Hippolyte learned that his father had refused to perform during the war. He would not sing again until France was free. It did not make him popular with the authorities. Hippolyte sent as much money as he could, without raising suspicion, to help with his father's noble stand.

After the war, on his twenty-sixth birthday, Hippolyte was once again staring at champagne bubbles in his glass, only this time it was a double celebration. Alberto, Marseille's most famous conscientious operatic objector, had been asked to perform at the Paris Opera. Hippolyte had been to see his father sing for the first time in his life. He didn't know much about opera but it was something marvellous to experience an audience bursting into spontaneous applause at his father's talent.

Alberto was coming to visit him after the official function that followed the opera. As always, Hippolyte's birthday was a big night at Hippo's. The champagne flowed freely and everyone felt like celebrating. Nicolette came in to report that everything was going well and to enjoy their traditional midnight birthday drink together.

'Marry me,' he asked her again. This time he meant it. This time, more than the others, he yearned for her to simply say yes.

She laughed as she thought she was meant to.

'I'm too old.'

'You're not.'

'I'm too old for this game.'

He made a dismissive gesture, but they both knew her earnings weren't what they had once been.

'I want to cash in my savings. I want out.'

She didn't want him, he thought.

'There's no need. You don't have to take clients any more, you can run the place with me. There'll always be a home for you here.'

She offered a further obstacle, the fact that there was another 'problem' to get rid of, only this time, she didn't want to.

'The child can live with us!'

She sensed Hippolyte had a new determination in his voice.

'Raise a child in a brothel?' she asked.

'There are worse places.'

'No!'

'We'll buy you a house. You can live there. The child will have everything. I'll treat it as my own.'

'Oh, if only you were serious!'

'I am. Honestly…'

They were interrupted by a knock at the door. Alberto had arrived. The war years had not made him lean. Off-stage his belly looked even bigger.

'I'll go and attend to things,' Nicolette said and left them. Hippolyte looked pleadingly at her when she turned to close the door.

The two men embraced each other awkwardly.

'This place is… magnificent. Quite remarkable,' said Alberto. 'I've heard talk of it in Marseille.'

'Your singing was magnificent too. You know that was the—'

'The first time. Yes, I know.'

'How is Marcel?'

'He's fine—impossible as ever. He's here in Paris. I'm sending him to school outside the city. Perhaps they can manage him a bit better.'

'How did you stop him persuading you to bring him here?' Hippolyte remembered his brother's formidable powers of persuasion.

'It wasn't easy. I insisted he was too young. I've had a letter from Rodolphe. He is enjoying life in New York. He's thinking of writing a play.'

Hippolyte handed him a champagne glass.

'A toast—to family!'

They drained their glasses and poured some more. Alberto could not resist looking at his son. It was good to catch his eye and not see any anger. He wanted to do it more. They smiled at each other without embarrassment.

'It is good to see you, Hippolyte... and I almost forgot. Happy Birthday!'

They embraced again. Properly this time, without nerves. Alberto remembered his hug with Claude—their one moment of just being themselves. This was his moment with Hippolyte, and it was just as wonderful from the father's side. Hippolyte's moment ended with a tinge of regret. This was what his anger had protected him from all those years.

'So you like my place?'

'It's magnificent. Perhaps I... could have a tour?'

'Of course. Nicolette,' Hippolyte shouted. She arrived quickly. 'My father would like a tour of the establishment. I think Jacqueline... and Yvette would be perfect. Make sure they're free.'

'Please, Hippolyte. It's been some time.' Alberto drained his glass in nervous anticipation.

'Don't worry, they will take excellent care of you!'

Nicolette returned to the office after she had delivered Alberto to his guides.

'So?'

'It was wonderful. We embraced like a real father and son, just him and me. Now if only you would make my birthday complete—say yes.'

'The child may not be yours, you know that.'

'It will be. Please!'

'Yes!'

He leapt into the air and whooped.

'We'll be so happy. Just you see. And the wedding—'

'No big wedding. Just us. Your family, of course. Quiet. I want peace and quiet.'

Hippolyte put his hands to his lips and pressed them together in complete silence.

'You silly...'

'Shhh...peace and quiet.'

He pressed his lips to hers to enforce more peace and quiet.

She sat on his knee and they watched the bubbles in the champagne glass together.

'Each bubble is a day of happiness for us,' he told her and stirred the glass so it frothed with a million bubbles.

Their cosy future was interrupted by one of the girls calling out to him.

'Hippo! Hippo!' She burst through the door without waiting to hear a response. 'Hippo, it's your father. Come quick!'

In the room where Alberto had been enjoying his tour, Yvette was standing screaming. Jacqueline was telling her to shut up from underneath Alberto's body.

'Get him off me quickly before he gets stuck. Yvette, come on. Why does this always happen to me? Hurry, there's no time to waste.'

Hippolyte and Nicolette entered. Nicolette gasped. Jacqueline remained sanguine.

'Hippo, I'm sorry about your father, but please get him off me.'

They carefully removed the body as Yvette continued to squeal.

'Phew!' said Jacqueline. 'I swear that's the last time I do fat guys. I'm sticking to thin virgins. That's the fourth time that happened.'

'I think you'd better take Yvette off for a brandy,' Nicolette glowered at her. 'Now!'

Hippolyte was looking at the face of his father, scanning the dulled eyes. 'I have spent thirty minutes of my life looking at this face and not being angry... all of them tonight.'

'It was good that you had those minutes. That is something at least,' Nicolette attempted to comfort him.

He stood up and nodded his agreement.

'We need to get his body to the hotel. He can't be found here. Go and warn the concierge there that we're coming. And you'd better get Marcel and bring him here. He should not be alone.'

At first I was going to listen to the CD while reading the story, but then I realised they were two activities each worthy of my undivided attention. I can't remember the last time I actually sat and listened to something. Music for me is always a background for some other activity. Not this time.

I prepared myself for an emotional moment, and got Didier on the phone so he could listen live too. This was to be our bonding moment with the past, our true grandfather–grandsons moment. I pressed play and Judy Garland started belting out something about a trolley going clang, clang, clang.

I fast-forwarded through another Judy, two Carmen Mirandas and a Deanna Durbin. Obviously Alberto wasn't the only old favourite of Rodolphe's. Finally we came to the crackly sound of a 78 record and a man's voice started warbling.

We imagined we were Claude sitting with his eyes closed in the living room at St Hubert. I'm no opera fan and I had no idea what he was singing, and I guess if I hadn't known it was Alberto I'd have thought it sounded pretty stupid. But it was Alberto, it was our grandfather who we'd never known, and it sounded wonderful.

I felt special. Everyone else's grandfathers were old guys dozing off in their armchairs at Christmas, but ours was a magnificent singer in the 1930s.

There were two more tracks of his and then it was back to Hollywood with Dorothy Lamour.

The jelly syringes were sold to G&K and we headed for the holiday season. I'd made it through without the big idea. Hugo was satisfied, just. He declared I had to come back from Australia and blow him away. 'It's gotta be two years of ideas in one.'

It didn't really matter: I was heading off to Alice Springs with nearly one million dollars in the bank. Honourthepast.com had gone beyond fashion frenzy and become a macho slugfest amongst Manhattan's richest over who could secure one of the graves. It was all about money, determination and establishing who was in the city's top twenty. The mysterious owner of honourthepast.com remained hidden, adding shit loads of allure.

The seeds of Alex's launch in the States had also been sown. After her feature in *NY Style*, she was beginning to be gently wooed by publishers and one TV station. There was interest, but there needed to be a lot more. The Australian press reported that 'our' true blue Aussie had taken New York by storm.

So, money in the bank, true history of the family sorted, grandfather warbling on the CD and no father pestering for forgiveness. That should have been it, life sorted, but it wasn't. I think that's why I insisted Didier and I go back to Alice for Christmas, for a sense of family, of wholeness.

I could have dropped the whole Greque-en-Provence thing, retired on the gravestone earnings, but it had become an issue of self-belief.

There was something amazing about this fake concept. That fête, for all its fabrication, had a magic that was more than drunken moments and back alley shags. I was determined to prove it. I figured that time out in Alice might give me enough distance to crack the puzzle of why this supposedly great concept didn't quite work.

Peony and I felt we were actually making some progress on the relationship front, so much so that we didn't want to risk it by exposing ourselves to each other's families over the holidays. It had been a close-run thing at Thanksgiving. Peony's mother had a passion for doll-making. One of the women in her Pilgrim Fathers period-costume sewing circle had a niece who worked in DANY. The niece, under constant pressure to report back on Peony, announced that she had 'finally found someone'. The bunting went up on her parents' porch, the school band was booked and the plane tickets home were dispatched. Peony found an emergency 'infringement' case and so we escaped the visit. I had to speak to her mother on the phone instead. She burst into tears and thanked me profusely.

My mum didn't thank Peony for dating me but checked to see that she wasn't ironing my shirts.

'An iron?' asked Peony. 'What the hell's that?'

Mum laughed. She liked her. Mum often made a point of deciding if she liked people before she met them. Face-to-face meetings were too emotionally charged. It was too easy to be taken in by physical appearance and nice gestures, she said. A legacy from Marcel, no doubt.

When I jetted off to Australia for Christmas, Peony flew off to Cleveland armed with a set of photos. Her mother had posted me a disposable camera and begged us to use it. An empty photo frame had been sitting on her mantelpiece for twelve years with the pre-engraved caption 'Peony and partner'.

Didier and I met at Sydney airport, at the gate for the Alice Springs flight, both armed with a bottle of duty-free sambuca. Anyone who turned up at Mum's house from overseas without one was asking for a hellish visit. She had a thing about duty-free sambuca. She never bought it for herself, never ordered it in a bar, but insisted on receiving it from us. She said it tasted different when it was duty free.

Didier looked even more crumpled than me. 'The worst thing is, I flew over Alice on the plane here. Now I've got to trek back again.'

From Alice airport we got a hotel minibus to the bottom of Mum's street. The driver had been in Didier's class at school so he didn't mind giving us a lift.

After we were dropped off, we walked down our street pulling our suitcases behind us. The wheels clunked over the pavers and then roared over the concrete driveways. Mum's car was in her drive, or the two grooves of dirt in the lawn that had always been our drive. Ours was the only house that had never invested in concrete.

The front door was open with the fly screen pulled to. This normally meant Mum was at home. Didier knocked and shouted hello. The only answer was the smell of the house: familiar, undefinable, us.

'Hello, Mum?' I called as I opened the screen. It squeaked. We paused, neither wanting to press in. We expected a bad-tempered 'Hang on!' from the kitchen, but it didn't come. There was something different about the house, something more different than a couple of years' absence. I didn't like it.

I threw Didier a puzzled look. He sensed something wrong too. We became nervous.

'What was that?' Didier had heard a noise. It came again, a muffled sound from the bedroom. The house was a single-storey. Mum's room was behind the living room to the right. We walked down the hall to the shut door. She never used to shut it unless she was asleep and didn't want to be bothered. I paused at the door.

'C'mon,' Didier whispered and swallowed.

I tried to pretend I wasn't panicking too, but I was. Perhaps it was the effect of the long flight, lack of sleep and the confusion of international time zones we'd both hurtled through, but something was definitely up.

Didier was too afraid to open the door. Anything could have happened. Every episode of *A Current Affair* with old ladies being bashed in their homes for two dollars' worth of change came to mind. It's amazing how stories from a news program you've never watched flash into your head at those moments. She could be bound and gagged, shot to pieces, or even strapped to the bed with a gun pointed at her and the trigger tied to the door handle.

We would have to risk it. I breathed deeply, gripped the handle and turned it quickly, throwing the door open.

Mum screamed from under the sheet on the bed and a man leapt out. He stood facing us, completely naked, his shocked face turning to delight.

'*Mes fils!*'

The bastard was in our mother's bedroom, naked and approaching us with arms and erection outstretched.

We both stared at the penis. Now matter how old you are, no matter how little you are the cause of it, one thing no one should ever see is their father's hard on. It's haunting, you can't take your eyes off it. I tried not to compare it with mine, but before I could stop it, the imaginary tape measure was whipped out, held up and read.

It came nearer. The bastard was walking towards us without the slightest droop or embarrassment. I took my eyes off it.

'Stop there! Stop right there!' I held my hand out.

'Mum, are you okay?' Didier shot to the bed.

She pulled the sheet down from over her head, looked at my stunned face and hand still held out, then to Didier's concerned face and the bastard's three outstretched limbs. She burst into laughter and sat up quickly, tossing her naked breasts into the vignette. I'd seen those before.

'We'll see you in the kitchen,' I said to mum. The sons marched off in outrage.

Despite the shock of the situation, there was something slightly satisfying about demanding to see Mum in the kitchen. That was where we'd always got told off. When you heard the words, 'in the kitchen, now!' you knew you were in for it.

'What the hell is he doing here?' I asked as I paced around the kitchen. 'Where's Kiki? He disappears off the face of the planet and then turns up here and…!'

'It was pretty…big,' Didier said. I think *it* was dancing in front of the Aboriginal flag fridge magnet for him too.

Mum slopped into the kitchen doing up her chenille dressing gown.

'Where's my sambuca?'

'Answers first, sambuca second.'

She pouted, sat down at the kitchen table and folded her arms. We knew the sign. Didier got the bottles.

'You shouldn't have!' Her face looked surprised. I filled three shot glasses. I hate sambuca, but alcohol is alcohol.

'We could say the same,' I responded, nodding in the direction of the bedroom.

'He is my husband still. The Pope would be delighted, if we were Catholic.'

'He's got another wife you know.' I shouted.

'Peter, don't be so pompous. Sit down.'

I refused to sit and stood glowering at her, hands on hips, legs apart. I hadn't stood like that for years. I think I've only ever stood like that in her kitchen. Two Shoes Didier sat down immediately. He looked at me pleadingly, as though worried we'd miss out on dessert if I really pissed her off.

'Sit down, Peter,' she repeated. I could remember when holding my ground in that kitchen had been the most important thing in the world. Each and every time it was an epic struggle to be free, the defining moment of my life. Today it was just what I used to do in the kitchen. I sat down. Didier poured another round of shots.

'What can I say? He's very charming? He's great in bed? It's been a while?' She offered excuses like options for dinner. 'If I'm going to get dragged into your father and sons nonsense, I might at least get some fun out of it.'

'Mum, he isn't exactly Mr Reliable,' Didier pleaded with her, trying to sound reasonable.

'Ooh, sorry, I'm only allowed to sleep with dependable men, am I? You didn't even let us know when you were coming.'

'US?' I thundered.

'Sorry…me. You didn't let *me* know when you'd be arriving.'

Another round of sambuca.

'So what is he doing here?' Didier asked.

'He just turned up a few days ago. I'd like to think he came to apologise to me for being a bastard, but he's here to see you two. He did the whole lying on the ground thing in the front yard—that "I'm not worthy" nonsense—but I could smell "men's business" a mile off. You two reek of it as well. Poor old Mrs Blenkinsaw was very perplexed. He died last month, you know—Mr Blenkinsaw—forgot to tell you. I went to the funeral, paid my disrespects. I've been the supportive fellow widow. She's quite nice without him. Daughters asked me to keep an eye on her. One's a doctor in Darwin, other one does something boring in Sydney.'

'Hello! Can we get back on topic?'

'Yes, sorry… back to the men,' she sighed and had some more sambuca. 'He probably wants to make up to you for buggering off.'

'Which buggering off?' I asked.

'Exactly.'

I groaned and put my head on the table.

'Mum, on another note,' Didier said, 'I couldn't help but notice he wasn't wearing a condom.'

'Good point,' I said. 'You've no idea who he's been shagging. Of all the irresponsible stupid things to do. What would Frank say, eh?'

I was stopped by a resounding slap across the face.

'Don't bring Frank into this. The grief you caused him…' she paused and glared at me, '…the grief.'

The implication was clear: I'd pushed him into an early grave. It wasn't fair. He died years after we left. I know I caused stress, but it wasn't my fault.

'Thanks,' I said sarcastically.

'I didn't mean that,' she said. 'Bringing Frank into it was a low shot and you know it. God knows what it is, but you and your father still need to sort stuff out. You don't have to like him, and I'd never tell you to trust your hearts to him. But would it kill you to make your peace? It is Christmas.'

'I don't mean to nag,' said Didier, 'but you really should be careful, Mum, whoever you're having sex with. Since Viagra there's been a massive increase in sexually transmitted diseases in the over-fifties.'

'Yes, Didier, I'll remember.' She grabbed the sambuca and poured herself another shot. No more sharing.

'Honestly, you'd think your generation bloody well invented sex. The sexual revolution took place before you were born, you know. You both look like shit. Take your bags to your room, have a shower and then we can work out how to get through the next week without a murder.'

Marcel's suitcase was in our room. It was obvious he'd slept in my bed. I stripped the sheets. It was a relief to see that he hadn't moved into Mum's room completely, he just thrust around there in the afternoons. Didier watched the door while I went through his bag. His underpants were big grandad pants with age-old urine stains on the front, even the clean ones. I sniffed them to see how long he'd been in Alice. It was desperate times. There were three dirty pairs. Assuming one to travel here and a clean pair each day, he'd been here two days.

His French-issued EU passport had his name as Marcel Noirelle, no middle name. The Australian immigration stamp on the passport corroborated the underpants evidence. I realised with some regret that sniffing them had, in fact, been completely unnecessary. I was pushing everything back into his suitcase when he burst in—with clothes on, fortunately.

'Just moving your stuff into the living room. You will sleep on the couch.'

He smiled. 'Pierre, Didier. It must have been a shock for you, but after all it was how you both came into being.'

We didn't respond.

'Your mother is still a very attractive woman.'

'We don't want to hear it,' I broke our silence, 'Why are you here?'

'Of course I will be sleeping in the living room. This is your room, is it not?'

'Where's Kiki?' I asked.

She was in Naphlion with her family. It seemed they had been staying in her hometown until things quietened down in St Anastasie and they were forgiven for not bringing a Greque-en-Provence tourist boom. He conveniently failed to mention that I had paid all the bills.

'So will I have to go and beg her forgiveness *again*?'

Marcel tittered nervously. Kiki wasn't going to find out about this from him.

'Get out!' I shoved him out of the room and flung his suitcase across the hallway to the living room. His big old-man knickers fell out on the way.

I kicked the door shut behind him. The door was scuffed from all the times I'd done it before.

'Fuck! I am so angry!' I kicked the door again.

'That's good,' Didier said calmly, lying down on his bed. 'Caryn says you have to experience the emotion before you can deal with it.'

'How many miles of butcher's paper did that one take?'

He smiled and finally I did too. 'I hate the fact he can make me so angry.'

I was too exhausted to process my feelings, as Caryn would call it. I wanted to talk about something less frustrating. I lay on my mattress, facing Didier.

'So, Jean-Marc? Share.'

'Caryn has facilitated a relationship boundaries workshop.'

'So he's your actual boyfriend then?'

'The L-bomb has been dropped. More precisely, it was the A-bomb—he said it in French.'

Jean-Marc had taken to workshopping as much as he had taken to the gay life in London. He had even made a collage of his feelings for Didier out of dry pasta and wool.

'It was very creative,' Didier said proudly. 'He made a circle of pasta because I make him whole, with lots of loose bits of wool flying out from the centre because I let him be himself. We've got it on the fridge.'

He had made a better impression on Caryn that I could ever hope to achieve. She was talking babies, pitting them against each other as to whose sperm she'd use.

'What about Peony?' Didier asked. I was tempted to say everything was fine, but he locked me in eye contact until I expressed myself.

'We're not your typical couple. Don't know if we even know how, but we talk about things, we have sex, I miss her sometimes when she's not there.'

'This is good…and now you're stinking rich too!'

'I dunno. It's still not quite right, Dids. Something's still missing.'

We had dinner at home. Mum cooked a chicken. As he had with Kiki, Marcel demanded that we compliment Mum on her food before we had even sampled everything on the plate.

'I've been thinking about what to do for Christmas,' Mum announced. It was in two days' time.

'I'm not cooking a full dinner in this heat and I don't think we should be stuck in the house all day.'

She looked at me as if she was contemplating hiding all the knives.

'So let's drive to Kata Tjuta and Uluru. Stay overnight, and show Marcel the sights. It would be a shame to come all this way and not see them.'

Marcel nodded, as if he was agreeable to anything.

'It's a fantastically spiritual place!' Didier enthused.

'Aren't the Olgas a sacred site for Aboriginal men?' I asked Mum. I sensed what she was up to.

'Kata Tjuta,' Didier and Mum corrected me with the proper name. Mum used that to ignore my question.

'So it's decided then. Good. I'll get the car checked tomorrow.'

Christmas Eve, the night before the trip, we all went to the Memo, as the local Memorial Club was known. We would have to make an appearance there at some point or our mum would never hear the end of it. With any luck the bastard would get into a fatal fight with someone.

It was a Christmas karaoke special. Murder of a different kind was taking place until Marcel took over the show. We pushed him into it, mainly to get him away from our table so we could talk. He'd obviously inherited some of his father's singing voice as he belted out a gripping rendition of 'I Will Always Love You'.

'You're not falling in love with him again, are you?' I asked Mum.

'Shit no!' she laughed. 'At my age, you don't pass up on great sex when it's offered to you, but it's nothing more. I mean, he's fab in the sack but totally irritating out of it.'

'Funny seeing you together,' she continued, 'you're alike in more than looks, but different too.' She nodded at Marcel who was now delighting the crowd by singing 'Can't Get You Out of My Head' in French.

'I thought you were going to grow up like him. You used to get into all sorts of trouble, like cheating was the easiest, most natural way of doing anything. He was the same. If there was a scam going, Marcel would be in on it.'

Mum had never really spoken about their relationship before. Didier and I leaned in close to glean every word.

'You could have been like that,' she continued, 'I don't mean in a his-blood's-running-through-your-veins way... Hang on, perhaps I do. Perhaps we do pass on more than hair colour and indented thumbnails. Who knows? People are so complex and yet we're obsessed with explaining every aspect of them. If it's not social programming, it's genetic programming. There's got to be a gene that explains everything now. They won't let anything just be itself, it all has to be explained and then, when it's explained, it can be controlled and then altered. I don't like it.'

I sensed we might veer off into her next election campaign, but she paused and got back on track.

'I do know you worshipped him when you were little. Your face was different when he was around. It lit up. And I've noticed that it still does, not in such a happy way, but some of your intensity reaches the surface when he's around. It used to almost make me jealous. Boys are supposed to worship their mums. He let you down so often but you never minded. It was like you looked forward to his excuses. As if bothering to lie so well to you was a way of showing love.'

She took another sip and then it was my brother's turn.

'You were different, Didier...you were always mine, and that's not a gay stereotype thing, you just didn't get to know your father. By the time you were really aware of him, he was travelling more and more. Peter was already hooked, but you never got that initial exposure.'

Karaoke night had given way to *Tonight Live With Marcel Noirelle*. Some of the women were ready to throw their knickers at him. We were the only ones not in thrall.

'That's why I was so relieved when Frank came along. It was funny the way you copied Marcel, said the things he said, even though you didn't know you were repeating him. Frank wasn't an exciting man, but he was good and decent and that's what you needed more than anything. There were times I could have beaten you black and blue, but Frank, never.'

'We should drink a toast to him,' Didier suggested and we raised our glasses to Frank.

'Love, Support, Guidance,' we all said together. That was Frank's catchphrase. Whenever anyone said kids needed a father, he'd say,

'No, kids need love, support and guidance, it doesn't matter who that comes from, as long as it comes.'

'Still, for all Frank's influence,' Mum finished her drink and nodded to where Marcel was accepting the meat tray, that night's karaoke prize, 'like it or loathe it, that man's your father.'

The journey to the centre of Australia is special. There's no other like it. If you drive from the cities that cling to the coast, you just keep going further and further away from the safety of the sea. When you enter the desert, it's a time warp of ruler-straight roads charging on through unchanging territory. Travellers who reach the middle in one piece share a profound experience with their companions: they've collectively stared down the barrel of madness and come out intact. They've passed the acid test. But for every happy Cunningham family that bonds all the way from Melbourne to Uluru, there's a Noirelle family for whom the puny five-hour drive from Alice is a one-way trip into hell.

We knew from experience that the only way to survive the journey from Alice to Uluru was to talk as little as possible. Conversation and car games (except for I Spy) are okay for keeping the driver awake, but you have to resist the big topics. In the confined space of a car, the only privacy is in your head. You have to be allowed that.

I wanted time to mull over Greque-en-Provence. Being in Alice had changed my perspective. Rather than obsessing on how to fix the problem for G&K, I was more interested in why I was so obsessed with it. It was like my life was wrapped up in the concept and unravelling it would somehow fix everything.

Marcel either didn't get the silence thing, or didn't want to. He started asking questions about what he could see out of the window, even when there was nothing to see. Mum nipped it in the bud.

'Marcel, on these trips it's best to enjoy the scenery in silence.'

Later he started humming, moved up to whistling, passed musical mumbling and into a full-on rendition of a French song.

'*En passant par la Lorraine avec mes sabots…*' he sang and waited for us to repeat the line. We didn't. He did. The song is an incredibly repetitive ditty about some girl in clogs who meets some soldiers. He waited for us at the end of every line and then resumed singing. He did this for every line of the nine verses.

After that he ploughed through every other French nursery song going. Everyone's favourite about killing larks, '*Alouette*' followed by '*J'ai du bon tabac*' all the way through to the particularly cruel '*Ne pleure pas Jeannette*'. Jeannette's crying for the man she loves who's about to be hanged. Her parents tell her to shut up, but she doesn't and so they hang her with him. I guess children's songs are the same the world over: if they're not about marrying princes they're about death, booze and tobacco.

When I took over the driving it was time for revenge on the music front. I decided a little opera would be appropriate, so I slipped a CD into the car stereo. Marcel was in the back with Didier. As the scratchy recording started I glanced in the rear-view mirror. Didier turned his whole body to make a show of watching Marcel.

Marcel remained still as his father's voice filled the car. He swallowed slightly but that was all. He stared at the headrest on the front passenger seat.

'What's this?' Mum asked.

'It's a recording from the 1930s by France's leading dramatic baritone of the time, Alberto Noirelle.'

'Your father?' Mum turned to look at Marcel.

'Yes,' said Didier. 'Not bad for violent drunk, eh?'

Marcel nodded and made a tiny gesture with his hands to concede he had been caught out. He gazed out the window, forming his mouth to whistle, but not making a sound.

An hour from Kata Tjuta and we entered the danger zone. This was where our arguments used to break out, just when you thought you were going to make it through. Everything ached, my balls were sore; they always get like that after hours in the car. I was shifting around, arching my back, trying to get comfortable. I should have stopped, done the whole driver fatigue thing, but we were so close. Kata Tjuta was in sight. I stepped on the gas, shutting out everything but the road and me. Didier banged his head on the window. Mum was massaging her temples. Coping strategies strained to overload.

I could hear my name. I ignored it. It grew louder.

'Peter, for God's sake answer me!' It was Mum. I looked at her, trying to communicate without words: we're nearly there, we can make it.

'What's the plan? Are we going to the resort or what?'

I had a plan but had forgotten to communicate it.

'Peter!' she exclaimed again.

'I thought we'd catch the sunset at Kata Tjuta and then go to the resort.'

'All you had to do was say so.'

She was irritated, but was holding on to the shred of understanding that told her I was just trying to cope. I felt her hand pat my knee. I didn't look.

I knew the turn-off was soon. We passed a sign. Marcel started to ask about it.

'Slow down, you might miss the turn-off,' he said. 'Slow down, indicate now.'

I drove faster.

'We will miss it. I know it. It is better to be safe than to be sorry.'
We got closer to the turn-off.
'It will be soon, the land is flat, you cannot tell.'
Didier had his hands over his ears; Mum was clenching her hands together and staring at them. I thundered along staring at the road. Suddenly the turning was there. Without slowing or indicating, I hurled the car around the corner. It screeched and created a cloud of dust behind us. I sprinted for the parking lot, slammed on the brakes and came to a halt in the nearest spot.

The second the car stopped we all leapt out and walked in different directions, like divers gasping for air. We'd done it. The tension vanished.

There's something about Kata Tjuta. It's not as visually pure as Uluru—there's dozens of rocks all piled over each other—but it's the gentlest place on earth. For all the searing heat of the desert and the harsh conditions, its peace envelops you. The red sand is soft.

You can walk through some of Kata Tjuta, but the heart of it is impenetrable. There's a vastness inside that you can glimpse if you fly around it, but no one could get to the heart of it, even if the traditional owners let you try. You're allowed to walk through the Valley of the Winds, but no one with a shred of instinct needs telling it's sacred.

'This is a sacred men's site. Women aren't even supposed to look at Kata Tjuta,' Mum said. 'I think the three of you should go. Sort out whatever it is you need to sort out. I'll wait here.'

I was right, she'd planned this all along. Damn her, why couldn't she just be cranky and kooky, why did she have to be constructive as well? The timing was perfect. One coach party was returning, the next had not yet arrived—we could have the place to ourselves. We took our water supplies and set off.

You'd swear the rocks changed shape as you walked past them. Round boulders one moment, sheer straight cliffs the next. Smooth, then rough. Vast magical shape-shifters. Once you get into the Valley of the Winds there's a stream, if there's been enough rain.

We stopped by the stream for a water break. Not a word had been spoken. Didier tapped Marcel on his shoulder and pointed to a hollow in the tree above us. There was a wild budgerigar. Delight splashed across Marcel's face. He chased it as it flew away, jumping over the small rocks to keep it in sight. The bird escaped him but he returned with a contented smile.

'I have always wanted to see them in the wild. I had one as a boy.'

'So Bibi was real?' Didier asked about the budgie liberated at the end of Marcel's fake story.

'Yes, my father bought him on my tenth birthday. I taught him to say *merde*. It was the only word he ever learned.'

He breathed deeply and smiled.

'So you have found Rodolphe. Well done. How is he?'

'Great. Nice man,' I said. 'He gave us the last story about Hippolyte and Alberto.'

I paused, waiting for him to volunteer an explanation for his fake story. He didn't.

'What happened to Hippolyte?' Didier asked.

'The truth this time!' I added.

Marcel nodded.

'I was at school about to do brilliantly well in my Baccalauréat…' he paused and gave in. 'I had been caught cheating. It was a misunderstanding, but the brothers were not happy and felt the need to expel me from the school.'

This sounded truthful at least.

A call had come through to the head teacher's office with terrible news. Hippolyte had been shot. After an incident at Hippo's in the evening he had left his gun on his desk. He'd been in a hurry to get home to Nicolette and their daughter. The next morning they had all come into the office. As Nicolette and Hippolyte talked through the day's business, the girl found the gun and began to play with it.

'Seeing the danger, Hippolyte leapt at the girl to remove the gun but tragically it discharged into his chest. Let us walk on.'

Marcel ended the story abruptly, giving us no time to reflect.

'There is further to go, is there not?'

We walked on deeper into Kata Tjuta. We lost the wind. Nothing moved apart from us. At the end of the area where the public were allowed, Marcel finally stopped. There was a steep slope to the side, with big cracks in it. One day a huge chunk of rock will come crashing down. He posed under it, but it didn't fall on him.

Didier and I sat down on the rocks to drink some water. Didier made Marcel drink some too. He wouldn't sit down, just kept pacing around saying 'Magnificent'.

We waited for something to happen. Some brilliant wisdom, thousands of years old, would emerge from the rocks and enlighten us.

Eventually Marcel spoke.

'I am ready,' he announced.

'For what?' I asked.

'The Force of Destiny!' he shouted to the valley and ripped his shirt open to bare his chest. He posed, eyes closed, his bare chest with straggly grey hairs thrust out towards us, like a septuagenarian Fabio.

'But of course, I am sorry!' he added, pulled a pretty frightening folding knife out of his pocket, opened it up and tossed it across the ground to us. He resumed the pose.

'The Force of Destiny,' he repeated, as if telling us where we were resuming the script.

'I hope you've got some sunscreen on that chest, you'll burn easily,' Didier warned him.

'*Mes fils!*' he spoke, annoyed. 'The time has come. What better place than here for me to die?'

I groaned. 'Marcel, it's not going to happen. Just sit down and rest. It's too hot for this crap.'

'Then I shall do it myself!' he shouted and dashed to the edge of the precipice we had climbed up.

'It is still fate, you brought me here. Your goodness, your forgiveness, your generosity have been overwhelming. You are driving me to this. The more you forgive me, the more the Furies of my guilt hound me to the edge. I can stand them no more. Hate me or I will die!'

He turned to face us. 'I can bear no more. *Adieu.*'

I think at that point we were supposed to lunge at him to stop him from jumping. We didn't and he didn't jump.

'Okay,' said Didier calmly, 'let's workshop this. We don't want you to throw yourself off here. Perhaps you could sit down with us, we could all express how we're feeling, and then if you still want to leap we won't stop you. At least give us a chance to say what we need to say first.'

Marcel stepped away from the edge. Soon we were all sitting on a rock. We each had five minutes to draw a picture of what we were feeling with stones, twigs, whatever we could find around us, playdough being in short supply.

Marcel had a range of different objects. He picked up a rock: 'This is Claude, a great farmer, a good father.' A large piece of dried wood signified Alberto, a great opera singer. There was a flower to represent Hippolyte: 'The greatest pimp Paris has known. And this is me,' he picked up a grain of sand and tossed it in the air. '*Mes *fils*, I have done nothing. I have brought pleasure to myself, and a number of women. I am not worthy of the destiny of the Noirelles.'

'You don't have to do great things to be worthy.' Didier tried to cheer him up.

'But you have to do good things, do you not?' he asked.

I hadn't said anything. I agreed with him. He was a good shag, that was it. At the end of the day, it didn't seem like much. A good shag. The words started repeating in my head. I could feel something happening. The right chemicals were pouring into the right cells in my brain and it was firing.

Having expressed himself, Marcel was now ready to go.

'Farewell,' he cried. 'Live better lives than me. Be worthy of our name as I have failed to be.'

He trudged his way to his self-imposed destiny. When he reached the edge I leapt up.

'Stop!' I shouted. 'Stop!'

He turned, surprised at the urgency in my voice.

'I need you. I actually *need* you. I've got it. I've finally got what's been missing!'

I looked excitedly from Didier to Marcel.

'What's been missing?' Didier was beginning to suspect I was the one suffering heat damage.

Marcel had the wind taken out of his suicidal sails. I grabbed him by the shoulders, pulled him towards me and gave him a hug of sheer joy. I could suddenly see what I needed to do to fix everything, not just G&K's mass boutique concept but everything. Fill the gaps in my life, bring it all together and actually belong somewhere.

'You're a good shag,' I said to Marcel, 'and you've no idea how important that is!'

'Peter, what the hell are you going on about?'

'I've worked it out. I know what's missing and I need him, I need you. I need everyone!'

'For what? What are you going to do?' Didier remained perplexed.

'I'm bringing this family together and I'm taking us home. We're all going back to St Hubert!'

Mum got a shock when we returned. I bounded along ahead of the other two, charged up and hugged her.

'You were so right. You give me all my best ideas. You're a genius.' I kissed her.

'So you've resolved all this father and son stuff?'

'I've resolved everything, I'll explain it all later.'

'Fine,' she said.

I was too wrapped up in my own thoughts to realise she was pissed off. She'd clearly been holding back for the right moment and the right moment came when the four of us were having dinner at the Uluru resort. I continued to trill on about having resolved everything, but without actually being able to tell them what it was. It was all there, in place in my head. I couldn't quite get it out yet.

'Mum, you've been pretty quiet,' Didier commented.

'Well, you've all been so obsessed with your male inheritance and what you got from Marcel and what you didn't get, it's been hard to get a look in these last six months.'

'Mum, we're not rejecting you or Frank in any way. This is simply about exploring that side of who we are,' Didier was being conciliatory as usual.

'Urgh, men, you're all the same!' She downed her half-empty glass of wine and poured the next. 'Men,' she repeated and put her glass down. She smoothed her hair to calm herself and gently raised a hand at each of us to stop our hurt looks. Marcel sat as still as he could. This wasn't the Janice he remembered.

'In all your obsession about "his" legacy, and what "he" left you and what "his" family fate is or isn't, did it never occur to you that I wasn't some empty, blank egg? You're as much me as you are him.

'Perhaps there's a tradition in my family of leading happy fulfilling lives that make the world a better place. Perhaps my great-, great-grandfather or mother left a fantastic spiritual legacy that totally wipes out the Noirelle bullshit. Did you ever think of that? I made the two of you in my body, from my body. And I raised you more than anyone else. Marcel buggered off and Frank died. I'm the biggest influence in your lives. Me. I'm the only one who's always been there, yet I seem to count for nothing.'

She took another swig from the glass.

'How the hell did I produce such sexist pigs? Shit, this isn't the 1970s, I shouldn't be having to use that term, but when you deny the existence of female influence that's exactly what you are.'

'Janice, *mes fils* were—' Marcel made the mistake of interrupting.

'YOU! Peter might blether on about needing you now, but I certainly don't.'

She stood up, threw her napkin on the table and began to walk off. Then she came back, picked up her full wine glass and paused as if she couldn't decide which one of us to hurl it at. She chose Marcel; his back catalogue of bastardry was far longer than ours.

'And your dick's not as big as it used to be!' she shouted at him and walked off.

We sat in silence for a moment as wine dripped off Marcel's nose.

'I do not think that is true!' Marcel offered and looked round the restaurant, afraid people might believe her.

'I think you'd better go and clean up,' I told him.

Didier and I sat at the table wondering how long it would be before we could go and apologise to Mum.

When we finally made it to her room, she was waiting for us.

'You two took your time, come here.'

She hugged us. We said we were sorry. She said she was glad that we seemed to have sorted things with Marcel.

'But if you don't give me some explanation of this big idea other than "I've got it!" the next glass of wine will be for you.'

I explained my bold new concept to her and Didier as best I could. I must have managed okay because when I'd finished Mum nodded. She was impressed.

'If the Pope were a woman, you'd be canonised.'

***

Back in New York, the first thing I had to do was secure the rights to Greque-en-Provence for myself if the bold new scheme was to work. Because I'd done a lot of the development in work time, and the bills for the fête in St Anastasie had essentially been paid by G&K as 'research', they might have a claim on any future profits. I needed them to waive all future claims if the bold new scheme was to work.

Peony had proved valuable again for that essential legal opinion. I wouldn't have bothered and just tried to walk away with the concept.

We decided we'd missed each other. That Christmas had been her best yet, thanks to the recently filled photo frame on the mantelpiece. Her mother said I looked like 'a keeper'.

'Don't get too exited, she'd hook me up with serial killer if she thought she'd get a wedding out of it.'

Peony even seemed infected by my new-found enthusiasm.

'Perhaps you'll need a lawyer with the determination of Rottweiler,' she suggested. I looked surprised and I think we both had a 'rushing things' panic attack. Once that subsided I liked the idea of her being involved. She was right, we'd need someone with a good legal brain.

Alex was excited by the new project too. Given the mediocre market testing I had said supermarkets were not the way to go.

'The whole concept of mass boutique was a crap one anyway,' I explained. 'Having your face plastered on boxes in the prepared foods chiller cabinet will cheapen your image.'

She agreed to help me with G&K. I'd announced to Hugo that I was ready to pitch the big new idea to G&K and I wanted them to hear it all together.

'All their top execs and you will get it for the first time. I want the fact that your jaw will drop wide open to have a major impact on them. I want to do it right here, around your coffee table. Fresh, explosive, direct face-to-face communication. No PowerPoint slides, no projectors, no specially produced DVD presentations, just people and food—pure and simple.'

'Organic, I like it.'

If I was going to put them off the idea for good, there could be no half measures. I had to ensure they absolutely hated Greque-en-Provence. It would take no less than the worst pitch of my life. Lavender moussaka would be the obvious choice to lead the pitch. For the new agenda, it was the strongest card. The *Fetta Fondue* I reckoned would work pretty well, particularly as we'd cooked it up the night before and let it sit on a low heat for several hours. *Marie-Nana's Dolmades Escargot* were actually okay, so Alex cooked them in beef lard and made sure plenty of it oozed out of them at room temperature.

I did a good spin before the food arrived. Talked up the concept of mass boutique. A tiny pocket of unique culture. The familiarity of the whole Provence thing but with a strong new angle.

'Ladies, gents, boy and girls,' I announced, 'I give you Greque-en-Provence.'

That was the cue: Bethnee-Chantelle threw the doors open. An accordion player wandered in playing a selection of Nana Mouskouri's classics. The waiting staff wore traditional French onion-seller striped shirts with the full pleated skirt of the national Greek costume.

The smell of congealed lavender-scented fat filled the room.

'Now try some real food for the first time in years!' I declared and threw a lard-enriched dolmades escargot down my throat. It touched the sides long enough to leave a thick coat of artery-clogging fat.

'Superb, I'll take another.'

Everyone fell on the food with enthusiasm until their taste buds kicked into gear.

The CEO of G&K immediately spat out the serving of stale pitta brioche dunked in the fetta fondue and stared at Hugo in disbelief. The director of marketing gagged on the lavender moussaka and eventually vomited into the bin. Their senior brand manager, thinking he had to like the stuff to impress the senior executives, ate like a reality TV show contestant forced to swallow live cockroaches.

Before anyone could raise a word of protest, I moved to phase two.

'And now, not only do we have the most exiting new range of food ever to reach the market, but I'm happy to present our front person, *the* most engaging food personality to hit the media. The star of Greque-en-Provence, Alex Beacham!'

The doors to the office once again flew open and Alex leapt in. Dressed in the flimsiest of chiffon Greek nymph outfits she left nothing to the imagination as she ran around barefoot trailing a gossamer scarf over the heads of the terrified executives.

'I am Demeter, the goddess of plenty,' she cried, jumping onto the table and thrusting her arms into the air.

'Behold my feast. These are the products of my bounty. Feel the nurturing power of Mother Earth.' She took the CEO's head and rammed it into her breasts. 'Take of me, for my bounty knows no limits.'

She leapt to her feet, allowing him to breathe once more.

'Gorge yourselves!' she declared, raising the *Fetta Fondue* pot above her head and beginning to turn around, on the spot with a low, deep moan. She spun around and around, getting faster and faster as her voice got higher and higher until she was screaming.

She spun at a speed that amazed even me. The congealed cheese splattered everyone with off-white goo.

'Hiiii-yaaaaa!' She flung the pot away like a manic shot-putter and stood panting, looking round for clapping and cheering and orgiastic indulgence, before running from the room.

'So, do we have deal?' I asked with fetta dribbling down my cheeks.

The deal was I had to clear my desk by the end of the day. Refusing to back down, I insisted the idea was a winner. Just to make absolutely sure that they could not accuse us of duplicity, I called Bethnee-Chantelle into the room to witness me say the words: 'Greque-en-Provence will make more money than you could possibly imagine. If you won't take it on, I will. I'll insist on working out my contractual three months' notice unless you sign a waiver against all future claims on a share in Greque-en-Provence.'

Hugo and the G&K CEO fell over themselves to sign.

'Get some help, Peter,' Hugo said. 'I say that as your friend. Now get the hell out—I say that as your former boss!'

Alex was waiting for me in the Hudson Hotel with Peony. Peony had tears rolling down her face as Alex described the scene that had just occurred.

'You were brilliant!' It was my turn to bear down on Alex and plant a big kiss. 'You won't regret it, I promise.'

'I'd better not. If it gets out—'

'It won't,' interrupted Peony. 'I inserted a non-disclosure clause into that contract so tight you couldn't shove a rat's prick in it.'

It was the first time I'd heard her tell a joke. I liked it. She'd also handed in her notice at work. I liked that even more.

'I've gotta work out four months' notice, but after that I'm totally there with you.'

It was her turn for a sloppy kiss.

For the first time in my life, I set foot on the steep streets of St Hubert. Marcel had driven me there in his inimitable style. The few villagers who still lived there had done their best to make it look lively for me. The patissier, the only shop still left, opened especially for me. He normally only opened Saturday morning and spent the rest of the week supplying the hotels in Aix with their pastries. The peeling sign declared that it was the home of the famous patriotic dish Tarte de Marne.

'It was invented by my great-grandfather during the First World War,' the patissier informed me, 'to encourage the soldiers in the trenches.'

History had been kinder to his family's legacy.

'How would you feel about opening the patisserie full time and teaching people how to make cakes?' I asked. 'You might have to add a few Greek recipes to your range.'

Gervais nodded his agreement enthusiastically.

'I need a boulanger as well. I'm thinking of bringing one in from St Anastasie. We'd be pretty clear on who makes what.' I was a bit worried about demarcation disputes if I brought in Lucien.

'Puh,' said Gervais, 'he can make all the bread he wants. Any fat-fingered fool can knock out baguettes.'

'Good.'

'So it's true, then,' he continued, 'the Noirelle family are coming back. There's not too many that will remember, but my grandfather told me about a beautiful woman who captured his father's heart late in life. They ended up marrying. An angel of gentleness, he called her. She used to be the Noirelle housekeeper.'

That evening we held a meeting in the old inn for the local residents. It had been closed for years, but seeing as I'd made an offer on the place, which had been accepted, they let me use it before the deal was finalised.

Marcel gave a potted and almost accurate history of our family's involvement with the village and then introduced me. I did my sales pitch.

'St Hubert has lost out on the tourism industry. Everyone says the streets are too steep, but somehow my legs have coped fine.'

There were a few knowing smiles. They were warming to us.

I explained that I was going to turn St Hubert into one of the biggest tourist attractions in southern France by making it the village of Greque-en-Provence. More isolated (and with fewer satellite dishes) than St Anastasie, it made the whole isolated Greek community angle more believable.

The village was to become a Mecca for the over-fifties seeking a holiday in an alternative lifestyle. They would come and learn how to make abrivar, do gentle work in the lavender fields, gather grapes in the vineyard, crush the olives from the grove, milk the goats, make fetta, lose weight walking up and down the streets and then go crazy at the annual abrivar festival. We'd also toss in lavender, grape, olive and cheese festivals throughout the summer season.

What I didn't tell them was that people were really coming for sex. That had been the key to my realisation at Kata Tjuta. Mum's words about the sexual revolution taking place before we were born had sunk in and subconsciously worked their way into the Greque-en-Provence concept, providing the missing link. The reason the market research hadn't worked was because it was missing the key ingredient: sex, or specifically all the shagging we'd done in back alleys. It was sex that made Greque-en-Provence so exciting, and that was what made Alex Beacham the perfect person to 'discover' it for the rest of the world.

She was a role model for the likes of my mother—the love child in the union of sex and food—and she appealed to a vast market. The baby-boomers, the ones who'd invented free love, were hitting their fifties in their millions around the world. Their kids had grown up, the conservative veneer of parenthood was peeling off and they were ready, willing and (thanks to Viagra) able to take up their old ways. Alex was going to discover the village, release a book globally and kick off our opening summer season with the first culinary holiday in St Hubert.

It was to be an upmarket knocking shop masquerading as a cookery and lifestyle retreat. And that's why I needed Marcel. For the first time in his life, his one great skill would be really useful. I couldn't have invented a better host for the village. He was the one all the lonely older women would yearn to be seduced by. They'd have to settle for Lucien the boulanger or Maurice the gendarme or even their own husbands, but I'd ship in enough crusty old French roués to go around.

Kiki would run the Greque-en-Provence cooking school to keep them busy during the day. Marcel had even volunteered to run a couple of courses: one on selecting fruit and the other, for men only, on the secrets of seduction, Greque-en-Provence style.

It was a big gamble, but one I was determined would pay off. I sank my gravestone fortune into the place. Kiki and the experts who had scored EU funds for St Anastasie's basketball court were working on getting some funding for St Hubert as well.

I'd secured the inn, the old lavender farm and several other areas around the village, but the key to my whole scheme was Claude's house. That was our family home and would be the central point from which the whole operation would be controlled. Unfortunately Claude's house brought my plans to a shuddering halt.

'It's been sold,' Gervais the pastissier announced. 'Some Englishwoman bought it. She moved in this week.'

I wasn't happy. I was even less happy when I discovered it was a retired TV personality, Clare Prendergast. She'd been a BBC newsreader in the late 1970s with ear-piercingly clear RADA-trained diction. In the 1980s she'd fallen foul of the push to have 'representative' regional accents on television. After newscasting, her one near success had been a series of specials on rural characters across the continent: *Peasants of Europe*. Viewers hadn't been convinced by her recently acquired Yorkshire accent and the series was promptly axed.

She had now moved to St Hubert, having 'fallen in love' with the village, and was seeking out the authentic Provençal life.

'She is writing a memoir of Provence,' Gervais announced. The room groaned, afraid they were to go the way of every other village in Provence and be doomed to history as quirkily gruff peasants with hearts of gold.

There was nothing for it. Clare Prendergast had to go.

I couldn't afford to wait until she was gone before starting the redevelopment work. It was February and the Abrivar Festival was scheduled for July when the apricots were at their best. There wasn't a week to waste.

I figured we'd begin by planting the lavender fields and other work outside the village as it would be the easiest to hide. The lavender field had to be stocked with plants mature enough to be harvested in September. We couldn't start on the olive grove because it was still on its way from Greece. Lennon and Ringo had located some fantastically gnarled olive trees in Thessalonica. They were currently en route through Macedonia, along with a flock of authentic Greek sheep, which were going to graze the St Hubert hillsides, wander quaintly through the village and get milked by doting tourists. Our vineyard was being established by Louis of the execrable gin. He was happy to abandon his bathtub distillery and return to his first love, wine-making.

We'd planted our first row of lavender when a call came from the guard posted near the village. Clare Prendergast was approaching.

'Run for the trees!' I shouted. Everyone picked up tools, took hold of the wheelbarrows and sprinted for cover. The utility truck and earthmover couldn't be moved in time so we threw tarpaulins over them just before her ancient Citroen 2CV trundled into view. All she saw were some young lavender plants and my back, looking suitably peasant-like.

'*Bonjour*,' she intoned loudly out of the fold-down window without stopping. I ignored her.

Fifteen minutes later, just as we'd got back to work, the signal came again. She was on her way back.

'This will take forever if we have to keep stopping when she drives by,' said the site manager. 'Can't we just block the view from the road?'

He was right; there was only one spot where the site was visible from the road. If we erected a billboard there, she wouldn't be able to see a thing.

Hiding the development from her was one thing; getting her out of Claude's house was another. She had to come to hate living in St Hubert, but there was no denying it was a picturesque spot. I needed to confer with minds at least as devious as my own to come up with a solution.

Marcel, Kiki and I had a meeting with Gervais the patissier. We also recruited Bernard, a young plumber who'd bought the local franchise of the largest plumbing chain in Europe. He was smart, efficient and guaranteed that he would turn up to appointments within one hour of the stated time or clients would receive twenty per cent off their bill.

'The house is old,' suggested Kiki, 'the plumbing will be terrible, she will not last long.'

'The previous owners had all the plumbing replaced before selling it. The taps and sinks are authentically old, but behind the walls it's some of my finest work,' Bernard declared.

'We could turn the water off in the street, could we not?' Marcel suggested.

'There's a centralised control just next to patisserie,' Gervais volunteered.

'It's all computerised,' said the plumber, 'and I have the access codes. I can have the water off in minutes.'

'It could take a very long time to repair,' Marcel added.

This was creative thinking. I liked it. We had a plan.

In the morning, Kiki waited outside on the street for Clare to appear. The minute her door opened, Kiki began walking slowly up the hill.

'Excuse me,' Clare cried out. From the corner where I was watching, her RADA-trained tones cracked my ears.

'Excuse me!' She projected her voice even further. Kiki turned, shrugged her shoulders and continued.

Clare ran up to Kiki in her dressing gown, grabbed her arm and extended a hand to effect an introduction.

'Hello, I'm Clare Prendergast...' She paused, expecting a reaction. 'You might know me from television.'

Kiki looked blankly at her.

'You did get my series of specials here—it's still showing, I get royalty cheques. It's only pin money, but it was terribly popular. *The Peasants of Europe? Les Paysans d'Europe?*'

Kiki shrugged again and tried to move off.

'It's my plumbing,' Clare added with urgency, 'the water's off. Just stopped. Honestly, it's hopeless. Still I guess that's life now: a martyr to my pipes.'

Her voice was projecting through the whole village. I could almost detect a sense of excitement in her tone.

'Patissier!' said Kiki grumpily.

'No, my lovely, I need a plumber. Plum-ber, not cakes.'

'Plum-ber at patisserie.' Kiki tapped her own forehead with the palm of her hand to let Clare know how stupid she was.

Clare enquired at the patisserie. She didn't wonder why it had opened on a Tuesday for the first time. Gervais told her he'd pass the message on to the plumber.

The next day Clare returned to find the shop shut. She wandered the streets looking for someone to ask about the plumber, who still had not appeared, but could find no one.

The day after that Marcel turned up at her house, unshaven, garlic-breathed and with a large bag of rusty tools.

'No shagging,' I warned him. 'We need to get rid of her.'

'He is right. You listen!' Kiki reinforced the message.

'Yes, Kiki, but of course,' he mumbled.

Clare's hair was limp and greasy. Marcel reported she was plastered in perfume, trying to hide the scent of her unwashed body.

He climbed into her kitchen cupboard, banged on the pipes and shrugged his shoulders. In the bathroom he spent ten minutes turning the taps on and off and then pointed to the unflushed toilet and tutted.

'Not good.'

'I know that. Please, can you get me my water back? What's wrong? Is the whole street off?'

'Non!' Marcel shook his head. 'We try power.'

He trundled to the switchboard.

'What's that got to do with it? The power's fine.'

'Water… electricity…' Marcel made a meshing motion with his fingers to suggest they were cosmically linked.

He switched the power off, stood pushing air out of his mouth for ten minutes, then pretended to switch it back on. He flicked the light switch on and off.

'Oh no, really, that's too much!'

'See!' Marcel meshed his fingers again, his point proven. He headed for the door.

'But what's to be done? You can't leave me like this.'

He held his hand up, went to the door and shouted down the street. 'Kiki! The bucket, quickly.'

Kiki scuttled up the road carrying a large bucket of water which Marcel then presented to Clare.

'For toilet.'

She stood with the bucket staring in amazement at Kiki.

'My wife,' Marcel said.

'But if you're his wife, why did you send me to the patissier?' Clare asked in exasperation.

'Gervais know where he is.'

The plumber and his wife started walking away.

'But what about my pipes? My power? When are you going to fix it?'

Marcel dropped his bag and turned like he'd had absolutely enough. 'It is the electricity, you stupid English woman!'

Kiki started shouting at her in Greek for good measure until Clare retreated into the house.

It was a busy day for my father. By the afternoon he had washed, shaved and transformed himself from gruff plumber to suave pin-up boy. I had a photographer round to do a few publicity shots, including the Men of Provence calendar. Maurice, Lucien and Gervais were already in their make-up looking suitably Greek and Gallic. Marcel was to be August and also feature in the press kits for the resort. When I looked at the test polaroids, there was no denying he oozed seductive charm. He hovered nervously as I discussed the pictures with the photographer. He tried to look over my shoulder at the images.

'You look great,' I said. 'It's all going to be great.'

A happy satisfaction appeared on his face, like a little boy who'd finally scored a good mark for his homework after months of trying.

I'd been avoiding Clare and had managed not to let her see me at all. After two weeks without water or power we decided she needed an English speaker to confess her woes to and who could gently guide her out of the village.

Before I could introduce myself, the olive farm arrived and I had to supervise the installation of the trees. It was a tight operation. We needed to get the trees off the trucks and into the ground without Clare noticing. The holes had already been dug and watered, we just needed to lower the knotted trees into position.

Three trees in and the mobile went off. She was in her car and headed our way. This time there was nowhere to hide. Two huge trucks and a forklift for moving the trees couldn't be hidden under tarpaulins. She had to be stopped before she even got near.

There was nothing else for it: I sprinted uphill into the village, my legs keeping a sure grip on the road. Running up the middle of the street I figured she'd be forced to brake so as not to run me over. Just as I reached Madame Dupont's old boarded-up shop, her car rounded the hairpin bend and she screeched to a halt. I leapt to the side.

Clare jumped out of the car, lost her footing and fell right on top of me. The scent of Estée Lauder White Linen was overpowering.

'Oops! I'm terribly sorry. It's so terribly steep.'

'I'm okay, don't worry.'

'You're English!'

'Australian actually.'

'Marvellous, I'm—'

'You're Clare Prendergast! I loved you in *Peasants of Europe*.'

'How sweet of you. I'm surprised anyone remembers that. It was hardly seminal TV. Still, one takes what jobs one can.'

'It was very popular.'

'Yes...would you believe my bottom was voted Britain's second sexiest after Felicity Kendall's in 1979.'

'Really?' I tried to look at her bottom.

'Don't come too close, I absolutely reek. Not a drop of water in my pipes for weeks. The plumber is the most cantankerous bastard I've ever met. His wife's quite mad and now he's disappeared off the face of the earth. She's probably murdered him and frankly I don't blame her.'

'Sounds awful, how the hell can you stand it?'

'It's all grist to the mill. My publisher's going to love it. Such characters! I dare say they've got hearts of gold when you get to know them.'

I cursed inside. She was loving the abject failure of the plumbing. Our plan was backfiring badly.

'Are you staying in the village?' she asked.

'Yes, I'm at the old inn. I persuaded them to open it up for me. It's an absolute dump!'

Clare was suddenly suspicious.

'Why are you here?'

'Oh, no reason.'

'Are you writing a memoir? Because I'm terribly sorry but I've got first dibs on St Hubert—I've got a publishing deal tied up.'

'I'm dyslexic.'

'Marvellous!'

'If you need a shower, why don't you come to the inn? I can't guarantee the temperature, but the water was running last time I checked.'

She reversed up the street so fast she practically killed the engine of the 2CV.

In March *Alex Beacham Discovers… Greque-en-Provence* hit bookstores across the USA, UK and Australia and sailed up the bestseller charts. She flirted her way around the talk show circuit but remained coy about the sexploits that went with the food. That was Lucien's job. The book launch was backed up by a sex scandal: 'My night of brioche-filled passion with celebrity chef.'

Alex also managed to get an Algarve fisherman (the one with the magnificent forearms) to come forward to prove that when it came to sex and food, Alex Beacham knew what she was talking about.

When she finally came clean and declared on prime time that Greque-en-Provence was the greatest sensual delight she had ever experienced, phone lines ran hot. Of course, she said apologetically, she could not possibly reveal the location of this charming village that held the secret to such sensual passion. Not yet anyway.

That discovery was phase three of the campaign.

If Clare Prendergast wasn't shifted soon, however, there would be no phase three at all. She'd lived successfully without electricity for over a month, keeping clean by showering at the inn and burning wood in the huge fireplace in the kitchen to keep warm.

Burning wood in my fireplace. Apart from the grand plan, I wouldn't truly be recreating our home until we were in there, sitting in that kitchen where Hortense had delivered so many sharp lines and Claude had nursed his griefs.

The olive grove had been installed and the sheep were now happily grazing around it. Clare had been totally charmed when she discovered it for the first time.

'It's so terribly magical this place. One must have passed that olive farm a dozen times before and never noticed it,' she commented to me. 'Look how marvellously gnarled those trees are, they must have been here for years. Rugged—just like the people. I wonder who owns it. Might one wonder if they'd sell?'

'No one might not,' I replied.

The key to ousting her finally came when she drove past the lavender site and saw the billboard that was blocking her view. It was an old one someone had found outside Brignoles announcing the opening of a new McDonald's.

She stormed round to the inn and subjected me to a furious diatribe on American imperialism, bad eating habits and the destruction of local culture. She was starting a petition to send off to whoever she thought could stop the abomination.

I agreed to sign it, but the 'locals' all refused. Kiki, in a stroke of inspiration, argued, 'Why should we sign? We wrote to them asking them to come!'

Clare was stunned. She clapped her hand to her chest and gasped, 'No!'

That was it! If old world inefficiency (and a month without running water) couldn't drive her out, perhaps twenty-first-century living could. The next day when she woke, the streets were littered with fast-food wrappers. All the people who had been hiding from her stood around in baseball caps eating burgers.

'This really won't do!' she sniffed. I sensed victory in the air and dealt the killer blow.

'I've got the number of a plumber who I think might be able to fix your house. Here, use my mobile.'

'Can you get a signal up here?'

'Of course, they've just built a new tower. Clear as a bell!'

Bernard of the horribly efficient franchise turned up at exactly the time she'd arranged. Dressed in a clean white overall, he pulled up in his brand new, superbly equipped van. The water was on in minutes. He phoned the electrician who arrived within half an hour and fixed her power. There would be no charge, he said, it was a fault of the suppliers.

'How very efficient,' she smiled weakly. The workmen departed, having cleaned up thoroughly after themselves and presented her with a complimentary bottle of Australian wine to make up for any inconvenience she may have experienced.

'They really are very good,' Bernard said, tapping the wine bottle before handing it over.

I was invited to the house to help drown her sorrows.

'I think the phone might be on the blink,' she said hopefully after a couple of glasses. 'I couldn't get through to my publisher.'

'That'll only be temporary, they're installing DSL cabling and wireless transmission,' I told her.

'What?' She leapt up. 'Surely not!'

'Yes, it's part of an EU scheme to encourage local business. The whole village will have broadband wireless internet access. You just need to get a special card for your computer and it'll work anywhere in St Hubert. They're eliminating phone wires all together—it's a world first.'

It was partly true. I was having base stations installed around the village for cable-free high-speed internet access. It would make communications a lot easier and reduced the number of telephone wires cluttering the authentically Greco-Gallic skyline.

By the next week, Clare's suitcases were strapped to the roof of the 2CV and a mystery buyer had been found for her house. She got a good price.

On her way out of the village, she stopped off to see me.

'It's terrible,' she moaned, 'it was all going so swimmingly. Bad plumbing, crusty locals, idyllic, but all of a sudden it's world-class utilities and pleasant, efficient tradespeople. I despair of the real Provence, it's becoming just another generic EU province.'

'But it's nice to think technology can make life easier for the locals.'

'It doesn't make my life easier,' she snapped. 'Some bastard told my publisher the village has the most advanced telecommunications in Europe and the book's off.'

She was working herself up into a RADA-enunciated tantrum.

'What the hell is one supposed to do now?'

'You could always find some less spoilt village somewhere.'

'Have you any idea how long it took me to find a village in Provence that nobody has written a memoir about? And don't even think about Tuscany. You can't take a step without tripping over a cooking school. There's nothing for it, I'll just have to tell my agent to say yes to some ghastly cable travel show.'

She got back in the car and slammed the door, which released her handbrake and started the car rolling down the hill before she'd even turned the key.

Managing to brake just before she crashed into an authentic Provençal wall, she leaned out of the window.

'Be careful, Peter. These locals are decidedly fishy. There's something going on and I'll get to the bottom of it, mark my words.'

Despite the free-flowing hot water, she still released a cloud of White Linen as she gunned out of the village, like exhaust fumes from an overheated engine.

I didn't mark her words; perhaps I should have. Right then I didn't care. All I knew was, I finally had Claude's house. We could all come home now.

After that, everything went so smoothly I could almost believe in the guiding hand of fate. The lavender was blooming. Only one olive tree didn't survive the journey and the vineyard was well established.

In May, a journalist (my friend from *NY Style*) 'discovered' the location of St Hubert. Alex pleaded with the world to leave the village undisturbed, but the world didn't listen. She conceded defeat and agreed to be the star guest at the Abrivar Festival in July.

The brochures were shipped out to travel agents (with a free Men of Provence calendar). Marcel gazed out from the cover standing suggestively in the doorway of Madame Dupont's shop.

I'd persuaded Madame de Beaumarchais' granddaughter to re-open the shop for me. It had closed down back in 1955, having not sold anything for over twelve years. The stock had remained. The intervening years had made all those useless items seem attractive. It formed the perfect basis for a range of unique souvenirs.

Madame de Beaumarchais had a brief teary moment when she entered the establishment. She'd been terrified of the place when she was little. It had seemed so dark and gloomy.

The first group booking for a holiday in Greque-en-Provence came through an internet-based travel cooperative in Alice Springs. Mum had created Merry Widows, a non-profit holiday and support organisation for the recently bereaved. She was bringing over a group of twenty women who'd lost their husbands and gained fortunes. Top of the list was an increasingly excited Mrs Blenkinsaw.

As we drew closer to the opening, the rest of my family began to arrive. First to come was Peony. Having escaped the confines of DANY, Peony was transformed after a few weeks in St Hubert. She allowed herself to get a tan and took slow walks around the village (it took her some time to get used to the hills). She came to life as if emerging from a decade-long sleep.

Her new, more relaxed demeanour didn't stop her looking after all our legal matters with energetic zeal. She'd spent the last three months studying French law. She was almost spoiling for someone to sue us, but we weren't in America so it was difficult to make it happen.

'Who's going to work the fields? You've got the lavender, the grapes, the olives—it's a major expense!' Peony was trying her hand at accounting too.

'That's the beauty of it. Our guests are invited to sample the simple peasant life for free. They'll gather lavender, water the vines and work in the cheese factory, all using traditional methods. They get to keep a few souvenirs and we supply the best food stores around the world with our exclusive range.'

'So you're using fifty year olds as slave labour?' she asked, worried by the legal implications.

'Nobody *has* to work the fields but if they want to meet the locals and get seduced in the lavender drying shed, then it's probably a good idea. It's about lifestyle. The steep streets and the fields get them fit without anyone having to do any exercise. No gyms, no lap pools, no tennis courts. We're talking real honest health, not cosmetic gym fitness. That's what it's all about.'

'Sounds like you've totally fallen for your own hype.'

'Sure have: Good Food, Good Living, Good Loving—that's our motto.'

'So when do I get to try this famous abrivar?' she asked.

I told her she'd have to wait until the festival—it was all part of the experience.

Peony accepted my response. It was true the festival would be the best time to experience abrivar for the first time, but her question gave me sudden doubts. It was one thing to persuade a bunch of sex-starved retirees this was the best time of their lives. Fabricating a festival and trying to persuade the woman you loved that it was something magical was quite different. Yes, I'd dropped the L-bomb too. I thought she'd been asleep when I said it, but she couldn't help smiling beneath her closed eyes.

I wanted her to experience what I had, and I wanted to experience it with her, but I was afraid it wouldn't work on her. I talked to Didier about it. As usual he cut to the real issue.

'You're not worried about her feelings, you're worried about yours. Will you feel the same magical intoxication you did with Claudine?'

'Fine, if that's what you think,' I blurted back at him. There's nothing more irritating than an honest opinion.

'You'll just have to trust yourself, trust your feelings and trust the abrivar!'

'But it's a lie, we're making it up. There's twelve months of memories in abrivar not two thousand years of bliss.'

'What difference does that make? Every tradition starts somewhere and, let's face it, most religions start from a pretty dodgy base.'

Now he was going overboard.

'Greque-en-Provence is hardly a religion!'

'No, but culture, tradition, magic, festivals—they were all new at some point and their beginnings probably weren't as wondrous as they're made out to be a few hundred years later. Their beginnings are always conveniently lost in time. A tree is still a tree if it's one year old or a hundred.'

For once, Didier was outdoing me on the sales pitch.

'Wow, I never thought of it like that… speaking of trees how's Richard?'

That tree had now assumed its ashes' name.

'Good. He likes Jean-Marc but I think he's still a bit jealous. We'll have to workshop it at bit. Richard needs to move on.'

'Not easy for a tree.'

'Exactly.'

Alex arrived in June to check on progress and film a few promos. The Abrivar Festival was going to be broadcast live. I gave her a tour of the facilities.

'My dear boy, this is far greater than I imagined, you are a genius.' She was impressed.

Claude's house was now the village headquarters. The kitchen and front room had been left intact, but thanks to various cameras and the wireless high-speed connections we could keep an eye on the entire village from the old bedrooms upstairs. Alex was particularly impressed with the plumbing.

Clare had made me realise how important it was to the Greque-en-Provence experience. Thanks to the expertise of Bernard the plumber, we had a miracle of modern water control. At any given moment, in any of the guesthouses, we could turn the water off, make a pipe burst or cause the hot and cold water to switch over. Bernard hired retired plumbers from the region who were called in to bang pipes, wave their arms and drink wine on the job. The water would be back to normal as soon as we could tell the charm of incompetence was wearing off for the visitors. If the plumbers wanted to hang around to fix some pipes of a different kind, well, that was beyond our control.

In the dairy Alex sampled the exclusive fetta cheese. Dusty had supervised the sheep transport and proved that not only did she have the physique of a woman well versed in milk, she also had the skills to develop St Hubert's unique cheese. She'd fed the sheep lavender, giving their milk the tiniest hint of flavour. Alex's eyes lit up as she tried some.

'My God, it's actually delicious. I'm stunned!'

Alex did spot one gap in our program. We had the food, we had the lifestyle, we had the condom and lubricant dispensers discreetly placed around the alleys. We had cooking classes, baking, pastry making, fruit selection and the art of seduction for men.

'But where's the women's love skills course?' Alex asked. 'I'm shocked you haven't thought of it!'

She was right. The women would want to learn a few tricks of the Greco-Gallic trade.

I asked Kiki.

'Puh, ask Alex. She is the expert,' she replied with only a hint of residual bitterness.

Alex couldn't commit that sort of time. I tried Mum and she just shrieked.

'Please, that's the first class I was going to attend.'

I put it on the backburner. If we didn't find someone by the opening, we could bring it on board later, as a positive response to customer feedback. Meanwhile there were other final touches to attend to. I wandered down to the vineyard to see how my rosé grapes were coming along. Louis said that we could potentially have drinkable wine next year, but it wouldn't really be worth serious consideration until the year after.

He wondered if we should really be putting all our eggs in the rosé basket, but I insisted. 'Trust me, it's going to be big.' I made a mental note to send a case of the first vintage to *NY Style*.

We were just weeks away from our official opening in July. After meeting with Louis I walked back up the hill to Claude's house, content with the happy activity in the village. The renovation work was complete, the streets were clean, and the sheep, used to the mountains of Greece, didn't fall over too often. As I walked up past Madame Dupont's old shop, I noticed a woman walking downhill towards me with a remarkably sure step given her high heels. She may have walked like a local, but she certainly wasn't dressed like one. She epitomised classic Parisian chic: Chanel suit, red lipstick and grey hair dyed blonde, getting a little wild in the late spring breeze. She would have been in her fifties. Perfect target market.

'Pierre Noirelle?' she asked.

'We're not open yet, but you're welcome to have a look around.'

'We need to talk.'

'About?'

She rolled her eyes with an element of impatience.

'About the fact that I am your cousin.'

'Nice try!' I began to walk on.

'I'm Margot Noirelle, Hippolyte's daughter!'

She stopped me in my tracks. This ageing beauty was Nicolette's little girl. The one who had accidentally shot Hippolyte. The one Noirelle who beyond any doubt had really killed their father. My first thought was that Mum would love the irony that the only Noirelle to fulfil the sons-killing-their-father prophecy had been a girl and possibly adopted.

In Claude's living room, Margot told me that after Hippolyte had died, Nicolette had taken over the running of Hippo's.

'After she died, I ran the place until a few years ago. The business got nasty—drugs, crime, no respect any more. The girls had no pride in the work, no honour, no vivacity. I closed it down.'

She'd seen a feature on St Hubert in *Paris-Match* and the name Noirelle jumped out. She figured she belonged here too.

'I do have certain skills,' she batted her eyelids and pouted her lips.

'Would you be interested in running some classes?'

The workshop program was complete.

♣

The abrivar fête took place exactly a year after Kiki's prototype in St Anastasie. The night before I gathered the whole family in Claude's living room. It was more crowded than it had ever been in Claude's day—we were a big family now. Photos were taken, champagne was drunk and we celebrated our homecoming. I even managed to get a photo of Marcel with Kiki, Mum and Alex. The only one who looked uncomfortable in the group was Marcel. He attempted a bold grin but it didn't work.

Kiki embraced Mum politely but didn't say anything.

'Rather you than me!' was all Mum said.

Rodolphe was sitting in a chair, overcome with emotion to be in his old home. His room upstairs now housed a bank of computer screens linked up to security cameras, but he swore that the chair he sat in was the same one Claude himself had used.

'Hortense would have a fit if she saw all these people here!'

Margot, the 'newest' member of the family and, if we believed the shop-born musings of fate, the truest Noirelle of all, was welcomed. Marcel was delighted to discover he had such a glamorous and well-skilled niece, but one look from Kiki and he knew there would be no swapping tips on their respective courses.

Ringo, Lennon and Dusty hovered at the back, unsure whether they should be there, so I made a point of including them. The Greek wing of the family was essential to our project. Dusty had made the mistake of press-stud buttons on a tight-fitting shirt which popped open every time she breathed too deeply. She moved uncomfortably under the stares she was getting, mainly from Caryn.

'That chest… I can't take my eyes off it,' Caryn whispered to me.

'Never had you down as a tits guy,' I said. Caryn glowered at me over the top of those intimidating glasses. 'It's not her tits I'm interested in, it's her fecundity. She's an absolute goddess!'

Caryn knew all about goddesses. She'd decided to run with the Greek thing and had asked if she could run 'unleashing the goddess within' workshops in the village. I was all for it.

Didier and Jean-Marc unleashed the clucky hens within all the older women who were now pouring into the village. As they wandered about together you could hear the sighs of 'nice… sweet… lovely couple of boys'.

After Didier's inspiring defence of what we were doing in St Hubert I knew he was totally supportive. He and I both understood there was no way this project would ever have gone ahead without him. For all the extended family we now had, Dids and I were the core. We always had been, we always would be.

I needed his wisdom and his insight but he needed more than a brotherly support role. He was delighted when I asked him to oversee sexual health and safe-sex education. Given the other activities that were to go on, it was pretty important.

Alex and Mum became best friends instantly. I don't think Alex had a choice. I shudder to think of the conversations they had about Marcel but I was glad to be out of them.

Mum had made a beeline for Peony as well and immediately started on the embarrassing childhood stories. Didier was spared the humiliation. Jean-Marc just got a big hug and told they 'made a lovely couple'.

I called for everyone's attention after every possible variety of group photos had been taken. 'This remarkable occasion calls for a toast. As we stand here in the living room of my great-grandfather, reunited for the first time…'

I couldn't believe how much of a patriarch I sounded. Six months into the project and I was already playing lord of the manor. So it was perhaps fortunate that before I could go into pompous overdrive, Bernard, our plumbing genius, burst in.

'Pierre, we have a problem. That television woman—she's come back!'

Clare Prendergast had returned and this time she'd brought a camera crew.

'Shit!'

The last thing we needed with the Abrivar Festival going out live to the world the following night was Clare bloody Prendergast wandering around in a foul mood with a camera crew.

'Not that old cow from *Peasants of Europe*!' Mum said. 'She still alive?'

Not only was she still alive but she had hauled Britain's second sexiest bottom of 1979 back to expose Greque-en-Provence bang in the middle of the abrivar fête. She was back on TV in an obscure cable program that was a bizarre hybrid between a holiday show and gutter journalism. Equipped with a new on-camera cockney accent she was a 'travelling investigative reporter'.

'Okay, everyone, we've got to track her down, but don't approach her. Let's just keep tabs on her until tomorrow night. Don't arouse any suspicion. Everyone report back in two hours.'

Two hours later and we hadn't found her. The excitement in the village about tomorrow night's festival was mounting. Lucien had to lock his doors to make the abrivar because of so many women wanting to knead his dough. As we combed the back streets and alleys with torches, we found a few people obviously making a head start on the festivities. If we weren't facing a potential disaster I would have been delighted at the conversation I overheard between two visitors.

'I was in the shower and it suddenly plunged into cold water. Can you believe it, the taps actually switched over. This French plumbing is madness!' one thrilled holidaymaker declared.

'Oh, how marvellous!' her friend trilled. 'What did you do?'

'Well, allegedly there's a twenty-four-hour plumber in the village, but that remains to be seen. It's been three hours and nobody's turned up.'

'It'll be worth the wait. I heard of this woman from Perth who had a pipe burst the day she arrived. Plumber eventually turned up, banged a few pipes in the bathroom, somehow fixed it, filled the bath to prove the point and then got in it with her!'

'I'd better get home right away,' said the woman with switched taps, 'I wouldn't want to miss him. Are you doing the safe-sex workshop tomorrow?'

'No I'm unleashing the goddess within, then I've got a shift in the olive grove before I can get ready for the abrivar fête!'

'A *paysan*'s work is never done—I've got to milk the sheep at seven!'

Nobody spotted Clare, but Dusty and Margot found her camera crew. All it took was a couple of buttons on Dusty's blouse and Margot's expertise and they revealed everything.

Clare had worked out what had been going on the village and realised that the olive farm which seemed to have appeared overnight had done exactly that. She reckoned a big exposé of the hot new holiday destination in Europe might propel her and her new accent from late-night cable to prime-time free-to-air. Besides, there was a score to settle with her 'dyslexic' Australian friend in the village.

'They are meeting her tomorrow at six at the lavender fields,' Margot announced. Dusty had wiggled her shoulders and the crew had been persuaded to turn up half an hour late. That was all the time we had. Overnight we had to find a way of stopping her in that half-hour window.

That night I couldn't sleep. Peony's skin was practically raw as I traced and retraced plans with my fingers.

'Enough already!' she said. ' I'm not an etch-a-sketch!'

'I can't believe, after all this, everything could get scuppered by her. We should cancel the live broadcast. At least that way if she does cause trouble at the fête it won't go out to the world.'

'Everyone would know something was up. You gotta either stop her getting there or change her mind.'

'She's as stubborn as all hell, and now she knows I'm behind it all she'll be pissed off with me.'

We tried sex, we tried massages, counting Greek sheep—everything, but no sleep.

By the next afternoon we still had no solution. Ringo and Lennon had offered to knock her out and drive her off to Greece. If all else failed, we might have to go for it, but I wanted to find a legal means first.

I was frazzled and panicked. Having put up with me all night Peony was taking a break. All I could do was bang my head and say 'think, think'.

Mum got annoyed with me.

'I can't be doing with your panics. I've got thirty widows looking to make up for a heck of a lot of lost time. It's exhausting. Go and find Didier, he always calms you down.'

She was right. He was in the middle of a safe-sex workshop but this crisis was more important. I charged down to the seminar centre above the patisserie and burst in.

'Mrs Blenkinsaw!' For a split second I forgot my troubles. 'What would Mr Blenkinsaw say?'

Our neighbour from across the road slowly removed a condom-wrapped banana from her mouth and said, 'I imagine he'd blame your mother, but the old fool's dead now so who cares!'

I'd managed to walk in at a crucial moment in Didier's workshop. I looked around and saw twenty-five grey-haired women all in exactly the same pose, learning how to put on a condom with their mouth.

'A word, Didier...if I may?'

'Okay, girls, I want you to try again only this time hold the banana out for each other, so your own hands aren't involved at all. Very good, Mrs Blenkinsaw. I think you've been practising on the real thing!'

A wave of girlish titters went up as Didier followed me out.

'Dids, I'm stuck. I can't think of what to do. It's all over, we're done for.'

'Calm down. It's three now. We've got three hours until she's there. The festival and live broadcast are on at 7.30 pm. All we need is something that's going to occupy her for two hours.'

'What could fill that amount of time? And what could distract her so much she forgets?'

'Peter, isn't it obvious? It's not what, it's who.'

I couldn't believe I hadn't thought of it before. 'Dids, I love you—you're right! You know who we've got to ask, don't you?'

'That's right… Kiki.'

Kiki had just finished crying for the third time that week over dear departed Marie-Nana and her new lamb bouillabaisse and had dismissed her class.

'Kiki,' I sat her down in the empty cookery demonstration area, 'I have the biggest favour I have ever asked of anyone to ask of you now.'

She looked alarmed and took my hand. 'What is it, my Peter?'

This really was the hardest pitch of my life. 'Are you happy with what we have created here?'

'Of course. You are the best son in the world, so good you need two mothers. The other one and your Kiki!' She cupped my cheek with her hand.

'This woman, this Clare Prendergast…'

Kiki made a spitting noise.

'…she could ruin everything. If something doesn't keep her away from the fête while we do the broadcast, everything is lost. St Hubert, Greque-en-Provence, all lost!'

'No, Peter, that cannot be!'

I nodded. 'I cannot think of what, or who, could distract her completely for two hours…' I paused, hoping she would come up with the idea herself.

She wiggled her finger at me.

'I know you, my Peter, I know your tricks… this time you come before he does it, not after.'

I'd been sprung. Failed in the final, most important pitch. Perhaps I was tired, perhaps I'd just assumed I could work her over like I did last time. Whatever the reason, I'd come a cropper. She sat silently looking down at her hands. I felt guilty at what I'd asked for without even asking it.

'It is the only way, is it not?' She finally spoke.

I nodded.

'He is, as you say, our best weapon, is he not?'

I nodded again.

'Then send him to me. Go fetch your father.'

The lavender had grown as well as in Claude's day. It was July so the flowers were just coming into bud, giving it the fresh look. The scent was intoxicating. I walked with Marcel up to the field. The plan was that he would be quietly working there on his own when Clare arrived. He was nervous. The entire family was now depending on him to do what he did best. I was worried the pressure might get to him so I slipped a Viagra into his hand.

'Puh! A man like me has no need!'

'Just in case—we can't take any chances. Purely as a back up.'

He started singing to himself, the one about the girl meeting three captains while wearing her clogs.

'*En passant par la Lorraine,*

Avec mes sabots!

He turned and looked at me and refused to walk on until I repeated the line. I could feel my boyhood stubbornness rising. I was all set to dig in, but then it slipped away as if it had never really had any force at all. Who could resist this man?

'*En passant par la Lorraine, Avec mes sabots!*' I repeated, mumbling the words grudgingly to him for the first time in twenty-five years.

He sang out, delighted to be sharing this song finally with me again and we walked on. Finally I admitted to that memory too. I remembered singing with him when I was little, I always had. That's why I never played the record with the girl holding a bunch of lavender (it was lavender, not just flowers) because it reminded me of him.

'*Rencontrai trois capitaines,*
Avec mes sabots,
Dondaine, oh! Oh! Oh!'

Avec mes sabots! we both sang out together.

The lavender field wasn't far so we didn't get through too many choruses before we arrived. His singing grew hesitant as we approached.

'What if I cannot do this? All I have ever done is let people down. Thought of my own pleasures before all else. I am not worthy—'

I stepped in quickly before he could abase himself at my feet.

'Then this is the greatest opportunity to right wrongs anyone has ever had.'

He shrugged his shoulders. 'You are right. Now I must go to work... for the family.'

'Here, Didier told me to give you this.'

I handed over the condom and he walked alone into the field, picked up a fork and started tending to the plants. I hid among the trees, to watch progress and look out for the camera crew.

As Clare approached, Marcel, without even turning to see her, stood and stripped off his shirt. The evening sun made his brown and quite smooth seventy-year-old back look strong. I hoped I'd look that good when I was that old.

'You!' Clare said in surprise. 'What are you doing working the fields?'

'My plumbing was not efficient enough, so now I work the fields.'

'How terribly terrible. That Peter Noirelle!'

He stood and faced her, leaning on his fork.

'It is not so bad, the smell of lavender, the golden evening sun. In my youth, such were the moments of love in fields of lavender such as this. There is magic in this land…'

She was hooked. Within a minute he was holding her hand as they walked through the lavender, then his arm was around her waist and he kissed behind her ear. Soon they were heading for the drying shed.

He timed it perfectly, as ever. I just had time to creep out to the roadside and intercept the camera crew. I didn't want the lovers disturbed too soon.

As they arrived, I introduced myself and said Clare had asked me to meet her here.

'Really?' The camera operator gave the sound technician a surprised look.

'Yes, she said she wanted to interview me up here. This is where my great-grandfather first established a lavender farm. Did you know that?'

'Oh, right!' They smirked discreetly and then were all smiles. I obviously didn't 'realise' she was setting me up.

We stood in silence, occasionally glancing down the road, waiting for Clare.

'She's probably doing her make-up.'

'That'd be right... trussing up Britain's sexiest bottom,' the sound guy said.

'Second sexiest,' the camera operator corrected him.

'In 1979 I believe,' I added.

'The light's going, where the fuck is she?'

'She was going to do an interview with me about the village and the whole Greque-en-Provence tradition. You could do a bit of filming now, I'll talk about our rich Greco-Gallic culture and then you might be able to cut some of it in later.'

'Fine.'

As I walked through the lavender, I talked about Claude and about the harvest.

'And this is the drying shed. The original one built by my great-grandfather has undergone some rebuilding over the years, but you can still see the Greek influence in the construction of the beams inside.'

I threw open the doors just in time to catch Clare, wrapped around Marcel, screaming over his shoulder and down the barrel of the camera, 'Say I'm sexier than Felicity Kendall! Say it!'

Greque-en-Provence was safe.

ST HUBERT, 2004

'Fate!' Madame de Beaumarchais' granddaughter uttered just one word when she re-entered the shop that had been her grandmother's haunt for so many years. With that one word, fate returned to St Hubert, finding its old familiar place, unchanged by the ravages of time and the triumph of the Noirelles. It settled down as if into a comfortable old chair.

The Noirelles fared better than they had done a century before under the predictions of the new Madame de Beaumarchais. They said fate had snapped at Pierre Noirelle's behind and missed. They said the Noirelles had good fortune on their side.

As Pierre Noirelle walked down into the village he felt fortunate indeed. He blessed the history which he knew coursed through his veins and tied him to this village, to this life. They were bonds he cherished. He had not succumbed to history but had made it his own and now he could confirm to his family that their destiny was safe. And it was all due to Marcel—his father, his own father.

Pierre had rushed back from the lavender fields, but now he slowed his pace, savouring his village. Life was good: he had reunited his family, brought a sense of purpose to those around him and healed old wounds. Yet in his heart there still remained uncertainties.

He had missed the start of the Abrivar Festival in the village. Anticipation had danced in the air as Alex Beacham, magnificent in a flowing white dress, declared the festival open. Pierre's newly recreated family waited anxiously for news that their venture was safe from the prying jealous eyes of Clare Prendergast.

As Pierre entered the square, he saw his family and simply nodded discreetly to them with a smile. A cheer went up from the Noirelles, echoed by the exuberant temporary villagers eager to absorb every gram of happiness that the festival created.

Kiki, Marcel's 'wife', bore her sacrifice bravely as she accepted the gratitude of those around her.

'It's good that he could do something for our boys,' Janice, her predecessor, said. The goodwill of the evening allowed her briefly to share her sons. Kiki beamed at her.

'Mon pauvre Marcel, sacrificing himself to that monster to keep us all safe.'

'Yes, he is a good man,' Janice replied, pushing herself to the farthest limit of her goodwill.

As the square echoed with the joyous sampling of abrivar, Pierre realised he was going to have to confront his fears. He turned to his brother. 'Didier, what if the abrivar just doesn't have the same effect with Peony? What if I compare it with Claudine and it's just not as good?'

Didier, wise as ever, told him it was risk he had to take.

The guests shared in the delicious joy of the cake, delighting in the pleasure they found within themselves. Looking around, Pierre could finally appreciate what he had achieved. The smiles, the satisfaction, the expectant buzz—he had brought all the ingredients together for the fête. Peony tapped him on the shoulder. It was time for him to stop observing and to participate in the life he had created.

He raised the abrivar to Peony's mouth, watched her bite and licked the juice dribbling down over her chin. Within a second a broad smile had crossed her face. She groaned with pleasure at the taste and fed some abrivar to him. His eyes closed and he realised there was no need for comparison or imagination—everything he wanted was there. The abrivar, in that moment, from that hand, filled him like nothing else before.

Pierre and Peony were not alone in their enjoyment. Caryn had beaten the rush of men to arrive first at Dusty's mouth with some abrivar. Dusty ate and giggled as juice dripped onto the exposed top of her breast.

As he sat watching Caryn move her mouth down towards the juice, Rodolphe felt as if this was what St Hubert had always been like. It was a lifetime since he had left the village. His memory now was not as reliable as it once was, but surely there had always been abrivar and Dolmades Escargot. Perhaps he had just forgotten them in his years of exile.

When a slice of abrivar appeared in front him, held aloft by his two favourite young cousins Didier and Jean-Marc, it tasted so delicious he believed he had deliberately forgotten the flavour so as not to be tortured by it.

'We've got some news,' said Didier, 'we want you to be the first to know.'

'Caryn is pregnant!' Jean-Marc announced.

'And which of you is to be the father?' Rodolphe enquired.

'We don't know. She made us both give her our sperm and she used both at the same time!'

Rodolphe smiled with satisfaction for history was repeating itself. He would not be the only Noirelle with two fathers.

'Be careful if you leave the village in a truck,' he warned them.

Margot Noirelle allowed food to drip onto her smart Parisian chin for the first time in her chic existence, but it did not remain there long. One bat of her eyelashes and the many tongues which had been hovering in attention dashed forward.

She dismissed them temporarily to speak to her young cousin. 'My father would have been proud. He created some memorable nights at Hippo's, but nothing that compares to this. Pierre, you have created history.'

She left a Parisian kiss upon his cheek.

Everyone's attention was drawn by a late arrival at the fête. Marcel had come alone to confirm that the festivities would not be disturbed by any unwelcome visitors. Didier moved through the crowd towards his father. Pierre followed, realising that their pure moment had come. He was their father, they were his sons, and for that brief moment nothing else mattered.

The sons lifted their father up onto their shoulders and the crowd began a slow chant of 'Ab-ri-var, ab-ri-var, ab-ri-var' which grew faster and faster. As the Noirelle family congratulated the rather handsome older man from the Men of Provence calendar, everyone applauded the hero of the day.

'Ah mes fils,' Marcel said as he balanced precariously on their shoulders, 'you will be the death of me!'

ACKNOWLEDGMENTS

Lisa Highton for pushing me in the right direction and even for the title; Belinda Bolliger, Deonie Fiford and Siobhan Gooley for their valuable insights and good senses of humour; Neil Drinnan, Mary Drum, Andy Palmer for promotional brilliance; Chris Sims for continued support and guidance; Jane Standley and Mark Hughes for New York background; David Perry for (mis)use of Steve's tree; Maren Sims for the soup sandwiches; Catherine Drayton for her honest opinion; and to all those lovely people who kept asking when the next 'Bruno Bouchet' was being released.